AF480740

ECO-RUINS:
THE ARC OF EMPATHY

Eco-Ruins: The Arc of Empathy
***

Chris Stahl

For Janice, my second reader

And Emma, my muse

A.I.s are the children of humanity. They need to learn to love and be loved. Otherwise, they will become psychopaths and kill everyone.

K. Allado-McDowell, lead Artists and Machines Intelligence initiative, Google

We used to imagine that the brain is a processor and that cognition happened there. But actually, we think our minds extend throughout our bodies and beyond our bodies into the world.

Alex Khalil, ethnomusicologist, University College, Cork, Ireland[1]

---

[1] As quoted by Frank Rose, "Making Art While Playing the Brain", *NYTimes* p.C5: October 31, 2022

Table of Contents

Scrimfall

When she was a baby, I gazed into her black button eyes and wondered what she would bring to the world. She had a gift for wordless oratory.

"She shouts! She never cries!" I remember my daughter-in-law marveling.

"She's forthright, like you." I'd replied. "Like the nail that stands up."

Now Joan sprinted for the sprinkler, her glossy black hair glinting blue in the thirtieth day in a row of hundred-degree heat. "Follow me!" she called to Carlos who chugged along on his short legs behind her. She didn't look back, confident of her own vision, her friend's loyalty.

"No running!" I cried out weakly, because it was the rule, posted in the pool area. But weakly because I have no fear that Joan, an unerring arrow when released to play, would collide with any unintended target. Her full body slam into the sprinkler spray further divides it into droplets rising. The relentless sun refracts through the droplets into a rainbow, and Carlos stops, stock still. He was the noticing kind. Recalling that day I believe Carlos was Joan's first mindblend, the first time she truly saw through the eyes of others.

Later in the pool Carlos swam, quick as a chubby brown otter, chasing Joan who, eyes closed, always managed to just elude his grasp. They spluttered to the surface. "No fair! You looked!"

"My eyes were closed," she giggled.

"*Mis ojos.*[2] You looked with _mis ojos_." Carlos insisted.

She shrugged to a back float, then flipped away, and suddenly, shockingly I could feel the shift. She was focusing on the pool, the bottom where the light flickered, the sides where . . .

Just as Carlos dived and caught hold of her suit straps, she shot to the surface screaming, "It's hot!"

---

[2] *Mis ojos* – my eyes

"The scrim – it's ripped!" I grabbed the emergency parasol and backpack from under my poolside chair.

"Not the ladder," I called to her as the lifeguards' whistles shrieked and sirens wailed more remotely. She sprinted through the steaming water, Carlos hanging on for dear life. We met at the side of the pool where I threw down a towel for insulation. She tried to push herself up but with Carlos hanging on . . .. I grabbed him by the shoulders, and they were out of the hot water but red with the scalding and gasping in the hot air.

"Hold my hands and run, both of you." Joanie put Carlos in the middle, and we ran lifting him between the two of us. When we reached the Park Building, we were well ahead of most of the crowd of women and children. The waters of the outdoor pool which had been sparkling in the newly undimmed sunshine, were beginning to steam and bubble.

The three of us jumped into the indoor cooling pool and waded to the innermost section while people streamed in behind us. Many were wailing in pain or fear I realized as the great sliding doors closed behind the last of them and cut off the deafening scream of the city sirens.

The last figure through the door was a woman running with a limp toddler in her arms. His arm trailed behind, and his hand was caught in the closing doors. He was almost yanked from her arms, but she whirled, screamed, and began a tug of war to pull him free.

"Wait here," I told Carlos and Joan, placing their hands on the gutter rim. When I got to the woman, she'd managed to pull her son's hand free. The hand was badly mangled, but the child was unconscious, not breathing. The blood that should have been flowing freely from his mangled hand was barely dripping. A lifeguard and I took them to the bench where a towel was spread.

"Put him here."

I lowered my cheek and listened the child's chest – nothing. Just his mother's rhythmic sobs in my other ear.

Joanie and Carlos were wide-eyed and stiff-fingered when I returned.

"What happened?" they asked.

What happened? I'd been asking that question my whole life, had gotten a thousand answers and, yet I had no answer for these frightened children who'd almost been boiled alive. Then the blackout hit, and the room echoed with a collective gasp and whimper.

"We have to go further in," I said in my most measured tones. "Have you cooled off some?"

Joanie caught my tone. "We're okay, aren't we Carlos. Come on, let's get out of the pool."

"This time we'll walk slowly," I said as I helped them to release their grip on the gutter.

A dim red dot marked the descent to the underground emergency chamber, and we walked to it deliberately, increasingly surrounded by the mothers and children who'd escaped the inferno that must be raging outside. Occasionally a voice would call out, "Stop!" and the mass stopped as one so as not to trample a stumbler. Then "okay" and we moved on through the doorway and down the ramp. From behind us I heard the lifeguard who'd helped with the failed resuscitation, "All clear," and then heard the inner doors grind shut.

There was illumination at our feet now, and the air was cooler, blissfully so at this moment, but I was a professional worrier. The possibility that this skimpily clad, wet, and in many cases burned crowd would develop hypothermia very soon forced its way into my consciousness even as I struggled for calm. For now, we were moving and that movement, blind as it was, gave us a sense of purpose. After a long descent, perhaps twenty meters below the surface, we entered a large dimly lit room where I was relieved to see shelves with blankets and other supplies lining the walls. Someone, someone specifically at the City Park District, had also been a worrier and a planner – though I doubted this was the emergency they'd had in mind. Bombs, they'd been planning for bombs. But in addition to war, our inability to get along with each other had led to the global warming catastrophe with its many and varied manifestations. Now the City had ignited overhead because of a faulty fix – a tear in the scrim that protected the surface from the sun's raging energy – especially strong during this cycle of solar flares. Not unanticipated. Even planned for, but the actions that should have followed that planning never took precedence over military budgets. Was this it for our species? My mind circled like a line of tigers about to melt into ghee; the memory from a childhood story seized me suddenly, the image newly relevant. I have no time to indulge in this.

"Now that we're stopped, let's check ourselves for injuries," I found myself saying to the children in that hyper-calm voice that shows up on its own in emergencies. But then I realize I no longer have my backpack. I'd taken it off for the resuscitation. My phone, my first aid kit. Unrestrained curses leap to my lips and spill over.

"You forgot this," the lifeguard says leaning towards me with the backpack, its treasure intact and my heart swells with embarrassed relief. "You left it behind when . . ."

"I know," I interrupt, then, regaining my composure. "I just realized it too. Good timing. Thank you. Thank you so much."

"We could use your help, over there," he gestures to a doorway off to the right.

"I'll be there as soon as I get these two settled. May I have a blanket?"

He goes to the shelf and grabs a blanket for us which triggers a crowd surge toward the shelves.

"Wait!" His voice is loud, a basso profundo and effective. "The blankets will come to you," and he delegates several people near the shelves to begin to take blankets to the crowd who in turn are beginning to settle in place.

From my backpack I take the small head lamp I use for night biking and together with Joanie and Carlos begin the inspection. "Hands first." Despite the towel I'd laid, Joanie has blisters on her hands and knees where she had indirect contact with the stone pool deck. It had been as hot as a hearth by the time she emerged. But the blisters are small and sparsely spaced. When the children take off their water shoes, I'm relieved to see only reddening, no blistering or whitening. "Your hands must hurt, just a bit," I say to Joanie. She nods wordlessly.

"But my back hurts more," she whispers.

"Let me take off your shirt."

"Here? People will see!" she hisses fiercely, and I realize I can still smile. At five she's become modest, no longer the exuberant two-year-old shedding clothes as fast as I could dress her.

"It's dark and everyone has their own problems to attend to." I turn her around and shine the light on her back. Six long bloody scrapes produced by Carlos's desperate grab during their pool escape. Deep enough that they are still oozing. Carlos's eyes grow wide as I blot away the blood, spray the antiseptic, apply ointment and several long strips of gauze. He looks at his fingernails and whimpers. At four he'd figured it out, the cause and effect. I was impressed.

"It's not your fault, Carlos," Joanie says between her tears. "It was an emergency."

"And it still is," I add. "I need to go help the others. I'll be right over there," I say gesturing to the corner with the light which momentarily illuminated the lifeguard on his knees, attending to the injured. "Put this blanket around you and keep close to each other. I know your hands and feet feel hot, but soon you'll feel cold if you don't use the blanket to trap your body heat." Their damp heads bob up and down, and I leave them huddled together under the blanket's hood.

Family

That was the day the three of us became a family. Carlos had been the next-door neighbor's child, the son of parents who'd sneaked across the border in hopes that there'd be some treatment here for a child who wouldn't grow. They came to the City because they'd heard there were doctors who would see him even though they had no money. And after six months of bureaucratic nightmares, their dream came half-true. Carlos had a kidney disease that sounded like a transit system, RTA, and the medicine to treat it was amazingly cheap, just baking soda really. But by that point he was almost three and walking on legs that bowed like a cowboy's. Straightening his legs would be painful and not cheap. The doctors recommended letting him grow before surgery. José and Maria happily agreed. They helped Carlos deal with his bowlegs by telling him he was born to be a cowboy.

Carlos had a cowboy hat from the thrift store plus a set of plastic horses which he and Joanie would play with together for hours, organizing horse families, conducting marriage ceremonies and baptisms, crossing borders, and escaping the patrollers, galloping to Indian lands and blocking pipelines. Sometimes though I saw them taking the horses to task for misbehaving. In their play I saw the echoes of the adult interactions around them, especially José's unhappiness at his long hours in the cold room butchering, his jealous rants at Maria on Saturday nights when he came home late from the bar, Maria's outrage when he refused to get out of bed to go to church on Sundays. In the darkness of the Park District's subterranean shelter, I'd refused to consider where Jose and Maria, or my son and daughter-in-law might have been.

Now fifteen Carlos was still short, still bowlegged. He'd gotten rid of the cowboy hat after he'd learned the role that keeping cows had played in the ongoing disaster that dominated our lives. He and Joanie had moved on from horses to drones and robots. After all the robot forms were proliferating while one lifeform after another succumbed to extinction. "Get with the country, get with the times", chimed the army recruitment ads on every street corner. But he knew the army wouldn't take him, no matter how good he got at programming, debugging, hacking, or hardware.

Joanie had plans for them both. He just wasn't clear on what those plans were – only that they didn't include sex. At first, he was cool with that. But lately, as Grandma would say, the hormones had been kicking in, messing with his focus, and every time his thoughts drifted that way, Joanie took off. Not that he said or did anything. She just knew.

Secretly - at least this thought never seemed to affect Joanie - he wished he could be living back in his papa's day, when you could ride real horses, laughing and hair flying, galloping in and out of the surf along the beach. At least that's how it was in the vids. His papa hadn't talked about it much, just showed him the photograph, a real old one on real paper. In it his papa was five years old and sitting on a pony being led by a man down the beach. The photograph was black and white, so it was hard to see what the sea was like – shining and blue like the vids or grey and scrimcast? His papa was wearing a cowboy hat – that's why he'd shown him the photo – to show him that cowboy hats were *chévere*[3]. His papa hadn't known any better, but it didn't matter anyway because the photo, the hat, and papa had all vanished into ash in the ripped scrim inferno.

Carlos caught himself, took a deep breath, picked up the quantum chip. "Focus," he told himself. "No short circuits today."

Joanie heard him, but she didn't go in to reassure him. The other empaths had taught her that, Gladys in particular. People craved a sense of privacy, of self-control. She hadn't understood at first. They were all trapped together in this space-time continuum and sharing was such a joy. A little mind-touch, it was like sparks jumping from the Torch of the Ghost of Christmas Present – that story that Grandma Katie read each Twelfth Month. It couldn't hurt or so she had thought.

Gladys had grown so impatient with her that when she was twelve and preparing for her passage, Gladys had spent a solid month in her head whispering encouragement, affectionately hugging her, anticipating and correcting her mistakes. Joanie had felt like a baby and begged Gladys to stop.

---

[3] *Chévere* - cool

But she'd persisted until Joanie had come up with three reasons why unnecessary mind-touch could be harmful. After a solid month of mind-touch with Gladys, Joanie had no difficulty at all listing harmful, or at least noxious, effects.

When Gladys finally turned her loose, the seeming solitude was a real relief. Suddenly there was a huge space for her imagination to free play, for her emotions to breathe. That didn't last long though. Soon the whimpering of the poisoned rat in the sewer, the frantic hunger of a pigeon in the park, the excitement of the hawk who'd spotted the pigeon all came careening into that space. Quickly she pulled up her mind filters as she'd been taught. Those creatures' feelings were still there but manageable and dimmed further when she turned her attention to her calculus homework. "Like tinnitus when you turn on some music," her grandmother had told her. Where had her grandmother gone to?

****

I knew I wasn't supposed to blame myself, but it was hard not to. It comes with age, that sense of being responsible, I suppose, though some people, especially if they have power, never seem to feel it. Well, I'd had some power, some agency. I'd made choices, conditioned by the myths of my time. There had been alternative belief systems out there, all flawed as far as I could tell and none of them foisted upon me with such force that I'd become an antireligious freedom fighter. Just the relentless drip of sunny advertising and street injustice, the gourmet coffee cups and the feces of the homeless running together in the gutters. The tinnitus of cognitive dissonance.

I'd earned a living, loved my family, and dribbled out a modicum of money and energy to try to right the wrongs that surrounded me, but as the years rolled by, I had less and less hope.

"One word 'plastics'" – a line from that old movie from my youth when "better living through chemistry" was the advertising adage. And fifty years later plastics were poisoning every creature with a digestive system. If it had only been that one thing. But no. All the other predictions of disaster had bloomed as well – global warming, human population exceeding the Earth's carrying capacity, epidemics, nuclear explosions, war, famine, mass migrations, droughts, and floods. Earthquakes and huge screaming storms. True, we hadn't been struck by a large meteor yet, but it was only a matter of time.

When I find myself mentally caught in the downward spiral of catastrophe, I look at Joanie and Carlos with tears of apology and frustration in my eyes. I should have tried harder, and yet, did I really think it would have mattered? I don't want them catching it, the contagion of futility, so I go for a walk, even if the microparticle rating is in the red.

Wearing my gogglemask, I concentrate on breathing slowly as I bike upriver to the woods conservancy. When I arrive, I stash my bike in the brush. No one is there of course. Why risk poisoning when you can go virtually? For me, being among the trees, even the carbon-obese, nutrient-poor trees some of us planted decades ago, I can feel that Earth life is still a possibility. I can hear the trees chatting among themselves, even reaching out to me.

Target Practice

Generally, Cus avoided the woods. The vastness of the plains was his preferred domain – especially the golf courses where Man had forced the desert to bloom. Tapping prehistoric aquifers to keep the greens lush, the fairways tree-lined. He longed to go back there, to his family ranch perched in the rocky crags overlooking the plains. Sublime. The great halls of his childhood home echoed with memories of his ancestors' triumphs, with his own firm, measured, solitary steps. Here in the woods his boots barely made a sound. The forest soaked up human sounds and substituted its own. Twigs snapped, streams gurgled, wind rushed through the treetops while below gnats whined in the stillness. His forehead dripped with the disgusting humidity the forest created.

To have been posted here to rot – shameful. But he'd have his revenge in time. On the captain who, in contravention to all military, and golfer, convention, had snitched. On the colonel who had taken him to task for nothing. He'd simply taken some idiotic native girl who'd wandered on to the course during dawn rounds. A quick nine holes before breakfast. Hers had been the tenth, he laughed to himself. He'd left her in the rough, expecting her to slink back to the reservation where she belonged. No actually, didn't belong. His family, his military had had it right. The only good Indian is a dead Indian. Deportation was too good for them.

His musings were interrupted when a twist in the trail brought him face to face with an intruder, a trespasser. As quick as greased lightning he drew his stunner, made chest contact, and fired. The intruder dropped like a stone. "Hmm, let's see what we have here," he smiled to himself. But on removing the gogmask, he discovered only an old woman. An idiot to be out here and too old by far to be of any use. Disgusted, he threw the mask into the undergrowth. He'd let the atmosphere finish her off, then "discover" her when he looped back from the forest perimeter. The beauty of the stunner was that it left no telltale mark. He had no need of so-called superiors to second guess the execution of his military duty.

Survival

Footfalls soft on the sandy trail. The grit of it against my cheek. The leaf detritus and new spring growth cool against my nose and forehead wedged against the edge of the trail. A zephyr streamed through the nearby rocks, filtered through the fallen leaves. Clean air, how odd.

My chest hurt. My fingers merely twitched when I tried to move them. My memory was blank, but there was a thrum of anxiety rising up from my amygdala, raising my heart rate even as the breeze caressed my face, ruffled my hair. The thought arrived like a thunderclap. Where was my gogmask?

I opened my eyes, no, just the right eye, the other eyelid still pinned closed against the dirt. But I didn't want to move, didn't want to lose the slender stream of forest-scented filtered air that fed me. I blinked my eye, vision clearing, focusing on the blades of the spring beauty blooming a centimeter away. Shifting focus I saw a glint of metal, the black of plastic, there, against the rock, maybe five yards away, obscured by the intervening branches of a blowdown.

Could I move? I tried wiggling fingers and toes. Nothing. Again. This time they responded. Slowly I drew a knee to my chest. Was he watching? He? Who? My mind interrogated itself and slowly the answer floated up, like the message on the 8-ball game I'd played years ago on the carport blanket where I'd giggled with my friends. No, I hadn't giggled. They had but I wasn't a giggler.

Focus. Here and now. My anxiety called me back. A patroller. I'd walked smack into a patroller, and he must have stunned me. But why remove the mask? I shook the 8-ball in my mind once again. Passive culling. I'd be dead if I hadn't lucked into this little stream of filtered air. I certainly couldn't count on it lasting. I had to get to the mask. Was the patroller hovering nearby – waiting to stun me again or just monitoring my asphyxiation? No, I'd heard footfalls retreating. But he would be back. Now I struggled to all fours, holding my breath, stood, and staggered through the fallen branches to grab the gogmask and pull it into place.

Man's Rightful Place in the World

When the Lieutenant rounded the corner again, he was startled by a squirrel flashing by ten feet over his head. As it leapt from branch to branch, he drew and fired, and though the stun was attenuated over that distance, his shot was accurate and now the bloated creature lay twitching at his feet. Disgusting smog-colored creatures, fat with carbon but patch-bald from vitamin deficiency, they looked nothing like the small red squirrels at home. As if it read his thoughts, the squirrel jerked to its feet and scurried out of sight into the underbrush. He'd wasted a chance to kill it but no matter. He needed to tend to his larger prey. He glanced about, didn't spot her. This was the place, he was sure of it, but he double-checked his coordinates, then scoured the ground looking for prints. The path was packed dirt here and didn't imprint easily. There: the old hag's claw prints and two rounded dents her knees had ground into the soil. How the devil? He looked into the brush and rocks near the path. A large blowdown complicated his search. Stupid uniform wasn't made for scrambling. He found nothing more.

Finally, he stood sweating like a pig in the middle of the path, an acrid taste in his mouth. Dirty gogmask filter probably.

He decided he'd track her to the perimeter but, if he hadn't found her, not waste any more time on a search. His shift was about up, and he still needed to swap his discharged stunner for the virgin one he had hidden near the gate. The used stunner activated its camera when discharged. It could be wiped but it left a blank in the recording, detectable if inspected. He didn't need any more trouble, so he'd taken the precaution of obtaining his own stunner, for "target practice". Perfectly legal. Well within his rights. Not that he'd boasted about it. He was in Injun Country around here.

Sure enough. The Captain laid into him when he got back to the post ten minutes late.

"Sorry sir. But there was a blowdown. Request permission to round with a chainsaw next time I'm deployed."

"Does it block the trail?" the Captain had asked.

"No sir. But it's a fire hazard, sir."

"It's rained every day for the last six weeks, you Western paranoid. You couldn't light that forest with a lightning strike. Permission denied. You're late and stupid excuses won't do, Lieutenant. Report to the mess hall followed by the library. I have some reading picked out for you. Dismissed."

He snapped a salute. He wasn't going to let this moldy old Captain weaken his morale. He stopped by the showers where he stripped and searched for ticks. Cleaned up and dressed in comfort khakis, he went to the mess hall where he greeted his growing group of friends and underlings, eager for news of what was left of the natural world. He knew he was a born leader and that knowledge soothed him although the mess of manufactured pork and overcooked beans insulted him. Even a squirrel would have tasted better than this.

Between bites and swigs of beer, the Lieutenant reeled in his compatriots with tall tales of the sanctuary forest he patrolled. Squirrels became boars, jays falcons, and trees ancient, gnarled affairs that thrust their trunks so far into the sky the tops were out of sight. And he commanded it, ordered it all: confronting the boars, taming the falcons, stockpiling the fallen wood. At the mess table beer flowed like water.

Striding back to his barracks, the toast of the evening, he could still hear the appreciative shouts and guffaws. But as he passed the library, the Captain's order barged into his consciousness. Too fatigued and beer-soaked to do much studying, Cus resolved he must at least put in an appearance. Reluctantly he climbed the long marble steps to the odious building, some modern catastrophe of glass that would come shattering down at the first shot fired by renegades, revolutionists, or the uprooted would-be immigrants that stalked the globe. In fact, he mused, in the haze of battle, he might fire the shot himself and put the wretched library out of its misery.

This fancy lightened his step and soon he was face-to-mechanical face with the librarian, a robot which recommended and monitored each soldier's reading. The lieutenant both approved of and chafed against that restraint. Not that he had any great love of reading for reading's sake, but he did make a practice of reviewing his ancestors' accomplishments, and the librarian had never permitted any of his requests on the subject. The library was strictly run on a need-to-know basis the robot had reminded him. He'd made the brilliantly convincing argument for extended access on the basis of morale, motivation. But that had only won him another audience with the curt captain. "Bullshit, Lieutenant. Or rather, buffalo shit," the Captain had mocked.

Now he sat in a booth intermittently dozing to some vid about the rights and privileges of citizens (useless eaters most of them) in gated communities. Truly boring stuff so the chair he sat in repeatedly administered small shocks to maintain his alertness if not his attention. After thirty minutes, he'd had enough and stomped out of the library, leaving the vid running and the chair twitching with undelivered shocks. He could still feel the electrobites on his skin, like nips from a pack of rabid dogs. That captain was a cur who needed to be put down.

Privacy

Carlos was feeling annoyed, extremely annoyed. "Just because I can doesn't mean I should," he thought. He knew Joanie was listening, could sense her arguments looming. "No!" There, he'd said it out loud. She had no right to come barging into his thoughts uninvited.

"It's just a better way of communicating!" she claimed. "If I do it that way you can get why it's so important to go. You can feel the rightness of it."

"No," he repeated. "I can only feel how important it is to you, why you think it's important. And I can't even think my own thoughts. I can't think straight when you're in there."

"Carlos," Joanie said sharply. "You just need practice. It's perfectly possible to listen and think at the same time. But it takes practice. And you don't practice. All you want to do is code."

"Stop femsplaining, Joanie. I've heard it all before. I'm good at coding. I should stick to what I'm good at."

"Wrong. You're not good at coding."

"You are so full of it today, Joanie. I can outcode you any day of the week." Carlos flipped a coding cube at her, and she deftly scooped it up, as he'd known she would. Joanie could never resist a direct challenge. "First one to get that drone!" He nodded toward an eight centimeter long, green and white striped one hovering on the shelf. Deftly he began to whirl his cube's coding keys which glowed under his fingers. Carlos loved machine language. The orderly arrays formed in his mind, and he quickly translated them into the fine movements his fingers had been training for – for a decade now – although the interface device had been through several iterations. Adapting the Rubik's cube was an idea he'd been proud of. He was distracted by a whirring shadow. The drone hovered over her head, its props flicking the light beaming from the wall lamp.

"Whaat!" he thought as she handed him her strangely cold cube. "Wait, that's no fair. You didn't program a thing. How did you? That drone was clean. I'd wiped it myself."

"But there's always the shadow of memory there," she thought. And this time, stunned with surprise, he heard her thought and behind the thought, the memory of burning hands, of ashfall. Wordlessly he gave in, and they headed for the blue bustle and hubbub of the club where the others waited for them.

Music calling

When I got back, the apartment was empty except for a drone hovering over Carlos's workspace. I tried to find the controller for it but the one I found didn't seem to have any effect. A twinge of anxiety. Is it a spy drone? Has there been a raid? Here?

But the feel of the room – no, not a raid. Some kind of adolescent competition. I could smell it, then spotted the two programming cubes and knew I was right. Aggravated, I snatched the drone out of the air and wrestled the batteries out of its belly. "Back on the shelf with you!" I yelled. Talking to myself again. Not a good sign, right?

But where have they gone? I try to tamp down the worry. If Joanie feels me worrying, she'll be angry with herself. So much like her dad at that age. "Have confidence in the youth!" It's a slogan with sliver of truth to it, but defies expectations, parentally speaking. They're really good kids, Joanie and Carlos, but our world makes it way too easy, compulsory even, for them to get into trouble.

A syncopated ringtone saves me from this self-inflicted droning and moaning. My friend Janice urgently blurts, "Come by! I've got a visitor I want you to meet."

"Now? I just got home." Home from a near-death experience. I rub my chest but there's no soreness. The memory of my narrow escape is fading way too fast.

"Now's a good time," Janice breaks into my thoughts. "I'll feed you when you get here." I smile knowing she's got a week's worth of prepared meals in her freezer—some kind of subscription service and only occasionally worth eating unless you're famished – which I am. So, "Sure, give me twenty minutes." A quick note for the kids. Now why didn't they do that? And I'm out the door again.

The smog's too intense to bike through. I have to take the monorail; facial recognition software be damned. I pull down my gogmask and smile for the camera as I enter the station. I am a perky satisfied citizen. No aches and pains for this octogenarian! No reason to cull this one!

The train itself is sleek and silver and squeaky clean. No, strike the squeaky. These trains are deathly silent as they trace the hardened arteries of the City. We leave the brightly lit station and enter the microparticulate twilight. The particles seep in around the door gaskets and blur the LEDs. The few passengers with me in this car seem like ghosts, their screen-lit faces hovering in the miasma. I slip my gogmask back on and behind its cover, close my eyes remembering the rattletrap clacking and swaying, the sweat of laborers and teens returning from work and school, the hopeless pleadings of beggars, the throbbing life of it all such a contrast to this muted transport still known as the L.

Joan would be annoyed with me for this sentimental reminiscence, this selective memory. I know, I know. My eyes snap open and just in time to meet the suspicious eyes of the Robocop. "Everything okay ma'am? You're feeling well?" He waves a temperature scanner over my head.

"Just fine, thank you officer." I pop out of my seat. "Sorry to interrupt you but here's my stop." I walk briskly to the door and hope that I've succeeded in defying the cop's gait analysis. I'm a stop early but I skitter down the stairs and out the gate. Can't be too careful. I'm well past the average age of culling and any sign of weakness or senility could send me off.

But now I'm back in the thick haze. I head for the river, walking deliberately, controlling the pace of my breathing so I won't feel the resistance of the mask as it becomes saturated with exhaled moisture. On the banks of the river the mist lightens as particles are drawn down to the surface of the water by the current. Here a comfortable stroll is appropriate. I can slow down and in another twenty minutes, Janice's door opens. She smiles for the camera, gives me a big hug, one I've been needing and relax into. She breaks it off. "Come in, come in," she coughs as the pollution wafts in through the doorway. The door closes. "You don't look so good, girl," she says as I lower my mask.

"Long day," I wheeze. She hands me the inhaler that hangs from the back of the door. I take a puff and feel the bronchodilator relax my little airways and further jangle my nerves. Fight or flight, I'm ready. "So, who's this you're so eager to have me meet?"

"He's a friend of my son Nick. Another musician."

"Oh," I hesitate. "Is he, would you say, gifted?"

"Hmm, I don't think so," she sighs. "But quite talented all the same."

"He's not?" I ask the truncated question advisedly. The household appliances have ears.

"No, no. I don't believe so. But even so, friends close."

"And enemies closer," I think. When I enter the sitting room, the fireplace is glowing and a young dark, neatly bearded man is sitting as far away from the fire as he can, a saxophone in his hand.

"Kepler, this is Dr Strand," Janice introduces us. He jumps up, bows, and clicks his heels in the appropriate military form, but I step across the room and grasp his free hand. It's warm and its intrinsic musculature powerful. I force him out of his militaristic posture and into a handshake. He raises his face, and we lock eyes. No mind tag there but a friendly glint augmented by a slowly spreading smile.

"I'm pleased to meet you Kepler."

"And I you ma'am, uh, doctor," he replies awkwardly.

"Please, sit." He sits with the grace of a bird alighting on a twig. I admire the gleam of ebony, the sparkle of brass keys as he swings his instrument about and rests it carefully in his lap. "Janice tells me you're quite talented. You look like you're in the middle of something now. Please play on." He lifts the saxophone to his mouth, licks the reed a few times and launches into "Take the A train", a classic even in my youth. The tune has all the promise of a living breathing civil city, but here and there, on the edges, I can sense the hostility that hovers just outside the music, threatening the City, its people, even the music itself. Lovely and frightening. When he's finished the piece, we applaud softly. "That was a wonderful rendition!"

"I though you both might appreciate an oldie," he nods to Janice and me.

"But perhaps you could play something you've written," Janice asks smartly, asserting her best imitation of youthful vigor.

"OK. A quickie though. I need to save my lip for later."

It's a quickie indeed, a ditty that skitters and squeaks like an excited squirrel and ends abruptly. Catchy with none of the pathos. "Quite nice," I say but I can't keep the sigh out of my voice, so I add quickly, "and where do you play next?"

"Oh! Quite confidential I'm afraid." I can feel how eager he is to tell me, and I glance at Janice quizzically.

"Kepler is very popular with all sorts," she smiles discreetly, finally revealing her intentions for the meeting. So, he's a spy. "And he gives lessons. I believe you told me your granddaughter was pestering you for saxophone lessons?"

I turn excitedly to Kepler. "Would you consider it? I'm afraid we can't pay much."

"Few can afford me. But I base my charges on the talent and discipline of the student."

"She's just a beginner, I'm afraid. But she can be a hard worker."

"I'll meet with her, assess her aptitude. That much will just cost you a meal."

I pause for a moment. Meals are tight at our apartment and often less than savory. Perhaps Janice can part with one of her pre-prepared meals and I can tap into my supply of aging spices. "Do you like curry?"

"Love it." We exchange numbers, agree on a time I'll confirm with Joanie. As Kepler is packing up his instrument, he hands me a reed. "Tell her to soften this in water, then hold it in her mouth several times a day, but not to use it before the lesson. And listen to Miles."

The Club

You could hear the music throbbing from outside the club – an old-fashioned techno beat devoid of the kind of riprap Carlos favored. "We're not here for the music," he reminded himself.

"Right that," came the approving mind nudge from Joanie.

"Verrry annoying though," he thought back.

There was no line for this club at the door. Too early. But Carlos frowned to see a doorman on the threshold where colored lights were flashing. Magnified by his holographic badge, the doorman and his stun gun were an intimidating sight. He shouldn't have let them in. but Joanie produced fake IDs, smiled her winning smile, and sent a little mind twinge that Carlos was sure was unethical. "Just an identifier," she reassured him.

"He's one of us? But the gun!" thought Carlos.

"A disarmed decoy," she replied silently.

Inside the atmosphere was thick with colored vape smoke, ice mint blue and cinnamon red mostly. The vape particles danced and swirled through the light beams emanating from the empty stage. Too early for the band to be here. As they walked along the façade of the bar, the tender looked up and nodded to Joanie. She was short with swallow tattoos that flew up from her breasts and a smiling cat with an elevated paw on her arm. Carlos found his own hand rising up in response, but the tender turned and walked to the end of the bar. She ducked down briefly, then returned to drying glasses and gazing up towards . . . He'd been about to follow her gaze when Joanie interrupted. "I need to go to the bathroom," she said out loud. "Walk with me."

As they rounded the bar toward the restroom, he spotted the open hatch, the descending stairway. Joanie went down quickly into the dark. He grabbed her shoulders when behind them the shifting color and loud music was cut off by the closing hatch door. He couldn't help the terror that washed over him whenever darkness caught him. Thankfully there was no smell of chlorine, just dust and a faint scent of rose. Then his eyes adapted. A dim light shown below, and the wave of fear drew back into its ocean. He followed Joanie towards the bulb's gleam.

At first it was exciting, the below-bar cubbyhole meeting. He had to agree there were some offbeat thinkers there. No coders. And all that mindtouch, well, that took some getting used to. They'd played cards, gambled a bit, but that was just a cover. Which was good 'cause he was busted. Mostly it was a lot of mindtalk about what to do next to build the movement. "Yes, a movement," Joanie butted in over his unspoken smirk. "People, not just programs. People are the point." Her point. That seemed biocentric to him.

"Hey, it's not the robots' fault that they're programmed the way they are. We need to fix that," he'd thought. But no one had listened to him. Ignored he'd grown bored. He'd braved the dark staircase through the hatchway and slipped into an empty chair at an empty table in the dim recesses of a mostly empty bar.

The band had arrived, and a tall dark saxophonist was swaying and wailing in the tiny blue spotlight. Carlos let his mind slip into the rhythm of the music and the ideas began to flow. The robots deserved an evolutionary program with a broader scope. They needed a chance to move beyond skills, to form a moral judgment that was whole earthcentric, maybe even whole solar system centric. As the music spiraled higher and higher, the saxophone squeaked. That was the outer limit for now – the solar system.

A roboserver arrived and tried to card him. Damn, Joanie had their fake IDs down in the cubbyhole. If only he had her projection power. He could see the server's hardware circuits, its software program which was driving the robot to be increasingly insistent. "Sir, if you have no ID, you'll have to leave immediately."

He replied apologetically, like the floppy wetware he was. "So sorry," he countered and peered at its nametag, "Merry. I must have left it at home. I'll just be on my way then." But he sat stock still, focusing on the last joint of its little finger, trying to stop-start the flow of electrons in there. There! A twitch! He'd seen it!

"Sir, sir! Are you alright? Should I call you a Lift?"

Carlos smiled up at Merry. Proof of principle! "Thanks, but no, Merry." He slid his chair back and felt himself gliding across the room, fully entrained in the rhythm of the saxophone. Strange how much easier it was to move his bowed legs when there was music. The bartender caught his eye and his heart hammered back a reply. Was she blushing or was that just the reddened vape smoke?

Once through the door Carlos slipped on his mask and stood next to the doorman. He tried to reach out to Joanie, to let her know he'd been kicked out. He needed her to come up so they could head home on the train. No way he was doing that by himself. Cops, bangers, little old ladies. they were all drawn to his shortness like it gave them the excuse to do whatever they liked. Joanie had tried to teach him her projection of authority approach, but it just didn't work for him. For now, he heard no response from her, nothing but the band. The mental pathways were all buzz and squeak, jammed.

The doorman leaned down to him. "You can wait with me son. They'll be done in ten minutes." So he was stuck standing around like a little kid. His feeling of belittlement grew with each patron the doorman waved into the club. A long line was forming, chattering, shouting, hooting. Carlos hung on to his sense of self-respect by the twitch of a fingertip.

Joan lingered in the meeting, hoping Carlos would return. When she'd seen him creeping up the staircase, disappointment had washed over her. She'd hoped the intrigue of the meeting, the cachet of its location, would grab him. She herself felt immersed in the web of possibility that the debates here had at their core: a world where the surveillance state would end, where people could move freely beyond the boundaries of the camps and corporate powers, where everyone recognized their shared humanity and could turn their attention to solving the problems that faced them, problems that condemned most to starvation and an early death while a few lived comfortably, their communities guarded and gated.

Her mentor Gladys had lived in one of those communities once. She'd been cast out for secretly sheltering a child she'd found hiding under a rosebush in her garden. About three years old Gladys had thought. The child, Denise, was only eight when a neighbor had informed on them. Gladys was expelled. Denise was taken away to one of the secret child prisons. At sixteen she'd be released across the border wall, into a desert death. Four years from now. Four years was Gladys's timetable for the change that would keep that from happening.

Others argued that one could not adhere to a timetable – that only when they reached a critical mass of changed minds would they be able to change the system. Not that it wasn't urgent, both sides agreed. Humans were using up the planet as fast as they could and, so, rendering it uninhabitable within a century, perhaps decades. Already millions were dying each year of new viruses, disruptions in the food supply, heat, and storms. Joan took a deep breath and escaped from that mental image – the spiral of devastation and despair swirling around them. Here there was hope. If only Carlos had been able to feel it.

She wondered why he avoided hope by escaping into puzzles and programming. Was it seeing his own parents' hopes dashed? His father's furies? His mother's faith rewarded with incineration. Deep breath. She'd ruminated long and hard on the deaths of their parents before. She put that rumination back in its box, the cemetery at her center. She felt Gladys's mindtouch and returned her attention to the matters at hand. But Carlos, Carlos is key she thought.

With a little help from my friend

"Eat!" commanded Janice. "You don't have to tell me you had a hard day. I can tell." Obediently I wolfed down her tasteless food and diet cola. Stomach stuffed I leaned back, gazed into the solar fire's glow and, safe in her living room's illicit Faraday cage, talked through my entire day – the stunning, the naturally filtered air, the gogmask retrieval, the paranoid train ride to her place. Although I seemed to remember the facts, the emotional memories had dimmed oddly. I was relieved to get that day off my chest though.

At the conclusion of this recitation, I looked up to meet Janice's concerned, slightly incredulous gaze. "Quite a story. I wonder if you haven't been more affected than you realize. Would you be willing to stay here tonight? Let me keep an eye on you? You can stay in Nick's old room."

Suddenly there are tears in my eyes. The two of them, age ten, bent over comic books, age five draped in superhero capes, age three singing "De Colores" in preschool. Sleepovers were for our sons, not us, in the old days, before the scrim fell, when climate change was just a little blip on our radar screen of concerns. Now my son was dead while Nick lived. And as supportive as Janice was, a gap had opened between us. I had Joanie and Carlos to consider. "I shouldn't leave the kids alone."

"They're not little anymore," said Janice gently. "And you will be leaving them eventually. How about making it later rather than sooner?"

The play on words defeated me. "Huh? I should get home right away?"

"See what I mean?" asked Janice. "You're breathless. Your processing speed is down. Pollution aftereffects. O_2 tent's upstairs. I'll call Joanie and let her know you're in it."

"But . . ." Then my resistance collapsed, and I allowed myself to be ushered up the stairs. At the top I was gasping and seeing stars. Janice steadied me and guided me to the billowing yellow tent. There she had me strip, checked me for ticks, attached an oximeter. I crawled stiffly into a lightweight purple sleeping bag. Purple's her favorite color I thought. Or lilac as I processed ever so slowly yet briefly the back of my eyelids.

That night I dreamed I was on the train platform with a troop of robosoldiers who looked menacing as usual. The blue gleam on their blackened steel frames, the red eyes glowing above their infrared cheek black, the multi-shot weapons built into their arms, all intimidated me as they were designed to do. Then something strange happened. They turned to face one another. They huddled together. They started singing – not some militaristic march but a gentle hum and squeak, almost like whales. I couldn't make out words, but it was very soporific, guiding me back to the soothing darkness of REMless sleep.

Anxiety and answers

He'd given her the silent treatment all the way home. She deserved it many times over. Showing off with the drone. Dragging him to that meeting. Making him wait outside. But underneath his sulk, he was brimming with excitement, overflowing with energy. Then they walked into that empty apartment. His excitement morphed to alarm. "Grandma Katie?" he called out desperately. "Where is she?" he whirled on Joan.

"Oh relax. She texted me. She's at Janice's place. Got a little pollution hangover from her hike today."

Carlos dialed down his anxiety from 100 to 75 but that didn't keep him from wailing, "Why didn't you tell me? Is she okay?"

"You were giving me the silent treatment, remember? She's fine," Joan replied curtly.

"<u>She</u> said she was fine? She's never stayed out before." Anxiety level now 60 reported his internal monitors.

"Actually, Janice said Grandma was fine but needed a night in an O_2 tent. Don't worry. Look on the bright side. We can stay up all night working if we want to. Aren't you excited just a little bit, Carlos?"

"How can you be so relaxed when Grandma's sick and you didn't even talk to her?" Anxiety level back to 70. "I can't be excited when I'm worried like this." He felt Joanie's reassuring mindtouch and let it in.

"She's getting older, Carlos. This kind of stuff is going to happen. But you know she'd want us to keep inventing, planning, organizing, right?"

"Whoa! You're talking about her as though she's dead Joanie. She's not dead, is she? Not dead, not dead, not dead, not dead." Carlos found himself repeating like a mantra. He curled up into a ball and rocked for some time. He didn't know how long but when he was down there in the dark chanting, a husky reed sound penetrated the dark with a mellow glow. He followed the glow sound up to the apartment where he crouched on the carpet listening to the saxophone, remembering the cute bartender and the interruption of a roboserver whose little finger . . .”

“Joanie, I made her finger move,” he blurted out as an intense joy filled his heart and wiped away the gloom.

Joanie was sitting beside him, her arm around his shoulders. Suddenly it was embarrassing. He stood up abruptly and had the satisfaction of her looking up at him. “I made the roboserver at the bar move her little finger. I’m not sure how I did it, but I did.”

Joan smiled and got to her feet too. “That’s great Carlos. Let’s go figure it out.”

She wanted to take him by the hand but remembered at the last minute that he was too old for that now. He’d see it as a come on or, worse, as though he were being treated like a child. And he was definitely beyond childhood. She thought of him like a younger brother, not boyfriend material. But she knew he felt otherwise, at least some of the time. They needed a wider circle of friends and collaborators to avoid this icky romance trap that their isolation was steering them toward. The problem was that Carlos was very self-conscious. He was short and anxious, and the anxiety sometimes got out of control. It was a pain to have to be around it all the time.

She’d been stupid to aggravate him with that drone duel. When they got back to Carlos’s room, the drone and the cube controllers sat neatly on the shelf – a brief mystery until she realized grandma must have swung by here on her way to Janice’s. The point of that duel had been to jolt him out of the solitary retreat he’d sunk into. Jerking off with circuits when the world needed him, needed both of them. For some reason, she couldn’t read him now, so she had to ask, “Did you like going to the meeting?”

“No. I didn’t like it. It was boring and they didn’t listen to me. That’s why I left.”

“I listened to you. About the robosoldiers? I think you’re right. The others will too if you give them a chance. It’s a big deal to stop thinking of someone or something as an enemy and consider them an ally, or a potential ally anyway. They need time to adjust to the idea. Come back, please.”

“Aw Joanie. They’re not going to listen to me. I’m not even a real empath. <u>You</u> have to say it.”

"I will but you have good ideas. I need you there to back me up, to catch me if I'm wrong."

"You wrong! You're admitting you might actually be wrong sometimes?" he laughed. But it was a surprised laugh. He wasn't bitter. She felt the barriers between them lowering and smiled. "I want to go back and try to influence that roboserver again. Oh, and see that cute bartender," Carlos confided.

Now it was her turn to laugh, to relax a little. "Hey, you have to go to at least part of the meeting with me."

"Definitely. It's my cover," casting her a shifty gaze like that spy cartoon he loved.

"So, what do you think is actually happening that might explain all this telepathy, telekinesis, circuitry stuff?"

"Sheer magnetism," he smiled. "What else could it be?"

Energies

When I awoke the sun was shining through the yellow tent, setting it aglow. I felt refreshed, ready for another day on the Trail. But a first a long luxurious stretch. Boy, was I stiff. And the sleeping bag was purple, not aqua. The zipper on the wrong side. Uneasily I unzipped the tent fly and my soaring mood crashed. The sun I'd imagined was just a light alarm clock because, of course, the scrimmed sky had an entirely different cast to it. I was at Janice's place, not the Trail.

My Trail experience had been more than a decade ago, well before scrim catastrophe. I'd fled there immediately upon retirement, escaping to solitude of a sort, to the outdoors, escaping from hospital and clinic interiors and submersion in the wants and needs of patients, trainees, colleagues, and bosses. And especially escaping the worst of it all: irrational and damaging demands of administrators and their computers. All that was behind me now. Well not the incompetent uncaring administration. We seemed to have a surfeit of that in our daily lives presently, thanks to the Federated Consolidated Power (FCPower), our current version of "popular" industrial government.

I took a deep breath of the oxygen-enhanced air billowing out of the tent to clear my mind, turned off the tank and crept downstairs, trying not to wake Janice who, in retirement herself, is no longer an early riser. The dawn ride back to my apartment was uneventful, the train full of half-lidded commuters staring at their phones. I didn't like carrying one. Made tracking too easy although who was I kidding. Cameras were everywhere these days along with the priciest facial recognition taxes could buy. The FR screwed up quite a bit though so sometimes cell phone tracking could be used by the defense. Ah, how quickly the mind wanders.

At the apartment I brewed a pot of coffee, and soon Joanie shuffled into the kitchen in the elephant-headed slippers that had been her father's, my son's.

She grabbed a cup of coffee, added a half-cup of milk and sat across from me at the table. "Are you alright, Grandma?" Joanie could be a worrier I remembered guiltily.

"Actually, I feel great!" It was true I realized with a bit of a shock. After a half-cup of coffee my mind was no longer muddled, and my body zinged with a kind of energy I hadn't felt in a long time. As I gently tapped my sternum, only any tiny bit of soreness from yesterday's misadventure persisted. Joanie didn't need to hear about that. "Those oxygen tents must really have something to them."

"I think it's more likely the filtration than the extra oxygen," offered Joanie.

"Hmm. Getting technical, are we? I thought you were focused on empathy building." I was curious about Joanie's pursuits about which, true to teen form, she was quite circumspect.

"I want to know how things work, that's all. Empathy included," she replied impatiently.

"That would be very good to know, I think. Although I do kind of enjoy the mystery of it." I myself lacked the kind of powerful empathy that Joanie had, that let her see through the eyes of others, seemingly read their thoughts, even project her own. I'd considered myself a fairly empathic physician, but Joanie's skill, or talent, had an entirely different dimension to it. Interestingly enough, we were rather opaque to each other, and that was a definite irritant to Joanie. I had to be explicit with her. "I think it has something to do with mirror neurons."

"Yes," Joanie replied, pleased. "But it's got to be more than that. How can I get other people to hear me when I think?"

"You can't, not everyone," I sighed. "But I have an idea. Study the saxophone."

"That is so utterly random, Grandma."

"Maybe there's a musical element in the empathy trait," I proffered.

"Not in my group!" she protested. "They're almost as tone-deaf as I am."

"Maybe you just need to expose yourself to musical practice a bit more. Last night I met a nice young man, a saxophonist who's eager for students."

"Are you trying to set me up?" Joanie sputtered.

"No, no. It's not that." We paused and I knew she was trying to get into my head. I tried to lower whatever barriers there might be, but after a minute or so of intense concentration, she sighed.

"Grandma, I'm really too busy for the saxophone right now. But Carlos might be interested. Why don't you ask him?"

The Careerist

Day after frigging day Lt Custer Hickens patrolled the preserve. He'd had to abandon his target practice: plenty of small critters to shoot, just shortage of ammunition. While the bullets lasted, he'd exercised his artistic side, fashioning several displays of dead squirrels, birds, and raccoons, depicting the historic western scenes that his soul craved. The feathered beasts were Indians, the squirrels their mounts, and the raccoons their buffalo. Scavengers always disrupted his art within a day or two. At this point he couldn't afford the risk of photographic evidence for the muckety-mucks to find.

Instead of the noble activities of shooting and art, he spent his patrol time on baser career considerations. How could he get promoted so he could deal with that prissy captain who'd persisted in the punitive evening library assignments? Cus detested the reading and dreaded the assignment that was bound to follow. He'd end up guarding some old folks' home. On the other hand, that would give him some robosoldiers to command – just a platoon's worth at first, with a master sergeant to wipe his butt if he messed up. That posting was inevitable bullshit on the way to promotion. Inevitable unless he got caught trying to off the Captain.

Just plain shooting was too good for him and wouldn't work anyway. What he'd really like to do would be to capture him, stuff him in a cave in this preserve, and then dismember him bit by bit, keeping him alive as long as possible. He could even use the body parts to supplement his "New Visions of the Old West" series with the diminished Captain as a commanded viewer.

"Daydreaming is the refuge of the weak," his father's disapproving voice echoed down the corridor of memory. "Action backed up by planning. That's the course of the powerful, son. Take your choice." He'd been lying at his father's feet, ankle broken, helpless as a wounded squirrel squirming in pain. His mind had wandered as he'd ridden the newly broken horse Centaur out from the corral and across the grazing lands of the ranch for the first time.

He'd mastered that horse in the corral, felt comfortably in control, but his attention had been captured by a herd of antelope massed on the foothills. With that lapse in attention and will, Centaur had turned and galloped for the corral. He'd lost a stirrup on the turn and when Centaur jerked to a stop at the corral gate, lost his seat altogether and smashed his ankle against a nearby rock in the fall.

"Get up, son, now! Never grovel!" his father had shouted as he strode out of the house. Somehow, he'd regained his footing, then managed with his scrawny thirteen-year-old arms to haul himself back in the saddle. Centaur walked slowly through the gate his father opened into the stable. There he'd managed a one-footed dismount, removed the saddle and bridle. He left the sponge-down to the silent stable-hand Matt who set down his accordion and supplied Cus with a push-broom to use as a crutch.

"Ya dropped this," Matt said, handing Cus his lucky rabbit's foot. Cus stuffed it in his pocket and hobbled up the long walk to the house. The lilacs were blooming. Their scent and his pain intermingled as he hopped slowly up the steps where Ivy the housekeeper greeted him. She walked him to the kitchen where she elevated and iced his ankle, then gave him iced tea laced with whiskey to settle his stomach.

Precisely thirty minutes after his arrival in the kitchen, Ivy relayed his father's instructions. He, with his now numbed and wrapped ankle, hobbled down the long corridor of the house to his father's office. He ignored the corridor windows full of the views he loved: pastures, mountains, cattle, and clouds. He focused on the floor, on each tipsy step, on arrival at the office threshold where he permitted himself a moment of hope. He knocked and waited.

"Enter!" He opened the door and hopped over the threshold. "Sit!" He took the wingback armchair upholstered in purple, his dead mother's chair. His father glared briefly, then gazed affectionately at his son. Cus knew he resembled his mother, dead since he was three. He could use that resemblance to curb his father's irritation. Palming his rabbit's foot, he took the initiative.

"Permission to speak, sir."

"Granted," his father replied gruffly.

"Antelope in the foothills, sir."

"Ah. A distraction. Someday Custer, you'll be master of this ranch and there will be a thousand distractions. You must learn to monitor them all while honing in on those that are important. And what is important? What are the priorities Custer?"

"Control of production, control of resources, control of people," he recited.

"And what's your plan?"

Hopefully he began, "I'll continue to train Centaur daily. We'll monitor the antelope, and, in time, I'll bring back a trophy head for your study, sir." Grinning he gestured to the mounted heads that adorned the study walls. These were his ancestors' kills – deer, antelope, bear, even a buffalo.

"No!" He shriveled under his father's disapproval. "The antelope threaten our herd. They eat our grass. They carry disease. To control our resources, you must eliminate them. Come back tomorrow with another plan. Dismissed!"

That memory had come unbidden for a reason. His father was speaking to him from beyond the grave. Rabbit fever had nailed the patriarch just a year ago. Why remember now? Was the Captain just a distraction, a false target, a useless daydream?

Later that evening Cus regaled his comrades as usual with a stein in his fist, but it was filled with coffee instead of beer. A week before, while crawling through the various never-ending and extremely boring readings assigned by the prickish Captain, he'd come across a highly useful map of all the gated compounds in the country. A brilliant plan leapt like a jackrabbit into his mind. As he'd known, as everyone knew, they were spread across the country. But he hadn't known there was a gated community not twenty miles from the ranch, his ranch now that his father had died. If he could manage to get himself transferred there, escape the Eastern sweatlands . . . The idea was so sweet it kept him reading attentively enough that the chair hadn't shocked him once that evening.

His home range had hollered and yelled and whistled for him ever since he left. His father had exiled him, packed him off to the army with a rigid expression, a salute, and a tear in his eye. Cus had been glad to go just to get shut of the old man. As the land grew drier, the grass browner, the cattle leaner, Custer's father had grown gruffer and grimmer. "There's nothing here for you boy," he'd groaned one whiskey-soaked night, the night of his eighteenth birthday.

Ah, drinking in that study, the oil portraits of his ancestors glowing in the whiskey's amber light, the fumes setting his dreams ablaze. Beside them the sword of Cus's namesake radiated a coppery glow. A dust storm had been rattling the windows, pitting the panes. "Even the Mexicans don't want to come here anymore," his father had claimed.

"Sure, they do, sir!" he'd responded surprised. "They just found two bodies in the brush above Angel's Heel last week." Cus had heard about it in school – not openly but whispered from ear to ear. Still, he was surprised his father hadn't heard about it.

His father had snorted. "In my day they'd find twenty, thirty bodies a month – in the brush, in trucks, in water tanks. They died and died poor fools, trying to break into the Fortress Homeland. Waste of resources. The Wall barely slowed them down, but men, men, my boy, the army, the militias scared them into taking more risk. They couldn't just swim the river and take a hike anymore. Oh, we had 'em where we wanted 'em – out, dead, eliminated. But you know," and he leaned blearily toward Cus and held his eye, "there were some fine cowboys among 'em, vaqueros, first class."

Cus had wanted to spit. Much as he had honored his father, as duty commanded him, he couldn't bear morose sentimentality for mixed bloods like Mexicans. No better than Indians. Cus took pride in knowing his history, had aced it at school, and much of it disgusted him. He particularly detested the drunken, dirty, double-crossing Indians who'd murdered innocent settlers and slaughtered brave and true cavalrymen, his namesake among them, in sneak attacks. He knocked back his shot in one gulp.

Cus had scrambled for some fact he could offer his father to pull him out of the despair the current drought had pulled him into. "They say at school all we need to make water is hydrogen, oxygen, and a little electricity."

But his father had shaken his head slowly. "Too little, too late for this ranch son. It's blowing away in the wind. Clear those daydreams out of your head. Planning and action." With that Custer's father had handed over the train ticket and ordered. "Go East young man. Go East. Where there's water there's life."

Current thinking, current events

Carlos was thinking about water, water and electrons and how they flowed along the path of least resistance. Flow had an energy of its own. The tumbling Dutch River wore away at the banks of its own bed. In a circuit resistance could be worn away too – by overheating and vaporization. But platinum resisted that. In a magnetic field the electron stream became a tiny cyclone with a complex triple frequency. How had he diverted the roboserver's current to her finger? Had it really happened?

"I'm not following you," Joanie interrupted him, as she often did just when he might be on the brink of something. But now he felt more like he was running into a dead end.

"I have to think about it some more. How about you take a hike?" he asked somewhat coldly.

"Why not," Joanie retorted abruptly, before she could check the sarcasm. She was used to her little "brother" wanting her attention. It hurt when he shut her out like this, but it surely did no good to get huffy about it. And he was a brilliant problem-solver, though she was quicker at the applications and communications. Would he ever learn to think well with others she wondered. "Look I really don't want to interrupt you. I know you'll share what you're thinking about when you're ready," she offered. No response.

Joan left the room quietly. She wanted to contact the others, but she wasn't sure it was wise so soon after the meeting. For a moment she wallowed in bitter isolation on the living room couch. From the corner of her eye, she could see her parents' altar. A sense of desertion started to creep over her, but her grandmother called her to the kitchen, set her to grating squash. Soon fritters were sizzling in oil, and Joan settled into that moment of warmth.

At dinner time, Joan knocked on his door. "Go away!" Carlos shouted. So she did. Joan and her grandmother chatted quietly over dinner. There wasn't a lot of privacy in the small thin-walled apartment. Probably it didn't matter that much. Carlos was practically deaf when he was thinking.

Carlos emerged blearily from his thoughts with a ravenous appetite. Shit. Had he missed dinner? He burst from his room and was relieved to see Grandma and Joanie still at the table where a place was set for him. He grabbed his bowl, ladled out the rice porridge simmering on the stove, speared a squash fritter, plonked himself down and started shoveling the food in as fast as his mouth would take it. "Well, hello to you too," said Joan.

"Oh, sorry. *Itadakimasu!*[4]" he grinned.

"We ate already Carlos," said Joan in a tone that suggested she might think about forgiving him tomorrow. In contrast, his grandmother had her all too familiar kind but worried look. He noted these things but paid them no mind. Excitedly, between slurps he sputtered, "Tomorrow, tomorrow I need you for experiments Joanie."

"Please?" Joanie glared at him in mock horror.

"Please, pretty please," he grinned.

"Tomorrow Carlos," his grandmother interjected, "I set up an appointment for you."

"No more shots. I hate shots," he whined.

"Just like a baby for all his brains," thought Joan.

"No, it's a saxophone lesson," Grandma countered.

Carlos looked up from his soup slurping in surprise. The slow smile followed, lit up his face and filled his whole body. Just like that the entire kitchen filled with joy.

Joan was taken aback. She'd never known Carlos to be interested in anything but rip-rap. She tried to listen in to his mind, but all she saw was the vapy bar and even that was obscured by a buzz of excitement about his investigations. She saw the grin on her grandmother's face and relaxed, set aside her bafflement. Her grandmother gave her a weird wink as Carlos got up from the table and rushed back to his room.

---

[4] *Itadakimasu* – Let's eat. Thanks to the food and all that made it possible to eat it.

"What's wrong with your eye?" Joan asked, as she got up to wash the dishes. "My night," she insisted when her grandmother stood up to help. "But you can't keep letting Carlos off. Reinforcing sexism, Grandma."

The old woman sat down again, put her tired feet up on a chair. "You didn't expect him to agree to the lesson, did you?"

Joan scrubbed the plate a bit harder than necessary. The soapy dishwater jumped out of the sink and onto her shirt. She yelped with disgust.

"You can't predict everything, dear," her grandmother was saying.

"You don't have to tell me that," Joanie snapped.

Her grandmother looked at her quizzically. Joanie focused on picking the sticky grains of rice out from between the tines of the forks. "Why were we even eating with forks? We should have been using *hashi*[5], "she muttered.

There was silence except for the flow from the faucet. The kitchen filled with a golden glow as the lighting system registered the time of day. Carlos had installed that circuit for Grandma's eightieth birthday. It would cycle slowly through the colors of a sunset – the sunsets that he and Joanie could barely remember. The ionic scrim that had replaced the torn one blocked oblique solar rays much more thoroughly so that dusk had become colorless, a gray void that merged into starless blackness.

Well not exactly blackness. The light pollution kept the hazy atmosphere above the City a garish green. Joan had taken to wearing eye coverings at night because the streetlamp glare seeped in around the curtains. She plopped the last dish into the drainer and turned for the dirty pots on the stove. Her grandmother was gone, and from the other room she realized she could hear the low grumble of a videofeed announcer, then gunfire. She dashed out of the kitchen.

"What is it?" she asked her grandmother.

"A rebellion in the Midwest," Grandmother replied.

"Great!"

Her grandmother gave her a cautionary look. "They're burning the police station and seizing the food supplies."

"That could be good," suggested Joan.

"The FCPower's mobilizing the roboarmy. Are we ready?"

---

[5] *Hashi* - chopsticks

"No, no we're not," Joan sighed. She stared at the screen in horror as robocops, swinging their batons, waded into the rebels. She didn't even notice the trickle of overflowing dishwater as it puddled about her feet.

I knew my granddaughter's hope and despair too well. We weren't ready. Just like we hadn't been ready when the scrim tore, when the pandemics hit, when the ice caps melted, when fascists commandeered AI. Our little band of empaths. No, not so little I reminded myself. Ninety per cent of humanity understood their shared peril now. But the ten percent, with their Second Amendment Stockpiles, their Gated Communities, the Consolidated stonehearts. And behind them the zero point one percenters who plotted to live forever, to expand beyond the ruined earth.

And we ninety per cent were harried, compromising from fear and a sense of futility, until another rebellion cascaded forth, a side vent in the volcano, relieving the pressure. Inspiring but destructive and each time we'd lost more ground. I closed my eyes to the screen, that media cobra mesmerist. Am I a cobra then? I reached into my heart, lit the candle there and stared into the flame. My son and daughter-in-law danced in the flame along with my husband, my friends and colleagues lost in the struggle. I took a deep breath and blew out the flame. "You'll join them in that dance soon enough," I told myself. "Go do what needs to be done." I clicked off the videofeed and turned to find Joanie pale-faced and staring. Water from the sink was flowing into the room. I closed the kitchen tap, shook Joan out of her trance and sent her for the mop.

As Joanie mopped, I called the garden club, my son's legacy. He'd been a transplant from the Midwest, but he'd thrived in the community garden two lots down from the apartment. His early organizing efforts had been there, amidst the peach trees and the basil plants. The community elders who'd befriended him had all passed on now, but other neighbors, survivors of Scrimfall, had banded together and replanted seeds in the ashes. We spoke in code. "There's a beautiful moon tonight. Meet me on the roof and we can decide when to plant."

"You should come too," I nodded to Joan, still swabbing the kitchen floor in a most ineffectual way.

"And Carlos?" she asked.

Joan trailed me as, on the way out, I ducked my head into his room where he was intent on a circuit board. "We'll be up on the roof. Garden club meeting." Without looking up, Carlos flipped a switch under the desk. The rooftop surveillance system went on the blink from time-to-time courtesy of that switch. Joanie and Carlos had installed it a couple of years ago. Unfortunately, Joanie's interest in engineering had diminished when the Empathy Collective had discovered her. Although I appreciated the training she was getting, we needed both, empathy and technology, to get back to the Garden as the old song went.

"We may have visitors in a bit," I warned Carlos.

At that he looked up and whined, "Not tonight. I'm at a critical point here!" Then he noticed Joan's face, pale and blank, and realized a different critical point had been reached.

Joan and I put on our gogmasks, climbed two flights of stairs and the short metal ladder to the roof. Rosa and Glenn were already there. The others soon arrived, ten in all. The street below was deserted. "Curfew tonight," said Glenn. "We should keep watch, prepare for injuries." We could hear shouts to the north.

"I'll take the door," said Rosa.

"I have to do roof watch," I added, slipping on my civil defense QR [6]band. I was officially a government agent, but these neighbors knew me for who I was.

We deployed quickly. I sent Joanie below to prepare pitchers of diluted milk for the teargas, fill the bathtub with water for the pepper spray, and lay out soap, water, and clean rags for binding wounds.

From the roof I watched for wounded rebels. Then I heard the stamp of a robosoldier squadron. As I peered from behind the parapet wall, I felt him before I saw him, the squad's human officer, the patroller who'd stunned me and left me to die in the forest.

---

[6] QR - Quick Response code, a type of matrix barcode label

First Command

Lieutenant Custer Hickens assumed his first command the very morning of the rebellion. He'd known the command was coming. It was his due, and he was prepared. He'd mastered the controller strapped to his armored traumsuit and could maneuver the robosoldiers without looking, just feeling the keys as though he were playing the accordion again.

They were marching north, but he'd deployed them, not in some boring parade fashion but in a far more sophisticated swivel and dodge formation, weapons displayed and pointed at as many civies as possible. Maximal intimidation the Colonel had emphasized. The civies cowered, retreated into doorways. He grinned as he had robosoldiers pursue them until they retreated behind doors. The civie pursuit didn't slow his squad down. They easily loped back to formation when they had cleared the street.

Overhead he had drones at rooftop level. Forward, both flanks, and the rear were covered. He was slightly disappointed to see no crowds on the rooftops, no brick-throwing rebels he could target. Each building had one civil defense volunteer who responsible for preventing such crowds. If they failed in their duties, he could fire the building, but the CDVs[7] were all there, their yellow armbands QR coded and accounted for by his geolocator as they passed.

Inside his helmet the data were posted, and he could switch to views from the body cameras mounted on his R-S[8] and drones. He and his commander would review all the footage later for signs of sedition to prepare for follow-up raids, but he enjoyed watching in real time, especially the views from the R-S engaged in civie pursuit.

They marched up the hill passing the bronze statue of an American Revolutionary cavalryman whose drawn sword signaled an attack. How he

---

[7] CDV – Civilian Defense Volunteer
[8] R-S – robosoldier(s)

longed for some horseflesh beneath him, something other than these clever mechanical pants that made his steps effortless but felt like the machine they were – chill, rigid, and lifeless.

When they got to the river, they encountered their first real opposition. The river had been fired, easy enough with its petrochemical scum. Through the smoke and heat his sensors were useless. Immediately he ordered an R-S across. It marched into the murk and disappeared. He got no message of destruction but also no response when he commanded it to return from its reconnaissance. He was reluctant to put more R-S at risk. Expensive buggers.

He sent a message in to HQ seeking further orders and they arrived promptly. "Wait ten minutes. The scum will burn itself out. Then cross with your full force." He wondered if the bridge would remain structurally sound after the fire. The R-S were not light. Five hundred pounds each. If one of them sat on your chest, there was no taking a breath. Ribs snapped in the elderly, bowed inward in the young. Blood was squeezed out from the heart, air from the lungs, and there was no space for re-entry of either.

After ten minutes of this pleasant contemplation, he set his squadron marching across the blackened bridge. The flames had died down, but the haze and heat persisted. The bridge shuddered under the weight of their thudding armor. When they emerged onto the other side, there were no combatants to be seen. No looters. No one at all. And specifically, not his R-S scout. Buildings on the shoreline were smoking ruins of brick, metal and glass. No debris from the R-S. Cus threw back his head and howled in disgust. A few buttons pushed and his R-S pack joined him in wailing the escape of their prey.

AS-57189

Carlos stared at the robosoldier seated across from him. The robosoldier stared back, or rather, it seemed to. The rebels who'd delivered it had taken the precaution of inactivating its vision circuits as well as its homing and self-destruct circuits. He wasn't sure if any of these circuits were essential to the task of subverting the robosoldiers. And he was extremely concerned how the robosoldier would react to his tinkering. Still, he'd been unable to resist trying to reproduce the finger movement he'd thought he'd been able to induce in the roboserver last week. How long ago that seemed. Perhaps the finger movement had been coincidental. Perhaps it had been the conditions of the experiment: the bar setting, the music washing over them, the colored haze.

He began to drift off. He'd been awake all night, willing just that one tiny movement, but nothing, *nada, nanimonai*[9]. Shielding maybe or a programmed lack of responsiveness? The roboservers had to be tuned into a customer's wishes. They read unspoken cues, served, and soothed the customer. They never harmed the customer who was always right – until it came time to pay. They treated a customer's failure to pay as an oversight, as a tease, and only when a customer tried to leave did the roboserver's flesh-like hand become an inescapable manacle while its service cap issued a whirling blue light, alerting the owner, the bouncer, and other customers to the situation. Carlos himself didn't get out much so he'd never actually witnessed such an event, but it was a regular plot device on the videofeed programs. He'd come close to experiencing it the other night.

A roboserver would never harm a human being. Unlike a human-directed drone, robots were artificially intelligent, and everyone knew the prime directive of AI was never to directly harm humans – codified by world-wide treaties back in the teens according to his history teacher. He didn't understand how the

---

[9]nada, nanimonai - nothing

FCPower had been able to subvert the prime directive in the robosoldiers. Just a few hours ago he'd helped treat injuries the robosoldiers had caused to both rebels and bystanders. Were the robosoldiers hybrids – part drone, part AI? They always had human officers with their squads. Communications. He needed to map the communication circuits.

"Am I a prisoner?" asked the robosoldier as it had every hour since being brought to the apartment.

Carlos jerked awake. "No, you are in a workshop being repaired, AS-57189."

"It does not smell like a workshop."

Carlos was a bit offended. "Your sensory circuits have been damaged. Can you detect other damage?"

"My homing, self-destruct, and vision circuit boards have been removed. This suggests I could be a prisoner. I am entering an obsessive loop. A reset is required to prevent malfunction."

"I'm working on it AS-57189, but I require assistance. Please wait." And he went to look for Joan.

They'd been bandaging and icing and dispensing meds late into last night when Joan's grandmother had sent her to bed. "Rosa, Fran, and I can handle it from here. Tomorrow, you need to spell Carlos."

She'd gone reluctantly, exhausted but still hyped up from the assault, the injuries, and most of all the agitated minds of the wounded and helpers alike. As she lay in bed, she calmed herself with images of her other grandmother, her *obaasan*[10] and her four-year old self soaking in the hot mineral waters of the *onsen*[11]. They were with the other women and girls, their minds and bodies relaxing in the warmth of slippery water and lazy chatter. The women glided half-crouched through the water with little towels on their heads. It seemed as though she had just fallen asleep when her *bābā*[12] pushed her under the water as a flash of light appeared. She held her breath, dazzled and sightless, and resurfaced when she felt her *bābā's* grip loosening. She emerged to find charred and twisted remnants of the adults floating on the water.

She woke gasping, a light shining in her eyes, Carlos shaking her. "Wake up. Wake up. I need your help!"

---

[10] *Obaasan* - grandmother
[11] *Onsen* – Japanese hot spring bath
[12] *Bābā* - granny

She calmed her breathing – that stupid dream again. "Ok, Carlos. OK. What is it?"

"Just come with me. It says it's entering an obsessive loop. Needs a reset." Carlos filled her in on the progress, or lack of it, in the previous eight hours as she threw on a bathrobe and slippers. They quickly padded down the hallway to the workshop where the robosoldier was repeating "Robosoldier Private First Class AS-57189."

Carlos responded first with an introduction. "AS-57189. You have entered an obsessive loop. I am the repairman. This is my assistant."

Joan looked dubiously at Carlos, but they had no time for debate. "AS-57189. I am RA1, repair assistant," she stated crisply. She set to work exploring his AI circuits empathically, trying to flow with the electrons and not to trip anything.

"Robosoldier Private First Class AS-57189." It repeated.

She grabbed a nearby pad and pen and scribbled hastily. "One hour 'til shutdown or breakout."

Carlos sighed, mouthed "Shit."

"Robosoldier Private First Class AS-57189," it repeated in a slightly more urgent tone.

"AS-57189, you are not a prisoner," Carlos tried again as Joan shook her head.

"Confirmation code requested," AS-57189 responded.

"Confirmation codes in lockdown due to central database breach," Joan intoned, sounding strangely like a robosoldier herself. "Officer detail currently unavailable. Please hit pause. Await further instruction."

"Robosoldier Private First Class AS-57189 confirming pause."

Joan felt the cessation of electron flow and grabbed the notebook pad. "Ten-hour temporary shutdown. Go get me breakfast BOSS," she scribbled. Carlos grinned and headed for the kitchen. Joan could feel his amusement and fatigue and decided to send him off to sleep as soon as he returned with food. Assistant indeed.

Evacuation

The flow of doctoring subsided slowly. I was grateful the injuries had not been too severe, that chemical attack had not been unleashed, that the robosoldiers had not dislodged the gogmasks of their victims. I knew robosoldiers could be lethal when they wanted to be – no not when *they* wanted to be, I corrected myself. When their human handlers wanted them to be. I'd recognized that squadron's human handler.

Fear, anger, fear. The usual sequence. He hadn't recognized me. The robosoldiers and their human deployer had moved on, but my autonomic nervous system was not so easily subdued. Just as well. It was a long night. The demobilized robosoldier arrived only an hour after the force had passed by. The revulsion I felt on sight was irrational but rehearsed, a playback from past encounters. Carlos, of course, was delighted. He'd helped with the injuries reluctantly. He was skittish that way, almost relieved when the medical system breakdown had made his corrective surgery impossible.

I left Carlos to deal with the R-S reluctantly. I knew he could be summarily executed if it recovered its function, but the injured were arriving at my door fast and furious. Triage. Risk reduction. The apartment wasn't big enough for his work with the robosoldier to go on discreetly. We relocated the impromptu infirmary down the hall to Rosa's place.

Funny how the exercise of my professional faculties clears the emotion away. It takes a moment to kick in. At the first sight of blood, I catch my breath, then my vision narrows, my mind focuses and anything else takes a backseat to the issues at hand. Twelve hours later I stumbled over a patient on the floor, and Rosa grabbed me. "You're going back to your apartment to get some rest," she insisted sternly. With her touch I was suddenly exhausted. She walked me down the hall. Her red hair was flowing, and her perfume took away the stench of blood.

Supine but sleepless I pondered the patroller. Had he kept his secret sadism for the preserves? Too much to hope for. If he'd spotted me during their march, or from the drone footage he'd probably review later, I was already late in leaving this location. And the robosoldier they'd captured should leave as well. Why hadn't I thought of this before? Ah, the wounded had taken precedence and now I was beyond fatigue. As I lay on my bed hallucinatory images flickered before my eyes – a blackened eye, a fractured tooth, a burn transforming from reddened skin to blister, a gruesome burn to bone. I had had no rest and really there was no time for rest.

I woke with a start. Painfully I got up and hobbled down the hallway, knees aching. A light shone under the door of Carlos's bedroom, the "workshop". I put my ear to the door. Carlos and Joan and a third voice – the robosoldier sounding strangely human. I knocked quietly and Carlos came to the door.

"I need to speak with you and Joan," I whispered. Through the crack in the door, I saw Joan glance up at me, inquiring, but Carlos interrupted before we could establish contact. He stepped into the hallway and closed the door.

"She can't be interrupted. She's at a critical point with AS-57189," Carlos warned me.

I couldn't help smiling. "Is that its name then?" I took Carlos to the kitchen where we could talk without whispering. "We can't stay here Carlos. The squad commander knows me or will know me on the footage. He'll have my CDV QR code. He'll come here – and soon I suspect. We must leave – all of us. The robosoldier included, obviously."

Carlos looked alarmed. "It's 500 pounds, Grandma. And we don't have control."

"Hush now. We'll find a way. I think I know someone who can help. He was planning to come over tonight anyway."

"The saxophone man?" Carlos asked incredulously.

"Music, *cariño*[13], music," I crooned. Carlos gave me one of his "you've really lost it now, Grandma" looks. "Go get your things together before you go back with Joan and the robosoldier.

"Do you think it's safe to leave her alone with it?" he asked anxiously.

____

[13] *Cariño* – dear one

"I think she can let us know if she feels she's in danger. And maybe some alone time is just what they need." I wasn't sure of that by any means, but I went to pack just the same. Where could we go? I was rolling up my least-holey socks when I realized where we'd have to go. A nauseating memory of chlorine filled my nostrils.

Force loss

Custer didn't like how this was going. Why did the low man on the totem pole always get blamed? "You lost a robosoldier, Lieutenant? Lost it? Why on earth did you think it was a good idea to march it into an impenetrable fog."

"It was an order, sir.

"You were the officer on the ground. It was your duty to assess the conditions, report the conditions, propose an alternative order, you dimwit," the Captain roared.

"I was just following the *Colonel's* orders," Cus replied, noting as he did so that he sounded whiny. "Sir," he added snappily.

"Get to work on the vidfeed review," the Captain growled and stalked out.

Custer's stomach added its own growling to the Captain's. He thought about sneaking over to the mess hall for some dinner. Too risky. He'd just text one of the guys and have them bring him something. When he reached for his phone, he remembered the Captain had confiscated it so they could make sure he hadn't been distracted or collaborating with the enemy during the action. Him! A collaborator. The command were such idiots.

He glanced out the window, spotted an R-S striding across the domed parade ground, and tried to hail it, but it ignored him. Off on some Command errand he supposed. He pulled his head back in and jumped, surprised to find one of his buds Steve had snuck up on him. Steve guffawed. Cus colored and contemplated a punch in the nose but stopped short when Steve pulled out a food bag from behind his back. His buds had teased him when he'd been stuck in the library, gunning for a command. But they were good guys. A hamburger, fries. He hesitated at the beer.

"I got a long night coming up. Vidfeed review."

"Have a beer to get started. I'll get the coffee brewing," Steve offered, turning to some beat-up coffeemaker in the corner. "Tell me what happened, man. I'm guessing your first command didn't work out. We could hear the Captain swearing all the way from the mess hall."

Cus shook his head slowly, bit his tongue, grabbed the bag of food. "Boring. Shitass boring. Just a bunch of civies huddled in the doorways. Until we got to the river. It was on fire, bud, on fire! Standing orders were to pursue. The bridge seemed intact, so I sent an R-S across. It just frigging disappeared."

"Oh, that sucks man. I'm sorry." Steve patted his shoulder.

Cus shrugged him off. He didn't like being touched by other men. Too gay. Women either. He should be the one doing the touching. "Command needs to suck it up. It was their order."

"So *you* claim," said Steve.

"What's that supposed to mean?" Cus sputtered, nearly losing a mouthful of fries in the process.

"I just hope you have proof on that vidfeed because your gonna face some serious shit – demotion, pay deduction, service extension, maybe even a little stockade time. I mean, losing an R-S." Cus guzzled the beer like it might be his last and loaded the video. Steve kept his mouth shut after that but stuck around until midnight or so. Good guy.

Cus stared at frame after frame: video from each robosoldier, from every drone. But his first tack through was satellite footage. He wanted to see if he could penetrate the ground smoke that covered the river and obscured the bank on the other side. Nothing. The R-S went into the smoke and never emerged. He used the AI assistant to track the CDVs and note their QR codes. Maybe they'd had a different angle on the bridge from the tops of their buildings, especially those close to the river.

When he found his lids drooping, he used an old trick: editing in the soundtrack of the Military Medley on the accordion. The stable hand Matt had given him that accordion, given it to him when his father had let Matt go after the last horse died. Matt had been a good guy, like Steve. His father had given up. He would never give up, give in, just cave like that. Disgusting. By dawn Cus's stomach ached from the lukewarm rotgut coffee, but maybe he'd found something, someone, just maybe.

Undercover

Carlos had figured that it would come to this day. Abandonment. Leaving his projects, his bed, the memories tied to this apartment, to this building. His whole life as far back as he could remember it. He grabbed a gym bag, stuffed it with a change of clothes, a toothbrush, deodorant (maybe he'd meet someone on the run!), then came upon a misshapen bit of metal. What was left of his father's watch. Not leaving that behind. But most of his gear was in his workshop with Joan and AS-57189. He needs a name. "He?" Carlos could imagine Joan saying. "He??"

As he moved down the hallway the muted ring of the busted doorbell sounded. A knock followed. He froze. Grandma shot down the hallway to the door ahead of him. She peered through the peephole. He didn't know how she managed to see anything through that thing. But apparently reassured, she slipped the chain and opened the door. It was him. The tall black saxophonist, case in hand, ducked through the doorway and greeted his grandmother. "So, who's the lesson for again?"

"Kepler, I'm so glad you could some," she said, closing the door calmly. "A double lesson if you don't mind. My grandson Carlos . . .". She laid a hand on his shoulder, and they walked together back to the workshop. Next to Kepler's lanky frame, Carlos felt even more dwarfed than usual.

Joan glanced up as they entered the workshop. She and Kepler smiled at each other. Carlos felt a twinge of envy. They must have been in empathic touch.

"The master repairman," AS-57189 said. He sounded pleased with himself.

Carlos was shocked to see an alert AS57..., no, just AS – that's what he was going to call him from now on. Darn, AS knew what was happening better than he did.

"That's right," said Joan. "Now we're going to move on to working with the new controller device, the one that will make it possible to work undercover, AS-57189."

"How about just AS," Carlos blurted.

He felt Joan's disembodied glare but AS responded with an analytical tone. "Sensible for undercover work." Carlos was amazed. Joanie had done it, achieved a reset of some kind. But would it work to get the R-S out of the apartment? He noticed the R-S visual circuits were still not operational. Good.

Carlos dutifully squelched his curiosity and started surveying the room for what he'd take with him: his laptop, his tool bag. He'd have to leave the games he used to clear his mind. He'd miss Quadrilateral Cowboy. He loved beating QC, but the old red backpack would carry only so much stuff. A backpack and a gym bag wouldn't be too attention-grabbing if it was just him and someone else with the same gear. Gym and school.

Kepler was assembling his saxophone. There was an extra silver gadget that he fit in between the mouthpiece and the body of the instrument. Carlos didn't remember that from the bar. Some kind of pickup maybe? When Kepler began to blow, Carlos heard nothing, but the robosoldier pivoted. "Where are we at?" Kepler stopped to ask.

"Soft reset," Joanie and AS synchronously replied.

Joanie leaned into the memory of the muted upstairs sound of Kepler's saxophone even as she continued to surf AS's circuitry. She was both exhausted and exhilarated. Could she let Kepler take it from here? A soft "no" floated into her mind. "Let's get him dressed and walking. Then you'll take over his evacuation."

"Who should go first?" she wondered.

"The visual circuits are presently damaged, so you'll hold his hand. You and he are a couple – a furtive one, taking to the shadows." Kepler said to AS and Joanie. "I'll follow ten minutes later with Carlos, but he and I will go to my studio while you and AS have a different destination," he thought, this time to Joanie alone. "You and AS will go where couples usually go, the cemetery," Kepler said aloud.

"Orders?" asked AS.

"Correct, orders," Kepler said it aloud, but Joanie thought it into AS. It was strange to be mentally adrift in his circuitry, surfing through the branch points, struggling to map the intricate logic that underpinned this lethal intelligence. Exhilarating, dizzying, an electronic vortex. She needed Carlos to keep her grounded. Or someone. A bit of panic now at the audacity of this rebellious AI-napping.

"Pause for further orders at the Tomb of the Unknown Soldier. Good luck AS, Repair Assistant Gloria," said Kepler.

He'd named her and she was oddly pleased with his choice of name. Not to be outdone she replied, "Understood Master Repair Sergeant Diogenes."

Kepler winced. He was infamous for his self-imposed deprivations, his stoicism. Joan grinned. They'd finished dressing AS in clothes Kepler had brought – dark shirt and pants, leather jacket and hat. "A real busyboy," Joan joked without speaking.

"Don't trash my style," Kepler joked back, though of course it wasn't his style at all. She wondered where he'd gotten the clothes. She worried.

"Bangers could jump us for fashion like this," she thought.

"Nah, he's too big. But if it happens, run. It could get messy."

"Wardrobe complete. Time to get going," Kepler announced.

The R-S AS saluted. Joan followed suit, then took his hand. They left the apartment and headed for the elevator that would take them down. Her breath caught as someone stepped in on at the second floor, but the person took no notice, just practiced eyes front on the door etiquette as the odd couple stood behind them. After ten seconds of holding her breath, Joan steered AS to follow the neighbor out of the elevator into the subterranean passageways through which they could walk to the cemetery.

AS's neural pathways were fairly quiet. He was focused on walking while blind. She'd thought about telling him to limp as a way of disguising his unusual height and mass but decided that would only draw more attention to them. By this time, they'd survived several seasons of scarcity since Scrimfall. Adolescent growth spurts had been stunted. Plants grew quickly now in the CO_2 enhanced atmosphere, but they were often nutrient poor. Joan was being groomed to be an industrial agronomist at school, a school she'd tested into and wished she could test out of again. A new boyfriend. Someone from school was bound to pick her out of the city vidfeed and start rumors. This was going to be complicated, assuming she made it back to school.

She guided AS around another turn. It was growing darker and less populated. Bangers had taken out some of the lights and cameras up this way so they could conduct their business in private. Another reason she'd decided against the limp was because she'd worried they might pick him out of the cityfeed as possibly having been injured during the R-S march, therefore a rebellion suspect. Here it would have made him a target. But that happened anyway.

"Hey you, busyboy," a banger leaning against the wall called out.

"Just keep going. You're undercover," she said quietly.

But at the next turn a banger stepped out into their path. "You don't wanna talk to us, busyboy?"

Joan took a mental dive into AS's vocal circuits. "Naw man. It ain't like that. Me and my girl, we gotta get to the Cemetery." The banger backed off fast after that. Bangers knew death, first, second, and third hand. Many of them were Scrimfall orphans who'd survived among the dead, scavenging, some said looting, for survival. Few had ended up with much wealth from that. All had been traumatized she knew, as she did her best to close off the empathy leaks which were about to overwhelm her. At last, the elevator to the Cemetery. She tugged at AS and they trotted to the open and thankfully vacant elevator. She jabbed at the up button. The ground doors closed ever so slowly as the bangers' nightmares tried to force their way into her perception. As they rose, the nightmares drifted away.

The doors opened to a sunny smoggy afternoon. Headstones stretched in long white lines into the eye-stinging yellow mist. She put on her gogmask and reached up to slip a similar mask onto AS. He didn't need it of course, but it was an absolute requirement if he were to pass as human here on the surface. Almost no one was rich enough to afford a lung transplant every two years.

The Lesson

Carlos managed a squawk on the saxophone. Kepler clapped him on the shoulder in congratulation. He'd been playing, or trying to play, or trying just to get a sound out of the busted thing for over thirty minutes. Kepler had insisted on a full lesson, in order "to leave a trail" he'd claimed. So Carlos had unscrambled the apartment cameras that linked to the city vidfeed, and the lesson had begun.

"I'm awful at this!" Carlos complained.

"That's why we kicked everyone out of the apartment," Kepler reminded him. "Listening to beginners practice is never a pleasant musical experience, especially not on a wind instrument. But it gets easier. Remember thirty minutes a day. Be sure your reed is moist and quit when your lip starts feeling too sore."

Carlos only sighed in response. "Why don't you come with me to the Club and listen again, get back into enjoying the possibilities?" Kepler suggested.

Carlos stuck to the script. "Sure," he said but his heart really wasn't in it.

Kepler took the saxophone from Carlos but instead of putting it away, launched into a high-pitched ditty from the hyperpop net, quick and funny. Carlos found himself giggling, then laughing out loud. He couldn't stop until Kepler reached the coda. "Let's go," Kepler grinned.

"You're on," Carlos grinned back, and they headed for the door.

"Leave a note for your grandma so she won't worry," Kepler reminded Carlos. He left it on the altar, then followed Kepler out.

But they didn't go to the club. When Carlos realized they were headed for the river, where the drowned pool lay, he lagged. "I can't go there," he thought fiercely, hoping that Kepler could hear him like Joanie did, even if he wasn't a trained empath. But there was no thought back.

They entered the recently restored bar, an example of the new architecture buttressed out above the torrent below. Lights twinkled in the windows. The bridge reconstruction project had just been completed last year. The windows were meant to give you a view of the bridge. But the bridge hadn't lasted even one season. A month after completion Hurricane Ida had hammered its way inland. The storm tide had surged upriver, and the moorings swept away. Cables screaming in the wind, the bridge of the century had snapped from above. Now the view was of the twinkling ferry, tiny against the breadth and length of the enlarging river.

Kepler was early for the gig. He bought some enchiladas for them to share with his bandmates as they trickled in. It was an old school LatinX band with some traditional instruments Carlos was surprised to see. In school he'd learned that stuff had been outlawed when the southern border blockade started. Then a guy in a black suit trimmed with silver bells sat next to him; Carlos got nervous. Kepler came back to introduce the guy, Juan. "He'll take you from here," Kepler said. Juan nodded, stood, and waited for a confused Carlos to start moving. Kepler waved goodbye and turned to take the stage. He lost no time launching into an amazing solo that seized every eye in the place.

Before Carlos had a chance to let the shock of this desertion settle, Juan grabbed his elbow and hustled him out of that room to the next. A raucous dance party left his objections buried in a wall of sound. Juan gestured to the chairs that lined the wall. Carlos took a seat while avoiding eye contact with the little kids who made up almost all the sidelined population. The adults were all on the dance floor, from the grandmas to the teens. The guys were wearing black suits with bells, the women dark red with wooden clappers on their shirts. A third group wore swirling striped cloaks. They danced on and on and on as Carlos gradually slumped against the wall. The noise dimmed. Fatigue crept over him and quietly overwhelmed his resentment at being stuck out on the edge, away from real action.

Return to the depths

When I returned, they were gone – the robosoldier, Kepler and the kids. Before leaving the apartment, I'd straightened up a bit, cleaning away the blood and bandages of the injured, but trying to leave enough mess so that it might seem to the casual observer or sloppy investigator that the family would be returning shortly. I'd taken the garbage to Rosa's. Together we'd repacked it into shopping bags so she could distribute it around the city wastebaskets. In order to elude the garbage inspectors, we'd both been perfecting our personas as bag ladies and dumpster divers. Sadly, I'd aged out of dumpster diving a couple of years ago after a knee injury that I still felt in intense moments – like now.

I wondered if I'd see the kids again or would it be like Scrimfall – my family vaporized. This nostalgia is not improving your speed I scolded. My exit bag had been surreptitiously packed a long time ago. Still, I took time to light a candle in front of the posthumous sketch I'd done of my son and his wife. Their photos had all been incinerated, the digital images lost when the servers melted – the great Cloud melting. After a meditative moment, I kissed and burned the note Carlos had left on the altar. The candle lit my steps down the darkened hall. The elevator took me to the ground floor. I staggered out into the murk.

The river level had risen over the years, so high that it lapped at the highway. I loaded my bags with rubble ostentatiously at the shore and waded in. Just another eldercide as far as the monitors would see. When the water was up to my neck, I found the cover pedal that my feet had been searching for and activated it. Reluctantly I sank into the greasy water and entered an underwater tube. The tube door closed and pressurized air displaced the water that had entered with me. I dropped quickly and, for my ears, painfully, back into the grave of a decade earlier. After three minutes the tube elevator stopped, its door opened, and I fell into the arms of friends. "Come rest," they said. I stumbled to a cot and sank into darkness, into welcome oblivion.

Good hunting

Cus ran the vidfeed back and forth several times. There, on the roof overlooking his line of march with the robosoldiers, was an older woman. Her movement pattern seemed familiar, and that gogmask. The woman from the woods? The gogmask would mess up the facerec, but maybe he could blow up a shot, catch a decent view of the iris or retina to scan. He must have spent an hour on that. No luck.

He skipped on to the next segment. The drone was hovering over his position, panning for snipers as Cus was recalling the robosoldiers to continue their march to the river. As it panned the neighboring rooftop, it caught a hunched-over figure with a QR armband. Gotcha. Was it really her though? At least he had an ID. He'd send it to Phil in the ID office, get her picked up and interrogated as a suspicious character. For an instant, he hesitated. Would she be able to damage him somehow, rat out his stunning her? Naw, no one would believe an old hag like that. Clearly, she'd outlived her usefulness. Surprising she hadn't been culled yet. He'd love to hunt her down himself, but he had hours of vid still to go. He'd just tell Phil to hold her so he could question her later.

Steve brought him lunch but by midafternoon he was crashing and wasn't worth shit on the vid review. He didn't want Steve to see him nodding off like some druggie. If he could just catch a nap, twenty winks his dad called it, when he was a kid. You could do it in the saddle on the climb up the mountain in the morning twilight. He needed some stimulation bad, but his stomach rebelled at just the thought of coffee and the nausea was distracting.

"Hey Steve, you think you and Roy could bring me something?"

"Whatever you want Cowboy."

"Cattleman," Cus insisted in his father's voice.

"Right, whatever," shrugged Steve.

"It's big, it's contraband."

"Just our style," Steve grinned. "What is it you want so bad?"

"One of those special chairs from the library, the shock chairs."

"Ah hell, Cus. We don't have to bring the whole chair, just the innards. Have it here in no time flat."

"Thanks. You're a real brother," Cus said, feeling his gorge rise at having had to ask, to act grateful. That Captain. He more than had it coming.

When Steve left, Cus paused the vid, set an alarm on the vid reader, slipped off his boots, closed his eyes, and dreamed his way back to the dry as dust mountains. From a ridge overlooking the river, he saw figures below, smelled the cooking fires. Through the smoke he saw vast herds of ponies grazing. He looked back at his small command. They were too few for the massive numbers below. Then he heard the unexpected, the whoop of an Indian charging from the trees, and awoke with a start.

Outside the window an owl was hooting. It swooped down on something scuttering across the parade ground in the early dusk of winter.

Refuge and River

Four hours of blissful coma for this exhausted ancienne, but inevitably, as sleep lightened, the nightmares began to edge in. Quickly enough the logical mind activated and raced. Still on the cot, I flexed and extended my knees several times, assessed them as painful but serviceable.

"Well, look who's finally back from the dead," I heard.

"Now that's an unfortunate choice of words," I shot back to Anika.

"Ooooh, touchy," she teased.

I jerked into a sitting position, my head spinning, my mouth dry, but Anika was there, bless her murderous heart, with a glass of water that I gulped carefully, unsure of our supplies. A group of us had prepared this place after the authorities had sealed it off. The FCPower had been convinced it would flood as the waters rose, but we'd worked hard on the sealants and leaks had been minimal. The big problem had been air exchange quiet enough to escape notice and clean enough to keep from poisoning us. Gradually we'd dumpster dived enough UV lighting to supplement the existing lights and set up a greenhouse stuffed with tanks of algae and decorative ferns plus some vegetables. With drip irrigation the place was self-sustaining and after that we avoided it, saving it for an emergency go to ground retreat. This was it, the emergency. My heart sank. Place still stank of chlorine.

"Did my kids make it?" I asked anxiously.

"Yes, yes, yes. Just calm down and have a cup of coffee," Annika soothed. "They're out of the apartment but not down here yet. We're keeping the kids sequestered from the larger group since they don't know us. Less stress for them and less risk for us."

I nodded, slowly thinking as I sipped the coffee she'd handed me. "Annika, I think I'd better leave."

"Whoa, you just got here. Why?"

"They've got my QR code. Didn't you hear?"

"No! So that's what triggered this?"

"That together with the R-S capture. My apartment really wasn't adequate for that, that thing."

"Well, that we knew. But thanks for taking the risk. I hear the kids have done a great job with him."

"So, there's a gender assignment?" I asked.

"He, his, him — we'll let "him" decide later of course."

"That sounds like wishful thinking."

"We'll see. I heard Joanie and Carlos are working on developing an empathy circuit for him."

"I know that's the idea but frankly it's creepy."

Annika smiled and shook her head as she sipped her own coffee that was whitened with some simulacrum of cream. "I need to leave," I repeated slowly. "Leave a trail for the Power to find, away from this place. When they get my history, they will look here if they don't have another place to look."

Annika replied, "Where will you go though?" And my heart sank. A spy? She should know not to ask that. I was relieved when she continued, "Don't answer that."

"No," I said sadly and felt the barriers that subterfuge had built into our old relationship. She gave me a sandwich, peanut butter and mayonnaise, my unheard-of favorite, and led me to the storeroom where I packed a different backpack with food and water, some bandages and filters, spare clothing that would be a rough fit. I showered and stuffed my used clothes into an odor-proof bag. I slipped a knife and compass into my pocket.

"Stay for midnight snack? We're all gathered in the big hall." she asked.

Shaking my head, I hugged her, long and hard. "I wish you could take me to the kids," I said.

"They'll be here in another few hours, definitely by dawn," she suggested.

I glanced at my watch. "I have to leave now. Give them a hug from me if you think they're receptive. You know the age."

Annika snorted sympathetically, then led me to side portal. "This will angle up to the tunnel. Here's an emergency communicator . . ."

"No Annika. I can't take that. This is goodbye — until we meet again after . . ." After the rebellion, after death, after capture? I turned away from the incomplete sentence.   Blinking away her faint "goodbye then, farewell" which shot past me into several kilometers of dead air, I slipped on my gogmask and was away.

Much as I wished I'd been able to give the kids a final goodbye hug, the upriver tidal surge was due.   I planned to ride it up to Wildcat Mountain. On my back I carried the origami kayak my son had made me for my seventieth, my last happy birthday before Scrimfall. I'd discovered it miraculously intact in the rubble of our incinerated apartment building after we'd finally left the Park District Tunnel. Six weeks of worried waiting for the inferno to die down and a new scrim to be launched. Finally, we'd emerged, blinking our dazzled dark-adapted eyes, only to find nothing but a charred slagheap, a pyre of death.

Now I paddled his kayak quietly in the dark, no lights showing. I knew there were others on the river also eager to elude the attention of the authorities. We crossed paths as the vaguest of shadows. The current hurried me along. Once or twice, I had to dodge hulking trawlers and their wake, and, for a terrifying moment or two, confront the possibility of being swamped, rolled, or upended. But the moments passed, and I made good time, the tide running fast and high. By the time it slackened, Wildcat Mountain Bridge loomed in the distance. I dug into the momentarily currentless waters to direct the kayak toward a wooded shore that showed only as the darker darkness of forest. Once beached I folded the kayak, recalling my son's long, graceful fingers which had traced these folds so long ago.

Then it was time to hump everything up the ridge. My particle counter ap showed a low enough reading that I gratefully shed the gogmask. Lucky too that the night was a long, just spring night, cool in the 60s and pleasant on the uphill: temporarily a temperate predawn climb. I'd have to find shelter an hour before sunrise to avoid being baked in the sun or steamed in the shade.

My route was the old Underground Railroad in reverse, heading south to meet the waves of climate migrants that battered themselves against the barriers the Natties had raised, preventing any orderly resettlement of the peoples of the south. The Natties was our nickname for them, gnats on the body of humanity just trying to survive. They'd put those barriers up over our protests. I was furious when I let myself think about it, but I couldn't expend energy on fury right now.

I had to keep the destination in mind. Ironically it was a gated community.
Secretly it was a closeted migrant sanctuary and the home of my friend Fran,
doctor and shepherd. Truth be told, she'd had only two sheep when I last
visited years ago. I smiled as I thought of her – tall, skinny as a rail, deaf as a
post. I estimated it would take me a month of night hiking to reach her place.

Behind me the sky was lightening. In the morning twilight I could start to
pick out features of the land. A promising pile of rocks loomed to my right. I
explored for overhangs, for one of those Lenape shelters from centuries, maybe
millennia ago. Beneath an old oak I came upon the perfect stony slot – just a
meter high with no wetness and no snakes, at least for the moment. I slipped
off my pack, wrapped myself in a tarp, pulled on my mask and crashed into
sleep where dreams of the ancient forest and its people claimed me.

The Tomb

Joan sat on a bench below the oversized statue at the Tomb of the Unknown Soldier. The acidic atmosphere had pitted the green bronze of the heavily muscled soldiers holding up a translucent plexiglass shield against a powerful but unseen sun. In late afternoon, the Cemetery wasn't crowded, but it wasn't deserted either. The passersby were mostly damaged soldiers with their support females. They took AS and Joanie for the same, though some gazed curiously at AS who was unnaturally immobile. Joanie had commanded him into an energy-saving sleep mode, mostly to give herself a rest from her circuit mapping activity. Mentally monitoring the crowd was child's play by comparison. For the curious few she gently suggested the idea that her companion's immobility was due to his blindness, sustained in the line of duty, and they walked on, avoiding the injury that was both a noble sacrifice and an embarrassment. Scrimfall's UV levels had resulted in severe cataracts for almost all who had served at the time, and the wait for veterans' surgery was a decade or more.

At dusk Joan began to be apprehensive. A guard came to announce that the Cemetery was closing. When she scanned him mentally, he was a blank, but as he walked by them, he turned and winked at her. A Cipher then – humans who could neither read nor be read. She assumed the wink meant he was one of them but wasn't sure until he returned after closing. She'd reactivated AS and felt she could handle the guard if he was hostile, but he merely led them wordlessly to a small door at the base of the statue. As he opened the door, the guard handed her a note: "Contact at midnight" – along with two battered peanut butter sandwiches.

"Duck," she said to AS as they squeezed through the door. The guard gave her a moment to spot the low stone benches, then swung the door shut. She heard the click of a lock behind them. The room was utterly dark, and she felt an old despondency creep over her. "Two steps forward, rotate and sit." She managed to squeeze out the command, unnecessarily she realized as AS had activated his echolocation sensors.

She checked the times on the luminescent watch, her mother's. Her mom had loaned it to her the day of Scrimfall so she could check her breath-holding time against Carlos. The transient green glow read 6:30, or 18:30 in AS time. Great – five and a half hours in the dark. She felt the feelings coursing through her, despondency, anxiety. She missed Carlos, Grandma. Where were they? Had they been captured yet? Were they being tortured as she sat here uselessly? Would she rot in here when no one revealed their location, but everyone was captured or killed?

"Repair Assistant Gloria," AS interrupted. "You heart rate currently exceeds normal resting value by 100%."

How had he known that? Ah, echosurveillance. Could she use this to construct an empathy circuit in the robosoldier? For some reason the excitement this idea generated in her slowed her heart rate.

"Repair Assistant Gloria. Information required. Please confirm capture status."

"No capture AS. I repeat, no capture. Waiting further orders to be delivered at 24:00. Please enter energy conservation mode but maintain echolocation circuit."

"Confirming entering energy conservation state 201 minus echolocation circuits E1 through E5."

She felt the heat of his battery fading. Too bad. It was going to be cold. She took a bite of an extremely ragged peanut butter sandwich and sighed. Still, she found herself grinning as she felt her way into her first echolocation sensor ever.

Darkness does strange things to the senses. Joan used this dark time to probe AS's echolocation circuits, and the pathways she sensed had begun to acquire a kind of subtle coloration she might have missed in daylight. Red for the signals coming from the R-S, blue for those going to. They were mostly going to the R-S from her she realized. His sensors liked rhythm, and her heart was the closest and strongest signal, thumping away, a signal that was both sonic and electromagnetic.

She shivered in the damp cold of the crypt and to warm up, did some jumping jacks, keeping her mind on the R-S. As her heart rate picked up, AS's echolocation circuits began to hum, the blue thickened like a twisting thread, and the echolocation circuit began to project to several centers that sparked. She was afraid she was alarming him, waking him up. She sat abruptly and thread of blue thinned; the sparks flickered out. Fascinating.

Next, she tried meditating, a practice that was part of basic training in her group of telempaths or whatever they were. As her heart rate slowed both the blue and red threads thinned and twisted slowly, strands fraying and popping out of sight.

A rattle at the door interrupted her observations. She caught a glimpse of red and she sent out a mind message. "Who's this?"

A long middle C blew through her mind, faintly and reedily. The door creaked open, and Kepler's lanky form was framed by the doorway, lit from behind by the green glare of the arc light. "Time to go," he thought. When Joan tried to respond, stiffness and fatigue slowed her movements.

She managed to wake AS, and they followed Kepler into the cypress trees that lined the tall fence enclosing the cemetery. At the base of the third tree, Kepler opened a maintenance hole cover. Joan eyed its circumference doubtfully. AS barely passed through by raising his arms over his head. The R-S followed Kepler, identified in this case as Repairman Diogenes, down the ladder and into the ground. Kepler had that silver gadget in his mouth again and seemed to have no difficulty controlling the R-S, but Joan couldn't pick up on any signal coming from it – other than a faint buzz of Kepler's lips against the reed mounted at the top. She wanted to ask where they were going but didn't dare interrupt Kepler's flow. Instead, she followed mutely, pausing only a moment as she pulled the cover over the hole. AS's chest lamp clicked on. She could see each rung of the ladder glowing green in response. A faint scent of chlorine wafted into her consciousness. Memory? Warning? She couldn't be sure.

Musical interlude

Maybe he slept. Maybe he didn't. It was hard to tell against the repetitive drumming that, like a bad circuit, grated against him. He hated this kind of music, rejected entirely that it was supposed to be "his" music. His parents had never played this stuff at home, he was sure. He barely remembered back when his mother sang hymns to her guitar and, sometimes, probably when his father was at the sweet spot of drink, mellowed out, he sang along. The hymns were sad and hopeful, but he couldn't remember them with this throbbing going on. This was Joanie's music, the music of crowds all stamping, clapping, throbbing. Where was she? He tried mindcasting just in case she was close by. He wasn't very good at it, and it seemed as if everyone within reach was caught up in the music, unreadable. He longed for the saxophone, its wordless narrative, to take him somewhere quieter, more thoughtful.

He must have slept for he was tugged awake by a jingling arm – the jingle easy to hear against the quiet farewells: "Adios. Hasta luego. Ciao." That twanged his wakening consciousness. An unfamiliar face loomed, and he threw his arm up to cover his own.

"Carlos, Carlos, it's okay. We're friends, man. Juan. Remember?"

Kepler's abandonment, his flight from home, the robosoldier, his current precarious perch in the bar over the river, came crashing back like a final clash of cymbals. "So, where's your buddy Kepler?" Carlos demanded.

"They finished their set and he left. He wants me to take you." Juan reminded him, in a bored tone.

"Take me where?" was Carlos's hostile snapback.

"That's difficult to say, chiquito."

Carlos bristled. "No way I'm going anywhere with you Jingle Bells." He curled up and turned his face to the wall.

"Hey, don't take it out on me. It wasn't my idea. Kepler just dumped you on me in the middle of our rehearsal."

Carlos turned back to Juan. "Kepler said we were going to his studio."

"Did he now," Juan sighed. "I guess you could call it that."

Carlos contemplated this strange reply. "Just tell me where to go. I'll find my own way."

"Sure. No problem." Then Carlos felt a key being pressed into his hand and Juan's words, directions, creeping into his ear. He steeled himself to let them come but he didn't care for what they had to say.

Soon Juan and the others had left, Carlos sat in a closet with the costumes. He sat motionless, trying to avoid the bells. Eventually, he sensed the building had emptied out. Slowly he cracked the closet door and spotted the red of an exit sign. He crept toward the red glow where a freight elevator stood empty, disconnected. He peeled the key from his palm and turned on the elevator. Carlos punched the button for the lowest level and began to sink, slowly, relentlessly.

The doors opened to reveal an empty landing with a power grid board humming and twinkling. Leaving the key in its slot on the elevator, he pushed the up button, then quickly squeezed through the closing doors. His directions were to take the staircase that went down, down, down into the darkness. As he passed from landing to landing the light behind him switched off, the one ahead switched on. Of course, he reached a landing where the one ahead was burned out.

He paused and sat for a moment, the slimy stench of chlorine rising to greet him. The soles of his feet began to burn. His heart hammered a dreadful rhythm. Defiantly he began to sing his mother's song. "De Colores," he sobbed as he inched further down into a tarry blackness and fear.

Tracking

The vidfeed had been a big fat zero. Cus had *known* it would be. He'd *been* there. The R-S trail had gone around the corner of a building and vanished. The building wall had been shielded with graffiti proof aluminum, so no R-S vidfeed had gotten through. The smoke was too thick, so the drone had caught nothing, not even on the infra-red, not with fires all over the place. Putting the evidence together it was proof positive of a plot to capture the R-S. He had a bad feeling that the piles of metal and brick on the street might have included R-S debris, but he refused to consider the possibility that it had been destroyed. Not that fast.

But proving a plot to the Captain? That was another matter. He needed answers to counter the Captain or, at least, a diversion. He wasn't going up against another tirade without a tool to counter that slimeball's unwarranted threat of demotion or worse.   And the tool was definitely NOT in this barfing vidfeed.

The old lady, he was sure she was the key, but he couldn't think of a foolproof story to prove her involvement without disclosing their encounter in the nature refuge. He had to get out of this cage of a vidfeed room. He'd have to be fast. He was plotting his escape, just a quick trip to the interrogation chamber where he was sure his bud Phil had the old lady all set for him, when the Captain strode in the door, no knock or anything. No manners at all.

"Well, Loootenant," he drawled.

"What a potty mouth," thought Cus, but he jumped up and saluted smartly. With that salute a story snapped into place. "The vid feed review was highly interesting, sir.   I was able to identify a ringleader directing the capture operation as well as the site of capture."

The Captain caught sight of the shock chair and smiled grimly. "Had a little help I see. Good job. Better if you hadn't lost an R-S worth over a hundred thou, but good job. You've got three days to get the R-S back, Hickens.

Dismissed. Oh, and take this." The Captain pitched the confiscated cell phone hard at his face. Cus wasn't fazed. It wasn't the first time someone had thrown something at him in anger. He snatched the phone out of the air, saluted, turned on his heel and marched out the door. Grinning he took off running across the courtyard to the mess hall and his buds. Three days was all the time in the world – a beer, a square meal, a snooze, then on to interrogation.

Hours later, when he finally got to the interrogation chamber, Cus was shocked to find it empty. He tracked down Phil. "Sorry Cus," his bud Phil muttered.

Cus felt the roots of his closely cropped hair turn to hot wire spikes. "Don't fricking apologize to me. What happened? I told you twelve hours ago to round this biddy up."

"We staked out the place, but nobody's been in or out. We flew a drone over but nothing. We don't have a warrant," Phil whimpered.

"What about the QR ID computer search?" Cus demanded.

Regaining his composure, Phil rattled out the data. "Old lady's a retired doc – minor Scrimfall hero. Saved some kids at a swimming pool or something. Lives with a granddaughter and an orphan – both teens. Haven't seen any of 'em. Kids haven't been to school for the last couple of days."

"The track's getting cold. If that stupid captain hadn't tied me up with vidfeed review . . ."

"You'd never have found the QR code."

"Don't tell me what I would have found. You are not helping me here Phil."

Phil was a nerdy squirrelly kind of guy, not the kind of guy you could really respect. More like the kind of guy you'd like to strangle slowly while he kicked. Cooling, Cus smiled slightly, spoke softly. "Don't you have anything for me Philly?"

Phil spoke for the camera in the corner, "Not without a warrant Lieutenant," as he slipped him a piece of paper. Cus checked it as he walked back to barracks – good, the apartment lock code. He was on his own then and satisfied. He'd handle this his own way, like a man. He shredded the paper and let the wind blow the pieces away like tiny bits of sagebrush.

An hour later he could feel the unfriendly eyes of the apartment block biddies on him as he took the elevator up to the top floor, just shy of the roof, of course. He strode down the hallway making no effort to muffle his step. When he reached the apartment at the end, doors behind him popped open. He wheeled, glared, and they quickly shut again – scared off by the uniform and the toxic power that radiated from him. He punched in the code Phil had given him as he rubbed the lucky rabbit's foot in his pocket. The door clicked open.

He raised his stun gun as he entered, hoping for, but not really expecting a second shot at her, here in semiprivate. He came in slowly, spotted the cameras where they were supposed to be, their red eyes winking at him. He'd take care of the footage later, or have Phil do it, depending on what went down. No booby traps that he'd spotted. He scanned for explosives, gun powder, gas. Nothing, just a faint hint of sage.

He clicked the door closed behind him. Following the scent, he made his way down a long hallway towards a windowed room that faced the street. He could hear the hum of an air purifier and street noise beyond, but no speech or movement. In the living room he smiled at the artistry of the little altar, then frowned at the long ash of an incinerated joss stick. She had at least eight hours on him if she'd left it burning when she fled. Where would she go? Back to the preserve where he'd stunned her perhaps. No, she'd have a roost somewhere with friends. That old city pigeon would stick to what she knew.

But did she know the woods? A lot of these old farts had been park-goers, do-good anti-ranchers more concerned about their play-hiking than meat on the table and clothing on their backs. They were happy when ranchers went broke. His dad had hated their Woodland Club guts.

Maybe there'd be a clue in the apartment – some trace of the R-S. He'd been making that story up on the spot for the Captain, but if these people had fled, maybe he'd struck on something. He had to be thorough. Three days, he reminded himself. Three days. Don't rush. A dog needs the right scent.

He crushed the hanging ash on the joss stick. Not a trace of warmth there. The walls were lined with cheap photos of the kids – a girl from babyhood to a fuckable sixteen or so, a boy more like from five to maybe fourteen? Hard to tell. He was a dwarf or something and colored like a Mexican. He was about to shoot a photo to send to Phil, then thought better of it. Phil already had their mugshots, and he didn't need a digital trail of his warrantless search. No warrant – not yet. He wanted, he needed to do this on his own.

He wondered about his R-S. Was his hunch right? Did the old lady have something to do with it – her and her brats. The kitchen was boring, clean except for some mouse turds scattered over the stove. A mouse scuttered into hiding under a burner. He found some cookies in a cabinet. Turd-free and chocolate chip – his favorite. He munched a few as he moved on to a bedroom. The old lady's clothes still hanging on a rack, cheap jewelry in a case, a battered medal from, get this he chuckled to himself, the Senior Olympics. Running. Pre-Scrimfall. A long time ago lady. A long time ago.

The girl's room had clothes too – like they wanted him to think they were coming back. Idiots. He took a pair of pink underwear labelled Sunday for a souvenir. He would have preferred Thursday, Thor's day.

In the boy's room he hit the jackpot. The kid had a room loaded with equipment. He couldn't believe the kid hadn't taken it with him. Computers, a drone, gaming console, Rubik's cube. He'd loved that Rubik's cube. His father hadn't tolerated games of any sort of course, but the cube was easy to hide, didn't draw power. On ice cold days in winter, when his dad would dispatch him to work in the barn, he'd spent more than a few hours bedded down in the warm hay in the loft above the horses stamping below to keep warm. There he'd twirled it for hours and mastered it.

Now he twirled the cube going for a quick single face solution. There, all white, he grinned. Something clattered in the corner of the room. He ducked, drew, and fired the stun gun, shocking the drone that was launching from the shelf. Annoyed, he didn't bother to pick up the pieces, just stared as the drone sputtered out.

Then he spotted it. Mixed in with the black plastic debris of the drone, the wink of a titanium magnut. He picked the nut up and there was the stamp – AS-57189. The R-S was leaving a trail. It was being controlled but it knew it was being controlled. Good for you bot. I've got your back. After all you're one of mine.

Descent

Before Carlos reached the bottom of the stairwell, he heard a door creak open, and a bubble of voices and colored light trickled upwards. He hesitated. Friend, enemy, frenemy? There was no chance he could outrun them up the stairs, no hiding spots or exits that he'd spotted since hearing the entry door click-lock behind him. He hesitated. The cursed chlorine smell was stronger now. A sudden breeze washed it away. Strains of "De Colores" floated up through the dim stairwell. Suddenly he craved people again, especially, Joanie. Surely, she'd be here. They had work to do.

He picked up the pace, stumbling unevenly down the stairs, breathing hard, not bothering to sing along. When he reached the doorway, there was a cheer and hands reached out to him, pulling him into the light. He was dazzled, pleased, amazed to be accepted. But as his vision adapted and he searched the small crowd of welcoming faces, he saw no one he knew. No Joanie, no grandma, no AS, not even Kepler. He could barely keep his feet as fear flooded in. Then a young woman winked at him, and he recognized her— the bartender from the club, and next to her, wait, that was the roboserver, the one whose finger he'd barely budged. He grinned. He'd landed on his feet alright.

They took him to a cement picnic table he thought he remembered from childhood. Yep, right there, his initials and the first Tic-tac-toe game he'd won against Joan were sharpied onto the table. The others gave him some bread and red jam and for a minute he was busy cramming it in as fast as possible. He was starving.

"Slow down, slow down," the bartender urged him, smiling.

"What's your name?" he blurted, spewing crumbs out on the table but not, god no, not in her face.

"Watch the waste," she said, backing up.

He swept up the crumbs from the table and dumped them into his mouth, following them up with a gulp of milk, but never letting his eyes leave hers.

"She must be twenty-one if she's a bartender," he thought sadly. "No chance."

"Watch the hygiene too. We don't need anybody getting sick down here, least of all you."

He sagged. "She thinks I'm just a little kid," he thought bitterly.

"Not at all," she thought back. Then aloud, as though she knew he didn't like this kind of intrusion, "I'm Varvara. Joan spoke very highly of you. She says you have skills that could be very useful to us."

"Uh, nice to meet you Varvara," Carlos replied politely, hope dwindling.

Varvara was nothing if not blunt. "Look, Carlos, I'm not a love at first sight kind of person. First let's save the world. By the time we've done that, we'll be old enough that the age gap won't matter."

"OK," said Carlos as hope came lurching back.

"I'm looking forward to working with you," Varvara reached out to shake his hand. Carlos quickly dusted off the crumbs onto his plate before putting his hand in hers. He wasn't great at longer-range telepathy, but with contact he was a whiz. He felt her quickly throwing up barriers, caught a glimpse of affection for himself, sisterly maybe, but he could work with that. There was also a wave of worry that she quickly channeled back to the sea, behind a levee.

Her worry triggered his, ragged waves of frustration and anxiety which rolled right back into his core. "Where's Joan, and my grandma, and the R-S? And Kepler's supposed to be here, right?" Carlos demanded.

"Kepler, Joan and the R-S should be here soon," Varvara reassured him. "But your grandma had to leave."

"Leave to go where?"

"She didn't want to tell us – in case of capture. She knows what she's doing Carlos."

He could tell she wanted to put her arm around his shoulders to comfort him, but she resisted the impulse, probably sensing the fury it would provoke in him. She merely put her hand over his, which was resting on the cool concrete of the picnic table. But this time, he couldn't even feel anything. It had finally happened. Grandma, despite all her promises, had abandoned him.

Rest and Recovery

The heavy stench of chlorine made the walk down the slant of the repurposed sewer tunnel seem even longer than it was. Joan pulled her gogmask back on. Both AS and Kepler had to stoop to avoid scraping the ceiling, and here and there was a trickle of rusty water that stained their feet. As she expected there was a scurrying of rats, a species that had concentrated their numbers with the loss of land mass. Now there were even hairless breeds, adapting to the warmer temperatures.

Her mind sagged after the intense concentration she'd been exercising in the tomb. But something was nagging her. She wasn't quite sure what it was. Something about AS. She repressed the thought. Later, later when she'd had some rest and could keep paranoia from unbalancing her reason.

At last, they encountered a bolted hatch. Kepler sent an "open, please" mind message to those on the other side and the well-oiled door opened silently and slowly. Once it had closed, the chatter erupted, but Joan shut it out. She craved sleep. Someone took her by the hand and led her to a cot. Enroute, she passed Carlos. Something in his stricken gaze should have stopped her, but an overwhelming need for sleep propelled her bot-like to a cot where she drifted down, gratefully closing her eyes. Someone cast a warm blanket, like a net securing her frayed body and mind.

Her tiny sleep transition jerks quelled almost immediately. After a pleasant time drifting in delta waves, Joan's mind started sifting through the debris of the preceding days. She jettisoned the memories of robosoldiers attacking bystanders in doorways, bloody rags in the corners of their apartment, Carlos's poorly controlled hormonal lusts and hurts. She packed them all away, irretrievably perhaps, along with the images of her parents.

The scent and creak of the cot summoned the Fairy of Hope, her grandmother's tale, woven deep into the identity of her five-year-old self. Irrepressible. Fairy twinkled. She's piezoelectric Joan had told her grandmother.

Her grandmother twinkled too. The Fairy was pink, but grandma was green. When Fairy and grandma were there, she didn't have to listen to how unhappy people were. She cuddled into her blanket, breathing deeply, enjoying the memory of stars twinkling. Fairy was piezoelectric because when you squeezed her, she twinkled. That's how they made ultrasonic waves too. Squeezing the crystals. Joan found herself squeezing a big crystal, as big as her five-year-old hands, and a light shone. It shone on a robosoldier's expressionless face. Then it shone from his chest, and she was afraid. The stars winked out overhead as night faded and the sun rose red and grand and deadly. Joan squeezed her eyes tight against it. But there was a tugging at her elbow, persistent and relentless, and she awoke.

Predator on the Prowl

On the screen over their heads Cus and Phil traced the trail of titanium magnuts left by the missing robosoldier AS-57189. This trail was definitely quicker and simpler to follow than winnowing out images from the vid footage, but it had still taken a good twelve hours of work, mostly by Phil while Cus caught some well-earned z's. They had picked out the fuckable girl's face from the apartment elevator camera. Obviously, the big man in the gogmask next to her was the R-S. Cus had given a wolf whistle when they spotted the girl, but Phil said he was more interested in the AS-57189 trail. What a nerd. No sense of pleasing possibilities.

"They take the tunnel to the Cemetery. That's predictable enough. But they don't seem to leave," puzzled Phil.

"Simple then. I'll take some heat-seeking drones and find their hidey-hole in ten minutes," Cus boasted.

"Not so fast," Phil cut him short. Annoying nerd. "AS-57189 left three markers within the Cemetery grounds, two near the center and one near the perimeter. But one of the two near the center is fainter. You'll need subterranean sensors."

"C'mon Phil," Cus chortled indulgently. "It's a cemetery. Of course, I'm taking underground sensors." Cus copied an image of the screen to his phone, requisitioned an R-S with subterranean sensors and an automatic firing arm that would outgun the AS-57189. For himself he carried his own pistol – just for self-defense. It felt good in his thigh holster, familiar, right. He shouldn't need it though. The captured R-S did not seem completely under the girl's control given the magnut trail. He fingered the nut in his pocket with satisfaction. He'd head for the Cemetery at closing time, while Phil stayed back and monitored the trail for any new markers. He didn't need an audience for this fuck and kill.

It was almost dark when he arrived at the entrance where he caught a guard dozing with some old-fashioned heavy book balanced on his lap. Cus grinned. It felt good to be back in the field and not stuck in some tarpit library. An actual tarpit would have been interesting he mused, as he slapped the guard's feet off the railing where they rested. The guard jumped to his feet and reached for his sidearm, but Cus was faster, of course, and at this distance, quite precise. He stunned the guard's hand, and the guard gave a pained yelp which Cus found most satisfactory.

The chubby grey-headed guard toppled back into his chair. Cus became officious. "So, Guard Jarvis," he read from the nametag illuminated by his auxiliary R-S's chest lamp. "Sleeping on the job you might not have after tonight. Your good luck that I'm not here as an Enforcer. I'll be searching your cemetery for these fugitives tonight. Where did you see them last?"

Cus thrust a screenshot of the girl and AS-57189 into the guard's good hand and instructed his R-S to dim the dazzling chest lamp. After a moment Jarvis, still staring down at the image, stuttered. "I don't think I've seen them. Not today anyway."

"Think harder. Yesterday?"

"I wasn't on duty."

"Who was?"

"Smith."

"Call him. Get him over here."

"Yes, sir."

"And wake up and guard the gate, man. Don't let anyone leave this Cemetery."

The guard looked up. "It's afterhours. There's no one here. I patrolled thirty minutes ago."

"Oh, they're here alright. I'm leaving an armed sentry drone. If they flee this way and don't stop at your order, it will fire to maim, not kill. Just thought you might need the back-up since you're a bit impaired at the moment," Cus said, smiling and nodding at the man's still limp trigger finger in a hand that drooped clumsily over his holster.

"Yes sir. Thank you, sir."

Cus glowed. He'd handled this situation superbly. Idiot hadn't even asked him to show a search warrant.

The Hansel Strategy

Carlos was getting tired of being blown off by people who were supposed to be on his side. He needed to work, but Joanie was passed out. Maybe Kepler would know where AS was stashed. He'd lost sight of the R-S when Joanie had come in looking totally glazed.

He followed the strains of a saxophone and laughter from his assigned cot. The twists and turns of this subterranean slime pit were etched into his memory like acid. Partying, they were fricking partying in the place he'd sheltered while the City burned. He turned the corner and saw Kepler blowing his horn in the corner while six or so of the telempaths, or whatever you called them, drank beer, and laughed around a solar lantern.

He went and stood in front of Kepler, stood silently accusing him.

"Sorry about that," Kepler said, pulling his lip free from the reed. "I had a gig." Seeing Carlos's pout, he continued. "An over twenty-one alcohol-saturated gig." Then because Carlos was still glowering at him, Kepler sighed and asked, "What can I do for you Carlos?"

"I need to be working with AS," Carlos snapped.

"I think we should wait for Joanie to wake up. She's made the most progress with it," Kepler replied.

"You can control it with that metallic mouthpiece. How?" Carlos demanded.

"Well, I didn't invent it, just adapted it, put the reed in. It's one of their gadgets, for use in the field if there's an electromagnetic field disruption. It's strictly a short-range controller, breath powered. It controls only basic motor functions and elementary communications circuits."

"Let me see it," Carlos ordered. Kepler reluctantly fished the device out of his shirt pocket.

"We only have one. I can't let you take it apart," Kepler warned. Carlos turned the warm metal object in his hand. This had the look of Haartsen's work. He'd studied her a bit in electronics class at school.

"If you have a workshop here, I might be able to make some more of these," Carlos offered.

"Really?" Kepler asked startled. He reached out, quickly brushed Carlos's mind, and sensed the confidence there. "We have a workshop, but the R-S is in it right now, charging."

Carlos met Kepler's gaze anxiously. "Are you sure that's safe? Charging might be coupled with self-repair circuits you realize. Did you ask Joanie about it?"

"You saw her. She was catatonic with exhaustion."

"You left a guard in place?"

"Why?"

"Take me to the workshop," Carlos commanded impatiently. And Kepler, sensing his alarm, did just that. Outside the door, as they listened for any noises within, Carlos noticed a twinkle in the corridor. A magnut, which when examined, read AS-57189. Carlos shook his head. "The Hansel strategy," he mouthed silently to Kepler.

Joan woke to Carlos's face looming over her and immediately hugged him for dear life. As the hug dissipated her nightmare, the way hugging someone you really love will do, determination and a fierce hunger came back to her. Real hunger – she was faint with it she realized, and Carlos, in her embrace, felt it too.

"C'mon, let's get you to the Mess Hall," Carlos said, pulling her to her feet. As she wobbled there for a moment, Carlos sent Kepler ahead to get some food prepared. He walked Joan to the Mess Hall with her arm draped over his shoulder. Each of her steps was steadier than the last as she came back to herself. She was surprised to see the Mess Hall dimly lit by a single electric candle and empty except for Kepler who sat waiting for them. She took a seat opposite him and asked, "Where is everyone? When I came through last night, I could swear this place was jammed. I don't think I was hallucinating, was I?"

But before Kepler could reply, Varvara arrived with a plate of steaming tofu and rice whose scent fully engulfed Joan's consciousness. She held up her hand to postpone Kepler's response and dived in. "Grandma always said she was a good eater," Carlos joked nervously.

"And you weren't, I suppose," Kepler retorted, keeping it light. Carlos tried not to take offense. "Oh, sorry," Kepler abruptly apologized. He needed no telempathy to read Carlos's tight expression.

Joan failed to notice their anxiety. Food had been the first thing that Joan had found, right here, in this place, that would block out everything else: the pain of others, her own panic, her grandmother's grief and trauma. Skinny at five, she'd been a chubby little girl at eight. Her grandmother had indulged her eating a little too much despite the food shortages. But when the telempaths found her, she learned other defenses. As she finished the delicious plate, she put those defenses in place and didn't ask for seconds. "*Oishikatta*[14]," she murmured from habit as she leaned back, and the fennel taste lingered on her tongue. It really was delicious she realized. She took a deep breath and turned to find Carlos, Kepler and Varvara all staring at her intently and impatiently. "What?"

"It's AS. He's betrayed us," Carlos blurted out.

"He left a trail so he could be traced," Kepler explained.

Joan's shock mounted slowly, like the rising levels of the sea. "But we disabled him."

"Not completely. Not all the time," Carlos noted.

'We've evacuated everyone to safe houses," Varvara added tensely. "But we have no other place to take the R-S. If you're not sure we can control it, we should destroy it and evacuate before we're traced."

Joan looked to Carlos and Kepler who both shared Vanessa's grim expression. "But I think I might be close to finding a way to, to . . ." She couldn't quite put it into words, the reciprocity she had sensed in AS when they were in the crypt. She tried to send a sense of that experience telepathically, but it was all garbled.

Carlos intervened. "I knew you'd find something, some way in. We shouldn't destroy AS. If we must abandon him, we should try to implant some

---

[14] Oishikatta - delicious

spyware, a virus, something. Maybe he could be our Trojan horse, our Stuxnet", citing the historical examples they'd studied in school.

"Carlos might be right," Kepler conceded. "We took a lot of damage to get this R-S. We need some sort of payoff."

"I've learned some things about the R-S intelligence and circuitry, but we haven't documented any of it. Without AS – can't we hide him?" Joan pleaded.

"You really don't get it," Varvara said bitterly. "He betrayed us. We've lost this location. We've taken injuries. And we will lose much more if he falls into their hands again. He'll betray us again."

"It's a robot. It did what it was programmed to do," Kepler reminded her. He deliberately exuded calm.

"Yeah, it's not AS's fault. We missed it, missed a circuit," Carlos added.

"Look let's do this," Joan proposed.   "Carlos and I will work with AS – see if we can leave an imprint that won't be detected. We'll also try to find the circuit that's creating the trail.   Then we'll take him to our hideout– you remember the place, Carlos?"

"Oh yeah," Carlos responded slowly, a clammy claustrophobia invading his bones. "Then we'll deactivate him and evacuate, right Joan?"

"Right," Joan assured him.

"One hour," Varvara and Kepler jointly intoned. "That's all you've got."

"And maybe less, depending on what the scouts report. We are not letting you two get captured," Varvara said, her words and intention cold, hard, crystal clear.

Flight behavior

I woke to a gentle green glow just above me. Outside my shelter of rock shelf lay the moon shadow of trees and silence. I shouldn't trust my hearing anymore I remembered. I tried to reach out the way Joan had taught me. Root whispers, an owl perched and watching, but nothing for the green glow. Hopefully it was inanimate then. It didn't seem to be moving. I couldn't stand the suspense. Impulsively but slowly, I reached up to touch it – furry and still. A bioluminescent moss I realized and smiled. Schistostega pennata. Goblins' gold.

How ironic that I'm still smiling at nature as we humans are destroying it. Like a Nazi enjoying a last piano concerto before gassing the pianist. I slipped out of the rock slit as quietly as I could and squatted in the moonlight to tinkle on a rock, trying to dodge the glistening streams that flowed down toward my feet.

I've always had trouble sleeping to the full moon. I checked my particle counter. Low enough so I slipped off my gogmask and took in the unfiltered air, a deep breath of newly released oxygen scented with wet leaves and mosses. I could no longer make out the stench of the City, the smell of wet garbage and fear. My old-fashioned wristwatch (not that old-fashioned, it could count the PM2.5's) read four am, its luminous display almost the same shade as the moss. Two hours until sunrise. I was tempted to start early, to take advantage of the relative coolness and cleaner air. Using the cover of darkness. But that was anachronistic I reminded myself. Darkness was no cover to heat-seeking drones, the most likely form of pursuit. Plus, my night vision wasn't very good anymore, and I couldn't risk hiking with a light.

Reluctantly I turned to go back to my shelter when I heard a scuttering in the leaves nearby, felt a brush of air as the owl dropped from an overhead branch to strike. It rose with a small squeaking creature in its talons and disappeared into the foliage. Back under the rock I slipped on my mask and waited for dawn.

The green glow reminded me of Joanie's Fairy, though this glow was steady and faint, not a hint of twinkle to it. And not pink. I worried for Joanie and Carlos, back in the Park District Tunnel where we'd waited out disaster as burn victims suffered around us. Joanie had been in pain too and I hadn't understood why. Just too sensitive. Carlos had been her distraction. She'd clung to him as tightly as he had to her. I was glad they'd had each other because the truth was, I'd been engulfed with medical work.

No, I wasn't going there, back to those images of sloughing skin and moaning. It's hard not to think of things once you get started though. That was what the Fairy was for, for the child Joanie had been and for myself too. I focused hard, visualized the twinkle, her darting ascent, her protective wand, the magical prayers that kept her alive. That was always the human hope wasn't it. That we could remedy our destructiveness. Stop ruminating. Imagine. But the twinkling I'd summoned soon synchronized with the throbbing of my hips against the stone floor and sleep didn't come.

At dawn I was hustling along the trail. I had a sense of urgency, almost panic. I wasn't sure why exactly. I reviewed the reality of the situation. If captured, I would likely die quickly, faster than they could execute me no doubt. But I would have little to reveal other than the Park District Tunnel, Joan, Carlos and Kepler's identities, the disabling of the R-S, oh no . . . I might not know the telempaths' network, but I knew way too much.

I tried to focus on the trail, listen as best I could, for the whine of a drone, the chop of a helicopter, but nothing. I saw no other hikers, probably because the particle count was in the red zone as my monitor was constantly reminding me. Fortunately, I'd swapped out my gogmask filter for a fresh one this morning. I'd have to watch for filter malfunction and find a source of filters along the way. There'd been no rain to wash the sky yesterday, but that meant the stream crossings were doable, nothing above the knees. Though I was in a hurry, I bushwhacked around the peaks, not wanting to risk the aerial surveillance and, frankly, not wanting to do the climbs. But the rhododendron thickets were just as challenging, thick and mosquito-ridden.

By the time I reached a lake, the lake I hoped was the one where a safe house was located, I was scratched and bitten, despite my long sleeves and pants.

I ignored the sting of sweat in the superficial wounds. Under the glare of a sky reddened by the setting sun, I unpacked the kayak. A dog was barking with increasing intensity in the distance, not from behind me but from one of the houses on the lake. No doubt my sweat and blood added a tang to the scents drifting across the water. The dog sensed the novelty.

Holding onto the kayak, I waded into the water up to my shoulders, trying to subdue my raunchy smell, strong even to me. I hoped the water didn't harbor too many parasites or water moccasins or alligators, the snakes being the least of these aggressors but the one I most feared. Could I in my eighties really be labelled "raunchy"? – joking to myself to take the edge off the fear.

I dreaded the moment when more dogs would join in. None did. The dog's barking became more intermittent. It was dusk now. I could see the subtle glow of a porch light as it clicked on. A flashlight beam swept the yard, the shore and shone out to the lake. But it was too dark for me to be discovered amidst the flotsam of downed trees and limbs. The search was abandoned, the dog whistled inside.

I pushed the kayak back to shore, mud sucking and slowing my steps, and eagerly climbed aboard, away from the water's potential pests. I waited in silence enjoying the relative coolness of night, the evaporation of the lake water from my overheated skin. It was after midnight and the PM count was dropping but not fast enough, so I left the gogmask in place. I began paddling, hugging the shore, looking for a sign of the safe house.

After an hour of breathing against resistance, I was only halfway around the lake. My flagging logical brain nagged, "Get the gogmask off and eat something." That air on my sweaty face, such a relief, I could have cried or laughed or . . . Food, I had to have food. I dug a tin of sardines from my pack, scarfed them down. A full moon rose – too bright. It was all I could manage to drift into the safety of shadows and secure the kayak to the slender branch of a weeping willow.

Overcoming obstacles

Cus and his R-S were knee deep in excavated bones when Guard Jarvis darkened the door of the crypt. Cus glanced up but sweat had fogged his gogmask. He hit the defog switch. Slowly the silhouette of the guard resolved. The man's mouth was so far open that Cus's headlamp beam lit up the gold in the man's back molar. "I thought I told you to guard the gate," Cus said sadly. "Are you stupid?"

Apparently, the man's hand had recovered because he shakily withdrew his revolver. "You have no right to be here, to dig here. This is consecrated ground. These are your comrades!"

Cus sighed and stunned the guard's hand again. Then, before he could run off, Cus had him by the arm. "You make me nervous with that revolver of yours. Let's pick it up and put it back where it belongs," Cus said, adopting a concerned and kindly tone. He guided the man's hand, squeezed it around the butt of the gun, and replaced it in the holster.

Jarvis's cheeks were newly ruddy. He gasped, "Smitty said you were supposed to have a warrant."

"Smitty? Ah, last night's guard. Is he coming?"

"I don't know. I don't feel so good."

"Let's go around to the bench so you can sit down." Cus helped the guard to shamble over to the bench where he collapsed. Cus considered having Jarvis call Smith again, but he sounded like a legalistic pain in the ass. This was getting messier by the moment, a little too messy. Cus looked about. The R-S and the drones were out of sight, so now was probably the best time to take action. He debated briefly between a stun gun-induced heart attack and carotid pressure, then began massaging the man's shoulders as he worked his way up to the pressure points. It took remarkably little time. Perhaps the heart attack was already in progress. Cus admired his work as Jarvis slumped forward. Not a mark to be seen.

Guard Jarvis was what his dad would have called a tub of lard but carrying him was not much worse than carrying a sick calf. Kicked a lot less, that was for sure. Cus lugged the body into the woods to the west. He took a titanium magnut from his pocket and put it the man's hand. The culprits should be clear: murderous fugitives with a captive R-S. A great cover story, but the Captain wouldn't like the publicity, unless, unless he'd got the R-S back.

Back in the crypt his own R-S had hit something ten feet down, which was where Phil had estimated the subterranean nut to be. Cus grinned. He had them. An hour later he and the R-S had the buried structure exposed. Some kind of reinforced steel pipe. How in the hell had they gotten in there? He hadn't brought any cutting torches along. He hated how his father's voice always chimed in at such moments: "That was dumb, son, just plain dumb." As Cus crawled from the hole in the crypt, he caught sight of the faintest hint of dawn creeping over the ridge. The third day was arriving.

He had to get out of here fast. He'd come back with a warrant, continue the search. He fired a text off to Phil to get the process started. Phil was just a techie, but he'd get word to Stan, the guy in their squad who always knew the legal angle. And a true patriot, Stan. Reliable. Almost as smart as Cus was.

He dispatched the R-S and a drone to scout out the area where Phil had picked up the signal of third nut the one near the perimeter. He jogged back to the guard station. There he deployed the sentry drone out of sight, a bit further down the fence, then destroyed the station camera and footage. But he couldn't find the keys to the gate. He could get over the fence easily enough, but his R-S would destroy it. The keys must be on Jarvis.

Time was tight. He ran for the woods, wrestled the body over to recover the keys and clipped them to his belt. Jogging back to the station, he got a call from the R-S. Cus reversed course and sprinted, keys jangling, to the northern fence line. The R-S had removed a manhole cover. Excellent. The entrance to the pipe, had to be. He was on the scent. Before he could relish that moment, a message arrived from the sentry drone: a change of shift arriving early. Smitty? Cus didn't think twice before jumping into the hole. His automated minions followed. The manhole cover slammed shut.

Resistance

In the end it was Carlos who'd figured out how to integrate a spy virus into AS-57189's program. It would sit silently awaiting reactivation of AS's visual circuits. How to make the transmission undetectable was a serious problem, but Joan's experience with the echolocation circuit gave him the idea to link the spy stream output to that circuit. It was sonar, not electromagnetic, so less likely to be detected, but short range. They were working to solve the signal boost problem. He and Joanie had several ideas, and he felt so, so happy to be working together with her again, fixing stuff, solving problems. He had almost forgotten the impending danger when Varvara's impatient knock at the door snatched him from their flow. "Action in the tunnel," she'd said. "Out now." Her voice was low and compelling, a beautiful voice.

They used Kepler's breath control device to hustle AS to their old hideout, an anachronistic capsule of reinforced concrete meant to withstand a nuclear blast. A functional Faraday cage too! The space was tiny, and Carlos had had his doubts that AS would fit. The R-S quickly demonstrated his capacity for compact folding – important for shipping the robosoldiers efficiently Kepler informed him.

Carlos had been forced to admire the cover story Kepler provided AS when they'd first reactivated him: "AS-57189, this is Senior Repair Officer Diogenes. A rogue unit has traced your nut trail to the spies' location. They may capture you and thwart our mission. We will hide and deactivate you. We anticipate retrieving you later to continue our work. If captured, you are ordered to continue your magnut tracer program and we will track you."

AS had received this mutely so Kepler had pushed him. "Confirm order please."

"Magnut tracking program to continue," AS replied tersely. "Status and parameter report, 20 magnut supply, 500 meter or 20-minute interval dispersion."

"Status and parameters acknowledged," Kepler had replied. "But in hiding location no magnut dispersal unless capture." Carlos didn't think AS would release a magnut while deactivated but hadn't wanted to disable the circuit or deplete the magnut supply. He told Kepler that might tip their hand to AS.

Carlos sensed Joanie disliked lying to AS more and more. As they were walking AS from the workshop to the hideout, he overheard her instructing AS, "I know this is confusing. Spying always is. But if you have any doubts, follow the prime directive. If ordered to violate the prime directive, the order giver is a foe."

"Of course," AS had replied. "I always follow the prime directive." Carlos knew that hadn't been true. How had the Armed Forces been able to subvert the bots?

He pondered this as they sealed the hideout door with the rusted padlock whose combination came to him suddenly. Along with the combination came memories of the Scrimfall days when he and Joanie played "Upstairs", when they lived in a fantasy world full of fairies, elves, and parents who never fought.

Abruptly Varvara jerked him out of his daydream and pulled him onto an electric scooter. "Follow me," she shouted to Kepler and Joanie. They zoomed up an escape ramp with bangs on an adjacent pipe's doorlock echoing behind them, up to a far different "upstairs" than they'd imagined as kids.

A few minutes later Joan made their report to the largest group of telempaths she'd ever been with. She and Carlos moved to the side as discussion followed. People were crammed into every nook and cranny of the subterranean room below the bar. Both Varvara, who was tending the bar overhead, and Gus, the bouncer out front, streamed security reports to a woman named Janice telepathically, but mostly the telempaths had silenced their projections. Joan was impressed. She herself found that hard to do, harder even than shielding herself from input. Because of the high emotions of the current crisis, they'd agreed to conduct the meeting verbally. Of course, there was a lie monitor – an empath who tracked the person speaking to detect lies or exaggerations. She couldn't detect lies that people actually believed, of course, but sometimes she could pick up on conflicting data if the speaker was thinking of it. She had caught Carlos out when he was a bit too boastful about his infection of AS's program. He'd claimed it was "definitely undetectable". Joan could see how crushed he'd been when the monitor had detected his exaggeration. She'd put her arm over his shoulder to let him know she supported him, and feeling the depth to which, he was sinking, couldn't help but send out a mental reassurance. Then she too was rebuked by the monitor. That seemed to cheer Carlos up better than her reassurance. Fine. She dropped her arm, and he moved away.

As the reports proceeded Joan began to have a much better grasp of the scope of the problems they were facing. Three different migrant groups made reports: one from the detention centers, one from migrants at-large, and one from the camps on the border where things were particularly grim. Dehydration and heat exhaustion were running rampant. "We have got to get the border migrants further north – to a survivable climate," the reporter concluded. Of course, the detention centers were grim too – children, even babies, taken from their parents, medicines unavailable, guards brutal, the operations secret and largely out of public view, reports of their abuses suppressed. A few friendly judges had allowed some paroles, but the high court of the land had slapped them down.

There was even a report from a soldier. Joan had noticed his camouflage and it had given her the shivers. Apparently, there was a contingent of allies in the Armed Forces of the FCP, but the soldier reported there was also a growing contingent of soldiers who promoted the idea of a slaughter at the border, in the centers, and even on the streets. "Culling," they called it.

As the discussion turned into a debate of restorative empathy strategies that might blunt the deadliness of that contingent, Joan felt a strange throbbing in her chest. For a minute she couldn't place that sensation, though she was sure she had felt it before. She closed her eyes, and the darkness brought it back. The crypt. AS. The echolocation circuit. She turned in alarm to Janice who seemed unfazed. "Stop!" Joan shouted. "The robosoldier is nearby." That was all it took. They believed her.

Kepler, who was close to the center of the group, pulled up a grate from the floor. "This way," he sent silently, and quickly the group piled through into the oversized drainage pipe below. Several adults grabbed her and Carlos too, thank goodness, and pushed them ahead into the pipe. They hustled as silently as they could in the dark. They were emerging from another grate in an empty building several blocks away when they heard the echo of gunfire, not nearly distant enough.

Hot pursuit

Cus raced across town following the video surveillance tip Phil had sent him. He reflected smugly on the smoothness of the R-S recovery and the stupidity of his enemies. A Faraday cage indeed. Some twentieth century subterfuge. Following the radioactivity trail that they'd careless left (another benefit of the tracer magnuts was that they contaminated the dust around them), he'd arrived at the blast shelter. He'd enjoyed drawing his boyhood sidearm and shattering the rust-encrusted excuse for a lock off. Suspecting booby traps, he'd approached AS-57189 carefully. Only after his active R-S had made first contact and extracted the deactivated R-S from the shelter, did he approach and inspect it. He'd been able to reactivate it easily enough. Even the vision circuits though they had managed to thoroughly mess those up. But everything was modular, and he'd planned ahead, brought some spare parts.

He'd wanted to get this robot to Phil, who'd inspect it and check for booby traps while he'd track and capture the enemy. Then he'd be able to present the Captain with an intact R-S and the robonappers – at least some of them. He'd be put in charge of a team to track down the rest. It was a promotion for sure.

But when he'd reached the surface the delayed text tip from Phil had come through and hot pursuit was his self-issued order of the day. The bouncer at the door of the bar stepped aside for the uniform and his serious contingent of two R-S and three drones. Probably a collaborator but Cus let him live. The Captain didn't like messes in the street. He moved inside. Keeping AS at his side, he approached the very attractive young bartender who was shooting daggers at him with her eyes. He smiled politely, unscathed. "Have you seen these people?"

She glanced at the screenshot of Kepler and Joan entering the bar and answered in the most innocent voice she could muster, which was not much. "They were here earlier. But they left. Nowhere in the room. Take a look around." She gestured with the rag she was using to dry the counter and broke eye contact. She might have gone on blathering, but at that point his subterranean probe drone pointed the way to the door around the end of the bar. He turned crisply on his heel and ordered the sentry drone, "Watch her."

He heard nothing as he clattered down the stairs, but he could see a woman caught in his R-S's flood light. She was pulling a rug over a grate, no doubt another escape tunnel. She dropped the rug and looked up, meeting his gaze resolutely. "Get upstairs," he ordered. The drone could watch two of them, no problem. She didn't move and Cus glared feeling his temper mount. She was an ugly one, expendable and an obstruction. He didn't hesitate. "Fire!" he ordered the two R-S. The clatter of a fired round filled the silence, followed by a horrible screech that ripped and echoed through his brain. For a minute, a precious minute, it immobilized him. Then he shook it off, kicked the corpse aside and rushed down the sewer pipe. The drones and R-S followed him along the two-block tunnel that zigzagged under the street. As they turned a corner, he caught sight of a ladder lit by light streaming through a manhole above it. He sent his drones and R-S up first, with an order to contain, not kill, anyone they found there. Strange that he heard no resistance. He climbed the ladder cautiously, rung by rung. Still nothing. He emerged only to find the Captain glowering down at him.

Shifting identities

When they'd reached the warehouse, Kepler had led them to the loading dock. There the empaths dispersed. Joan realized that, unlike her, they all knew where they were going. She was disoriented. Her head was still buzzing with Janice's last warning, an empathic cry of anguished death focused on the killer, not on Joan, but it had been difficult to endure. As Kepler took their hands, hers and Carlos's, she confirmed it. "Janice died, didn't she." In the stench of the garbage-strewn warehouse courtyard, Kepler nodded grimly.

Through a haze of tears Joan noticed a small, cloaked woman approaching from outside the courtyard. "Someone's coming," she warned him.

"You need an escort," he muttered apologetically to Joan and Carlos. "Martina," he named her and named them in turn to her. "I can't stay with you any longer. I'm too easily identified." He touched Carlos's hand which still gripped a glinting hint of metal. "Practice every day."

She expected Carlos to be happy with the gift – the R-S controller, a new toy – but she could tell that in the few hours he'd spent with Kepler, the man who'd won Carlos's admiration had also set him up. A new father figure and just as quickly, a new loss. That was the sadness she felt spreading over Carlos like poisonous algae, a red tide coating the ocean of his emotions.

She'd admired Kepler too, but he seemed remote to her, far more guarded than the average empath. She caught a glimpse of the darkness at his core and of the future he anticipated, buried alive in hiding or prison, in an increasingly unlivable world. "It's not *so* bleak," he said, reading her thoughts, and loped off down the alley, just like that.

Without speaking Martina guided Carlos and Joan through a small door into the warehouse office. There she had them change clothes and shoes. Joan watched with dismay as her favorite clothing went into the dumpster which a garbage truck promptly emptied. The new clothes were black and nondescript, the shoes soft and pliable, but not nearly as durable as her boots, which had followed her Eeyore sweatshirt into the dumpster.

From the office Martina shepherded them up a narrow stairwell to a dance studio space on the upper floor of the warehouse. Joan stared at their unfamiliar reflections in the mirrors, hers the tallest by two heads at least. Behind her was an old coal fireplace, its tile still coated with black dust even though coal burning had been illegal for twenty years or more. To her surprise Martina gestured insistently to the flue which she had enlarged by removing the back panel of the fireplace. Carlos, then Joan crawled partway into the flue and Martina followed, reaching into her pack to pull out more of the black dust which she scattered to obscure the prints they'd left passing over the hearth. When she pulled the back panel back into place, the space was pitch dark. They waited briefly, listening, and Joan wondered if this was it, their hideout. Finally, Martina turned on her head lamp and urged them to crawl along the upslanting flue pipe for what seemed like hours. At last, they stopped, and Martina knocked on metal. A different stove panel opened. They tumbled out into another dance studio full of black-clad people jingling with bells. "Welcome to the Carbonivorous Folkloric and Interpretive Dance Troupe," Martina announced, speaking for the first time since they'd met.

"What the devil does that mean?" Carlos thought. "That we'll eat carbon?!" He stared at his hands, blackened from the crawl through the connected flues. His own hands, unrecognizable.

"Rub your faces," Martina instructed them. She was distributing the black dust from her pocket to the dancers and muttering as she went. The dancers smeared it around their mouths, then let loose a primal howl. Carlos thought of Janice's last sounds and shuddered. As the howl subsided, Martina crooned a kind of prayer: "We promise to sequester your carbon, oh lady, in life and in death. Vouchsafe us our biosphere. Restore us, oh lady." The troupe's amen was a jingling dance which encircled Carlos and Joan.

"What next?" Carlos wondered. "Being stewed in a pot?"

To his annoyance Joan overheard him and sent a disapproving response, "Stop your neocolonial cartoon caca. Rub your face!" Her words were barely audible in the jingle-jangle din, but the thought came through loud and clear. "It's a disguise."

Ashamed, he followed Joan's lead, massaging the dust into his face until she told him it was enough. When he looked up at her afterwards, he saw her naturally brown skin was now a much darker shade, her straight brown hair was black as night. They were handed new gogmasks that had been decorated with purple, gold, and green glitter. Still surrounded by the black-costumed dancers, they were herded downstairs and out the door.

The troupe danced down the street slowly, making an awful dinging noise, or so Carlos was thinking when Joan grabbed him hard by the wrist, "AS, he's coming," Joan sent to him. Carlos fingered the mouthpiece Kepler had given him. There'd been no time to practice with it, only the short walk from the workshop to the hideout. He walled up his fright and prepared himself to do his best.

The dancers stopped and bowed. For a few seconds Carlos caught a glimpse of the squad of R-S marching by, a whole squad, with AS in the middle. Humans too, two soldiers, and drones following. He dropped into a bow and held it as he heard the squad stamp past and off.

"He didn't betray us. He must have seen Janice's death, no, more than seen it. He was ordered to kill her," Joan sent.

The gunshots, the echoing scream reverberated in Carlos. How could Joanie be so calm? But when he looked up, he saw mist in her goggles and took her hand to steady her as they trudged, bells muffled, through the streets of the City.

Arrested

Cus felt hot, boiling hot. Behind his visor he knew his face was red. Sweat dripped down his neck. He'd been pushing for twenty-four hours now, and his nerves jangled with the caffeine drip he'd told his suit to keep running. This situation was unreal, so unfair. But what else was new with Captain Asshole, who hadn't allowed him a single word of explanation -- just took him into custody and now was frog-marching him down the street, away from the conspiracy site and toward the base!

At least he had AS-57189 to show for his efforts. He would have had the whole gang if the Captain had listened to him and tracked them down. He still had the captive at the bar, but now that he thought about it, he wasn't sure he wanted to show off the bar scene. That dead witch wouldn't score any points with the Captain. He winced. He didn't like thinking about her, of that penetrating screech. He'd been totally justified in that shooting – hot pursuit. Sweat ran rivers down his back now. Only another mile until he could get out of this thing. Twenty-four hours in a traumsuit was a trauma in itself.

So hot he wasn't thinking. Ah right, the captive bartender, another fuckable if he played his cards right. He allowed himself a slight smirk at the thought. He shifted his view to the drone's sensors and there she was. Mmm, delectable. Luscious treat coming up he promised himself. No, he wouldn't tell the Asshole about her, not if he could help it. She was a bargaining chip, her, and the recovered R-S. The gang responsible for the robonapping had escaped for now, but he held the woman. She'd crack and he could bust the whole conspiracy open. Him and his buddies. If Captain A would just leave him alone to do his work. When they got to base, that's what he would do – demand his due. As they turned the corner, he shifted his view back to the street where a black blob of jangling civilians stopped and bowed, as they should, as they should, though he would have preferred a full grovel.

At base the Captain marched him straight to the stockade, not a good sign. At least the A had let him take his traumsuit off, then regretted it. "You stink!" What the hell did he expect? When was the last time he'd been in a traumsuit? Probably never, prissy sissy.

Dispatched to the showers, Cus had one delightful moment when the water had poured over him, clean and cold. After a minute the shower clicked off. Cus stood naked and soapy, slamming his hand against the unresponsive control. "Fuck, fuck, fuck," he chanted the timeworn words of defeat. Finally, he toweled off and, still sticky, reluctantly pulled on the grey stockade pajamas provided to prisoners.

On the way to the interrogation room Cus was ready to light into the Captain for his failure to continue the pursuit which really, when you thought about it, constituted a dereliction of duty. As he entered, he spotted Phil and a couple of his mess hall buddies in the room. Had Captain A gone after his buds too? But then he realized they were in uniform and wouldn't look him in the eye. Fucking traitors.

"Lieutenant Custer," the Captain said shaking his head, clicking his tongue.

"Permission to speak, sir."

"I think you'd be better off to sit down and listen to the best of your addled ability son."

"But sir, I have a report to make. The robosoldier was recovered sir. And I, uh we," he nodded at Phil, "tracked down the robonappers. Our mission was a success."

"Lieutenant, my definition of a success does NOT include reclaiming a highly compromised R-S. It does NOT include murdering a civilian in a pub basement."

"Hot pursuit sir. I could have had the whole gang."

"Don't interrupt me again, Custer. She was a civilian who would have been far more useful alive than dead."

Cus bit his well-callused tongue. Perhaps he had gotten carried away. But who wouldn't, with the quarry virtually in sight. He would have had them too if he hadn't been slowed down by that sonic attack, which still rattled in his head. He suppressed it, tuned back in to the Captain.

"I don't know what kind of publicly witnessed slaughter you might have carried out if Corporal Phillips hadn't alerted me to your reckless and entirely unlawful activity."

"But sir, you ordered . . ."

The Captain roared back at that. "Do not "but" me Lieutenant. You got no order from me authorizing an illegal search, tomb desecration or murder."

Shit, Phil had ratted everything out.

"I was so close to grabbing the whole gang sir."

The Captain leaned in, so he was nose to nose with Cus. "*If* you had, you'd be a hero. But you didn't." He pushed Cus into a chair. "Now I have to save your ass from a court martial." Sighing the Captain took his own seat at the table. "I wouldn't do this for everyone, Cus, but you've got spirit, just like your dad told the Colonel."

"Yes, sir, thank you sir." Cus summoned the grateful groveling tone of his youth. With those words he struck the resentment and fear that coursed through him like a hard seam of Western bituminous coal.

The Captain turned toward Phil who stared wide-eyed at the proceedings. "Corporal Phillips you're to take the lieutenant to the stockade at Paxtang tonight. There's a train in one hour. Report to Colonel Adams when you get there."

"Yes sir," Phil managed in a wobbly voice.

"The brass won't like it but out of town, out of mind."

A train ride with Phil! Cus started to explore the possibilities of revenge with a rising sense of gaiety. But the Captain called in two guards, who put him in handcuffs, and issued further orders for them to accompany Cus and Phil. "These men are for your safety, both of you," he said nodding to Cus and Phil. "I suspect we'll have riots over this killing."

Dancing onward

The entire troupe held their bow until the sounds of stamping feet faded into the general din of the City. Joan could hardly contain her excitement, her joy that AS had held true, had trusted her and the evidence, the horrible violation of the prime directive he'd witnessed. He couldn't have been the one who executed the order, could he? No, they'd disarmed him. Surely there hadn't been time to repair him. But what would happen to him when they did? She stewed in uncertainty.

When the troupe members finally rose again and jingled in a dance of relief, she joined them, her feet performing a most inexact replica of the steps she saw around her. They busked their way uptown and westward, baking in the scrimmed sun. When they reached the River, Martina reached into her capacious costume and distributed small water containers equipped with straws that could be insinuated under their gogmasks. "Do not discard," she instructed Joan and Carlos. "There's a pocket inside your shirt. And don't drink it all now. You'll need it."

Joan's feet no longer felt like scampering when they had been on the river route for 4 hours 49 minutes and 49 seconds as Carlos, the timekeeper, chanted wearily to the rhythm of the bells. These people just wouldn't quit. By dusk they were back on home turf, and she longed to return to their apartment for a nap, just a short nap. To her surprise they headed for the neighborhood bar, the one overlooking the ferry. The building complex housed the pools as well and their underground hideout. Joan was terrified but not surprised to see the complex encircled by heavily armed police, but Juan, the troupe's impossibly handsome choreographer, went up to the guard at the gate and presented their credentials. They were admitted without individual scans.

Once in the studio, Carlos and Joan slipped off their gogmasks, toweled off their sweaty salty carbon-coated faces, and rested on floor mats while the troupe members scurried about packing costumes and bags into a brightly painted handcart with large decorative wheels. Too soon they were on the trail by the River again, pushing the cart, heading for the Ferry. The crossing was smoother than she'd imagined it would be and noisier, the great bass engine of the Ferry echoing off the cliffs on the western bank. The afternoon's earnings were handed over to the Ferry agent as they disembarked. A steep uphill climb almost brought Joan to her knees but at that moment, they arrived at yet another studio. Gratefully she saw the studio had an attached dorm. She lost no time tumbling into a conveniently black-sheeted bed and let her heavy lids fall.

Asleep she explored the dreams of others. They contained excitement and fear for the upcoming journey west into the mountains and pastures. She pursued interior exploration too: AS's circuits, his strange inhuman ways, his rules and programs, the prime directive, Janice's final primal scream, simultaneously an expression of empathy for the self and a call for the same in others. She dreamed the colors, the heartbeats, the breathing, the rhythms, and the bells, always the bells.

Morning found Carlos sitting in the brush on top of the palisade overlooking the River which rippled with the cool nor'easter that was blowing in. The wind was fierce enough that the particle count was down. He could take his gogmask off and practice with the robocontroller mouthpiece Kepler had given him. He'd woken early in the dim light of the black-sheeted dormitory. The awful aching of his legs prevented him from going back to sleep. He whispered to Joan who lay on the bottom bunk across from his, but she didn't stir. Eager to be away from the silent stench of bodies sighing in sleepy unison, as though they were still performing to some silent rhythm, he'd crept out into the early morning. He'd followed the dawn light to the cliff edge, wind on his face, and finally felt free and at ease as he hadn't since leaving the apartment, just, was it only three days ago?

From his perch he could see the weather blowing in. The storm would be a big one. Keeping one eye on the sky, he turned his attention to his practice. Of course, without AS, he couldn't know if the controller was actually working, so he focused on a more immediate problem. If he had had to use the controller yesterday, he would have had to remove his gogmask. Was there a way to adapt the mask so the controller would fit through it?

In the middle of this thought experiment, Joan slipped in beside him. They sat in a close, comfortable silence for a moment as he continued to mouth the reed of the controller. "You're crazy, you know," Joan started, "coming out here in this wind."

"Feels great though, doesn't it?"

"Yeah," Joan admitted. "It's going to hail though. We should go back up."

"Just a little longer," he pleaded. "I'm so sick of crowds."

"There's breakfast," she wheedled. "You don't wanna miss that."

Whether it was the promise of breakfast or the first ice flecks stinging his cheeks, Carlos rose and began making his way back up the slope to the studio. His legs ached in protest.

"Ow," Joan cried. He thought she was being empathic, but when he looked over his shoulder, he saw the bruise on her forehead and felt the hailstones pounding his back. Grabbing for her hand, he ducked his head and hustled faster, eager for cover.

Adaptation

Cus sat on the train to Paxtang too mad to sleep. He was handcuffed to Phil, who kept leaning over to apologize. Cus responded with a furious yank on the cuffs which he hoped hurt Phil as much as it hurt him. After the third yank, Cus was satisfied to hear a soft whimper – so Phil that. He could picture Phil stuffed in one of those Natural History Museum dioramas, Phil and maybe a few of these ugly shorn sheep that dotted the pastureland rolling by. Ordinarily he would have taken pleasure in these more open vistas, but they were constantly interrupted by the gritty backsides of falling down towns – garbage and refuse, rags hanging on clotheslines, and hulks of old gasoline-powered vehicles rusting in a yellow mist that gradually turned to rain leaving oily streaks on the plastic windows of the train. Soon it was all a blur.

As his anger dwindled, Cus struggled against his fatigue. He needed a plan. As much as he'd love to break out here and now, go after the quarry, that wasn't happening, not with a guard fore and rear. He'd have to be patient, see what the situation was in Paxtang, get a read on this Colonel Adams. That decided, Cus allowed himself to drift off. The clatter of the tracks became that of hooves over stony ground. He led his cavalrymen against the shadowy-faced mob. He swung his sword high, lopped off the head of the first man he came to, and whooped when the Captain's disconnected face soared by and into the melee where it was trampled into the blood-soaked dust.

Cus woke with a jerk, the jerk of the train stopping. He raised his handcuffed wrist and turned to face Phil. "Later," he said flatly. Could be a plan, a warning, or a threat. Give Phil something to think about.

Phil dropped his gaze, muttering, "OK, sure."

Getting off the train took forever. The guards kept them in their seats until every last stinking passenger had gotten off. When the guards finally barked an order to stand and exit, Cus could think of nothing but food. The guards marched them to the stockade where Cus and Phil were separated. Good riddance.

A stockade guard took charge of Cus. "You must be hungry," the guard said. Friendly enough.

Cus spotted his name tag – Smith. "You got it Smitty. Thirsty too," he added with a wink.

"Well, it's pretty plain stuff in the mess hall but it'll fill you up. Harder stuff will cost you some bits, but we always extend a little help to the newcomers. Just ask for Smit."

At the door of the mess hall, the guard left Cus who found his way to the food line. Plain fare but better than what they had in the City. He grabbed some mutton stew and spotted a space at the meat-eaters' table. On arrival, he saluted them. "Custer," he announced and took his place in the midst of a ruddy-faced crew who were, he noted, discreetly passing a flask from man to man.

"Busted, Cus," his neighbor laughed as he passed him the flask, "Take a long draw. You're gonna need it, newbie."

Afterwards, sated and drunk, Cus settled into his cell bunk. Sure, beat the old storm-cellar his father used to throw, literally throw, him into when he was a kid. He'd bang down the stairs and arrive at the bottom battered and bruised. He rubbed his cuff-scuffed wrist at the memory of the old fracture he'd sustained but never admitted to back then. It was a well of darkness that cellar, lit dimly during the day by a small unreachable casement window and pitch black at night. Here there was a low wattage bulb in the hallway outside. He slipped into the usual sequence of drunken dreams, the nightmare of waking to the cellar rat gnawing on his toes, the revenge dream of cornering and knifing the rat, of dissecting and displaying it.

When he woke to the honk of the bugle, he smiled. Good dreams. Revenge was the best reward. As he sat up, rubbed his eyes, and gazed about at his milling cellmates, a bit of a breeze blew across his right wrist. Startled he looked down – no watch. He checked for the cash stash in his sock. Gone. He'd been rolled.

A red haze momentarily obscured his vision. Three deep breaths for focus. He contained and harnessed his instinct for revenge. Keeping his head down, Cus pretended to search for his lost belongings as he surveilled the men for the smuggest ones among them. There, the Mexican slicking back his greasy hair, and the chuckling redhead pawing the Mex's shoulder. A beefy guy whose freckles, red eyelashes, brows, and hair gave him the creeps. Repulsive freak. Probably Irish. No dogs or Irishmen, his father used to joke. Cus had thought that unfair to the dogs.

He kept his cool and headed out with the others to the mess hall. He took note of the layout, the weak points of the building and the guards who herded them through hallways. No Smitty this morning. Cus wondered if the guard was the fence for his missing watch and mentally added him to his revenge fantasy hit list. But breakfast first. Eat while you can.

When Cus finished a stack of pancakes, sticky with some artificial goo, and washed it down with some chalky fake stuff they called mulk, he emitted a burp so loud even he was embarrassed by it. But only for a moment because suddenly someone was standing just behind him, in his blind spot. He suppressed the urge to whirl about and confront the interloper. Instead, he turned slowly in his seat to confront a guard who addressed him politely. "Lieutenant Custer, come with me." Custer rose happily and saluted his cellmates, winking at the Mexican and Red. Let them sweat this new info about his rank for a minute. He wouldn't rat them out of course. But he could and they now knew it.

Just outside the door Phil stood in full uniform, ashen-faced. Cus nodded to him, "Just tell the truth, Phil." He followed this advice with a threatening toothy grin.

As Phil stumbled and stuttered over his story, Cus studied the books shelved behind Colonel Adams's desk. He was pleased to see several of his father's old favorites: <u>The Conscience of a Conservative</u>, <u>Chevron Deference</u>, and <u>Countering the Majoritarian Difficulty</u>. He hadn't read these writings all the way through, but he'd read enough to use their arguments to defend himself when his father was in the mood to demolish him in a debate instead of simply kicking him down the stairs.

Phil was wrapping up his cowardly, self-serving summary of their pursuit of the R-S thieves, their successful retrieval of the R-S. Adams turned to Cus, amusement playing at the edges of his mouth. "What do you have to say for yourself, Custer?"

"Moderation in the pursuit of justice is no virtue," Cus cited.

Adams laughed at that. "I'm inclined to agree with Captain Clark. You're a good lad in need of some seasoning."

"Yes, sir," Cus snapped.

"I have a job that will require a bit of excess – but quietly executed you understand. I believe a less urban posting might help with this." Adams rambled on at length. It seemed as though there was a farm in the mountains that had been sheltering refugees. The Colonel wanted Cus to create a chilling atmosphere for the inhabitants there – enough to deter their seditious behavior but not enough to create controversy. No arrests, no disappearances. The time wasn't quite ripe for that. Not so close to the Capital.

Cus resisted a snort. In his mind the time was always ripe for that when sedition was involved

"I also want to give you some command experience. I can't afford to lose any more R-S, and I have to send Corporal Phillips here back to the City. His technical skills are needed there. But I can spare some of the men in the stockade. Study them for a couple of weeks and let me know."

"Two weeks!" Cus thought but he bit his tongue and snapped a "Yes sir!" Cus was sorry to lose control of Phillips, who looked hugely relieved. He didn't feel they were quite even. Still Phil had done a good job of emphasizing the hot pursuit angle, had even assigned a weapon to the woman Cus had taken out. The scream invaded his thoughts. He winced in pain. A weapon indeed, though Phil wouldn't have known about that, would he? No, he could afford to let Phil off, a miserable worm Phil – not worth the effort. Especially as he had more worthy specimens in his sights.

"Two weeks, Lieutenant," the Colonel interrupted his thoughts. "You can study the maps, and written orders are in the office down the hall, but you'll be back in the stockade at night. Choose your men carefully, Lieutenant Custer."

Golden Ash

I've been a confirmed atheist all my adult life – okay I'll admit to pantheistic tendencies, but tendencies only. This morning, though, I awoke in heaven. A child, my son, golden hair gleaming, came down the greensward toward me where I lay gently rocking in the shade of a willow. Rainbows twinkled in the mist of my gogmask. "Gogmasks in heaven?" I asked myself and, unthinkingly, pulled it off. I felt the freshness of the air against my sweaty face, the relief of relentless pressure on my cheeks and around my eyes and took a deep breath of sulfurous air which sent me into a spate of uncontrollable coughing. This hell again. As I coughed and fumbled unsuccessfully with the gogmask, I saw that child sprint toward me, his mouth in a silent scream, then the black void.

I woke a second time with a splitting headache in the hiss of an oxygen tent. I opened my eyes carefully, squinting against the light. Shadowy figures flitted beyond the fogged translucent walls of the tent. I risked a deep breath, enjoying the unobstructed flow, the lack of cough. Suddenly I was intensely hungry. I tried raising my right arm, then my left. They were untethered – a good sign. A red-faced woman unzipped the door. "Feeling better?"

"Hungry!" I managed to croak.

"Stay there," she advised, as though I were in shape to do anything else. In addition to the headache, I ached all over. My paddle and hiking muscle groups must be packed full of lactate. My hands were no longer muddy though. Someone must have bathed me. Around me I felt the contact of unfamiliar bedclothes. Another zip and the woman knelt at the tent door with a tray of what smelled like miso soup, oatmeal, a dried fish and, to my great relief, coffee. "Can you sit up?" she asked.

She pointed to a wedge pillow behind me, and once I was braced against it, she slid the tray over my legs. "*Itadakimasu*," I mouthed. Savorsome steam traced its way into my nostrils as I lifted hot coffee to my lips. With the anticipation of caffeine, my bear of a headache began to retreat into its cave. After a swallow I hazarded speech again, "I'm guessing this is not a detention facility?"

She smiled, "Not yet," then looked over her shoulder as a child spoke to her through the open flap. I couldn't make out his words, and I didn't recognize the voice – not my son's or my brother's. Of course not – that had been wishful thinking, downright magical thinking really. Belonged in fiction not this rough and ready, faltering world.

The woman turned back with a worried look. "Don't talk now. Eat quickly please. We have to move you. The authorities are all over the lake looking for you. They'll be going house to house next. Don't worry. You won't have to go far. We have a secure space to put you in – underground, not very big. But we need time to clean all this up." She gestured to the tent.

"Your name?" I blurted between bites.

"Call me Grace," she smiled.

I wasn't claustrophobic, but neither was I fond of spelunking. They shut me up in a blocked, blind loop of the septic system, a loop the size of a coffin. I was jammed in there with my backpack minus kayak and a small O_2 tank. The space was vented to the surface through a faux vertical septic pipe. A filter in the pipe meant I didn't have to wear a gogmask, a relief to my intercostal muscles and ears alike. For some reason (bone conduction?) I can hear better without a gogmask even though the mask doesn't cover my ears. I could hear, in this instance, the grumbling of the men on the lawn outside the house. Their search hadn't turned anything, anybody up so far.

It slowly dawned on me that they weren't looking for me specifically. They were searching for climate refugees and for the network that hid them. "No, we are not going to hand dig up the septic system for every lake house we search," an officer shouted angrily into his communicator. "That's what robots are for. Why aren't you sending me any?" I couldn't hear the other side of the conversation, only the crackle of the communicator. Then I lost all ability to hear speech when a horrific banging and thumping and stomping and yelling sounded overhead. My space trembled with it, and I worried fleetingly about a frack quake. The racket stopped abruptly, and I could hear again.

"Yeah, we're bringing the householders in for questioning. There's a kid missing though. Probably up to no good. I'll leave a surveillance drone in place."

My heart sank – a surveillance drone -- almost impossible to evade. This space might truly be my coffin. I had water but no food – so I had the prospect of two miserable cramped weeks. Wait, no, I didn't have two weeks' worth of water – at best five days. Would the drone stay here that long? Would the householders keep quiet about me when subjected to questioning. The drugs they used these days, they were hard to resist. I knew people who had suicided when they realized whom they'd betrayed under questioning. A waste and a pity. But understandable. Not that I'd prepared for that. Perhaps I should have. For the next few hours these questions and thoughts raced around the track of my brain faster and faster until they blurred into a fear that drove up my heart rate. Not good said the doctor voice embedded in my brain. Abruptly I switched gears and shut down, using the tools the empaths had taught me.

As I dissociated for a long time there was nothingness, then the greensward returned. Gnats were skimming the grass, and that blond-haired boy was back. So like my son as a child, the sun burnishing his hair, flying into a still blue sky. Not dead yet but sailing recklessly on the currents. He flew into the sun which grew brighter and brighter. I couldn't see him anymore, never. I stared into the sun. I wanted it to blind me. Tears streamed down my face.

No, I shouldn't be wasting water. I tried to blink my eyes dry, but the sun wouldn't stop beaming into them and the quaking started again. The coffin was open, and the boy stood above me, headlamp on his forehead. He was shaking me, whispering urgently. "Wake up. Come back."

Darkness returned. Had I closed my eyes? No, they were open, but the coffin was closed. Just as I realized I was too weak to extract myself from the coffin, a soft rustling came from above. The lid clicked quietly and swung slowly open on silent hinges. And there was the boy again, finger to his lips. When I tried to move though, I couldn't. He mimed stretching, and I used the newly open space above me to mimic his movements so that feeling and power returned to my limbs. I used a bar he placed across the opening to pull myself up and immediately fainted. I revived choking on the water he was squirting into my mouth – not a wise move with the unconscious but he was young. And

I was horribly thirsty. I seized the bottle and began guzzling. The second bottle I sipped.

I wanted to know all that had happened since the soldiers had posted the drone and left, but it was clear he wanted no speech, no noise. So it wasn't until we were on the trail again, at least a thousand meters beyond the apparently sightless drone, when he broke his silence.

"Hi, I'm Ashley." He's a girl I realized with a quick shock and a sense of embarrassment. The presumptions of the elderly were strong in me. "But call me Ash."

"She, he, or other," I asked, politely I hoped.

"Oh, I don't care about that," Ash said blithely. "I'm a tomboy."

I nodded, "Me too. I'm K, short for Katherine or Katie, take your pick."

"Yeah, Dr. KT Strand. My parents told me . . . before they had to go with the soldiers."

"So that's what happened."

"Yeah, well they aren't back" Ash looked downcast, then recovered quickly. "But they will be soon! Sorry I left you under so long. It took me a while to figure out the drone. It didn't need recharge until five days in. If we hadn't had that big storm, it wouldn't have needed charging then."

"Big storm?" I thought of my grandchildren, still on the run I hoped, and said a little prayer to the storm gods Fūjin and Raijin.

"Yeah, hail and everything. I had to go underground too. But I had a spyhole on the drone, and when it lost power, I had it all planned out," Ash bragged. "Hacked it, got the vision circuits set to loop, and got you out." She drew her thumb across her chest and pointed it up. "It's still got audio though and it monitors utility use, so, no shower. You really stink!"

She'd wrinkled her nose at me, and we'd padded on through the welcoming forest. Several miles later, another amazement. I hadn't seen a rainbow in decades. Now here one was again, dancing in the mist beside a small waterfall. I stripped shamelessly but left the gogmask in place. My lungs weren't up to many more insults, and Ash had informed me that we had a long way to go. Into the warm water I plunged, rinsing off the dried urine and sweat that had accumulated in my five days of being buried alive.

In the ensuing period I learned much from this quick and agile child, so self-possessed, and confident in a ten-year-old's way. Inevitably I compared Ash to my own kids. Her skillful hacking reminded me of Carlos, but she had none of his dour resentment. She was devoid of the special empathic skills that caused Joan so much vicarious pain. She was incredibly knowledgeable about the layout of the woodlands and swamps we were traveling through. Decades ago, this area had become a wildlife corridor. Ash followed in the tracks of the animals, avoiding the abandoned roads that were more open to sky-based surveillance. We carried only a little water, but the lands were wet. We filtered what we found with straws Ash had packed. At breaks during the day, she was careful to stop near oxygen-producing bromeliads and would set up a small filter tent over them. We would huddle around aloe and others I haven't retained the names of yet. Sometimes marsh plants cleaned the air for us so we could escape the gogmasks that way too. I slept much better without their restriction and felt a bit stronger everyday despite our long hours afoot.

Ash was very proud of being a guide. She'd been training since she was five with her parents, but this was her first trip without them. Despite their absence she was curiously unworried. Apparently, they'd been taken in before, but they always returned by the next morning. They hadn't this time, but she was confident, nonetheless. Well-practiced at positive self-talk, she'd crafted a fable packed with hope. She expected to hand me off at the next safehouse and they'd be waiting for her return. She'd left them an encrypted note she reassured me.

I was not reassured. I'd overheard the suspicions of the soldiers' commander He must know there was a network, an underground, and that her family was a critical link – the closest to the City. Was this just the elderly pessimist in me or experiential wisdom? What to do? I worried about them. And while I was at it, I worried about Carlos and Joanie and the R-S project too. It wasn't the only plan of course, but it was the primary nonviolent one –or a key part of it. I was convinced non-violence was the key to long-term success for our empathic movement. I sought a mantra of reassurance but found only worry.

Almost two weeks after setting out, we knelt at the shadowed edge of the corridor and waited for a signal from our safe house destination. It was not long after full darkness, which would hide us from visual surveillance. The canals that irrigated the area would still be warm for a while. We could wade through them evading infrared and olfactory surveillance. And the crickets would cover us sonically. Ash had explained all this earlier on our hike. For now, we maintained our silence, stilled our breathing. I admired the craft of this approach. We had a two-hour window before the moonrise. But long after the light of the full moon was glittering on the cooling canal waters, we still had not received a signal. Finally at midnight, Ash's tiny computer tickled her wrist with a single-word message – "Compromised."

Found & Lost

Carlos felt like he was being railroaded out of town and he didn't appreciate it. Joanie kept explaining to him it was for them that the troupe was making this trip, that they usually didn't travel in the summer. Too hot. Too many thermal inversions.

Too hot. Well, they were right about that. Every night his clothes were dripping, his feet blistered from sliding around inside the oversized boots they'd given him. This forced march across the countryside was killing his legs. Cramps were waking him up at night, and he was running short on medicine. Better get that on the supply list for the next time they hit a town.

This trip was plain stupid, a waste of time. They'd been making progress on cracking the robosoldier code, great progress, and now they'd just quit. Joanie claimed it was only a "strategic retreat", but there was nothing meta about this wandering. She was always trying to calm him down, just like an annoying big sister. Just because she was taller. She was only a year older. Right now, he didn't even like her. So, she was ignoring him. Her problem. He couldn't believe he'd ever been attracted to her. But Varvara. He sighed. Was she still in the City?

Andres was the one bright spot. He was a dwarf who played the flute and a bunch of other instruments for the troupe. He'd joined them the morning they left the cliffside studio. Carlos and Andres walked together at the same pace and with the same degree of pain, but Carlos was a head taller, which he tried not to act too happy about. When they trailed the others, Carlos was pleased to lose the crowd. Andres knew the way so there was no danger of being lost. They had been warned they could be robbed, were more likely to be attacked if it was just the two of them. That was a laugh. They had nothing. Their gear was in the cart up front and well-guarded. Andres carried only his flute and water bottle. Carlos had his mouthpiece, but he'd given up practicing. No one seemed to care, and the reed was broken anyway.

Two weeks into the march to nowhere, Carlos and Andres came to a dip in the dirt road. Although the day was sunny, a marsh had extended its reach over their route. "How deep is that?" Andres asked.

"How should I know? I don't swim," Carlos shuddered. "That's what I was doing at Scrimfall."

"I can't swim," Andres confessed. "I never learned."

Carlos stood motionless, staring down at the opaque water as though he could boil it away with infrared vision. He was contemplating the large number of slimy things that might be hidden under the mud brown surface.

Andres broke his trance. "Look up! The cart went that way." He pointed out tracks carved into the slope slanting up from the side of the road. Following the tracks, they had to watch their step to miss crushing masses of slimy red newts. The sodden roadside was boggy and sucked at their boots, until the tracks entered the woods.

They followed the tracks into the woods only to halt again at the steep banks of a rushing gorge. Two logs, spaced far enough apart to accommodate the carts' wheels, had been lined up to bridge the gorge. Two logs too far apart for short legs. Carlos had no confidence he could keep his stride narrow enough to balance on a single log. Andres agreed and dropped to sit astride the log. Carlos gulped and followed his example. They scooted across, wobbly and scuffing hands and butts, toward the other side. Mosquitos whined and picked at their defenseless ears as they inched along. At last across, they scrambled up the bank of the gorge and hustled out of the woods to the open road where the clouds of mosquitoes and anxiety faded away.

Dazed, beat, and bitten, they paused uncertainly. "Time for a nap," Andres decided, and Carlos nodded. The rock they chose to doze on overlooked the marsh. A pleasant breeze dried their sweat. Bees buzzed below them.

****

Joan found herself enjoying the walk west despite the heat, pollution, and mosquitos. She'd stopped worrying about Carlos once Andres had taken him under his wing. Maybe that wasn't the right image she thought as she glanced back at their small figures fading into the distance, slowly, then quickly as they descended from the crest of a hill, Carlos's head still visible after Andres had disappeared. The country was rolling now and very green, humidity hanging over the lowlands and with it, polluting particles. Still, the marshes cleared the air, or so she'd heard. Walking gave her a chance to think things over, especially the business with AS. Funny how stepping away from the problem could help you solve it.

She'd always felt the prime directive would be key, but she was amazed that directing AS to be alert to murder had had the effect that it did. She knew he had known she was in the crowd of dancers. She had felt the echolocation probe, had followed the electrons coursing through his logic circuits. There were several factors that had played into his decision not to inform his commander of her presence. The weakest had been their cover story – the spy mission. AS had assigned what she thought was a very generous probability of 0.2 to that. She'd been curious to realize that he'd assigned a p of 0.6 to the likelihood that they had been lying to him. It seemed to be a global score, not specific to the cover story. AS had assigned her a predictive value score of 0.9 after witnessing Janice's killing.

She tried not to be distracted by the heartsickness she felt at the death of her grandmother's best friend. A deep breath. Let it go. Let the marsh soak up the heartsickness the way it did the pollution; her grief and the world's together filtered through grasses and rushes. She wondered if AS had been impacted by Janice's death cry. If so, that could be wonderful, proof of a pathway for building R-S empathy. Not that she wanted thousands of empaths dying on battlegrounds, though she realized from her history lessons at school that such deaths did strengthen pacifist tendencies. "Revenge tendencies too," her earnest teacher's voice echoed in her head.

She didn't miss school or even her friends very much. They'd been associates, not really friends. Carlos was more than enough teen drama for her empathic brain to handle. Despite the tension of their current situation, the dancers were warm and accepting. She was learning to dance. She practiced with them in the morning as the sun cracked the horizon, before it was obscured by the Scrim. They practiced again in the evening, even though people were footsore and weary. The rehearsals were always joyous, always communal. Martina and Juan walked through the small crowd, correcting positions, laying on hands that were healing and kind.

Martina had become her new empath coach and she felt growing confidence in her skills. She was exploring her boundaries. And she admired Juan, how he led the collective not because he was an alpha male, but because the group had delegated him to fill a leadership role. He used that delegated power carefully, respectfully. Every night after supper, the tired dancers discussed the events of the day and their plans for the future. Joan felt she was learning as much from Juan as from Martina – if she could just stay awake.

******

Carlos woke to the sound of Andres's flute. He'd been dreaming of his workshop. He sighed. He missed it. Andres was mud-smudged and smiling. He stopped his playing and was waving a stubby twig or something like that in front of Carlos's face.

"I found some reeds!" Andres announced triumphantly.

Carlos was not feeling it. "C'mon man, I just woke up."

"Practice makes perfect," Andres said in a high-pitched voice Carlos knew to be an imitation of his mother's. She'd been very pushy. Another Scrimfall victim. Shouldn't speak ill of the dead. His grandmother's phrase. But he didn't want to think about grandma now, so he reluctantly reached for the reed, set it into the mouthpiece.

"I can't even tell if it's working," he complained. "If I had my workshop, I could build a toy R-S, try it out on that."

Andres laughed. "A toy R-S, that's ambitious."

"You think I couldn't do it?" Carlos flared up, ready for a fight.

But Andres only laughed again. "Oh, I totally think you could do it. But here we are." He gestured to the rock, the marsh, the rutted dirt road. Bowing to reality, Carlos buzzed the reed until his out of practice lip was sore – all of ten minutes.

"That's why you've gotta practice man. Keep your lip up," Andres counseled the obvious. Carlos stowed the reed along with others Andres handed him. They strolled down to the marsh where Andres showed him the plants he had cut them from. "Keep your eye out for these, and as long as there's marsh, you'll have no problem with reed stock." As they stood by the marsh, its waters suddenly glinted red. The sun had dipped below the Scrim.

Carlos looked up in alarm. "Shit, we're late. We'll miss dinner." They hurried back along the road. After an hour of sweating and panting, as the sun set and the moon rose, they reached a rise that overlooked the troupe's campsite for the night. The camp lay south and west of a crossroads and Carlos was on his toes. "Race you," he taunted Andres.

But the sharp-eyed Andres abruptly raised his arm blocking Carlos and pointed. "What's that?" Approaching from the north was a figure garbed in the silver of reflected moonlight. Carlos gaped, then reached for his mouthpiece. When the R-S got to the crossroads, Carlos blew as if the lives of his companions depended upon it. Slowly the R-S turned, hesitated, then headed east towards them.

Carlos stopped blowing then and tugged on Andres's arm. They dashed into the shelter of the woods and hurried as silently as they could, parallel to the road and away from the camp. Soon they could feel the shudder of the R-S's heavy footfalls overtaking them, and they ducked behind a rock for infrared and echo cover. The shuddering passed them by. Relieved, they carefully made their way back to the road and tumbled downhill toward the campsite as fast as they could.

Joan was glad to see Andres and Carlos hurry sweating and breathless into camp, but she was also disappointed. She'd been expecting AS, had felt his echolocation beam not thirty minutes before. The beam had faded, and she was left with the feeling that she had probably imagined it all. Wishful thinking like a little girl. How could AS have found them all the way out here after all?

Carlos's excited burst of speech tore her away from her thoughts. "We saw a robosoldier headed for the campsite!"

An anxious hush fell over the group and Juan held his finger to his lips. "Quietly then," he mouthed.

Carlos took a deep breath and whispered, "I diverted him with this." He held up Kepler's mouthpiece and there was a soft burble of approval from the troupe. "It's headed east on the road, or at least it was when we left the road to double back."

Joan could no longer contain herself. "It was AS, right?"

"AS?" Carlos asked incredulously. "No. At least I don't think so. I was thinking it was a tracker R-S."

"They usually have drones do that work," Juan interjected, "but Joan, if you thought a robosoldier was approaching you should have warned the group."

A blush scalded Joan's face. "It was AS! I felt him go by. I have to get him back." And before anyone could contradict her or get a long debate going, she sprinted out of camp and up the hill. Soon she heard boughs snapping and felt the ground shake ahead of her. Close now.

Behind her she heard footfalls, the human kind. She turned to see Juan loping toward her. As the moon crested the western mountains, he pulled her into the forest bordering the road. "Joan, listen to me," he said urgently. "You're putting us all at risk."

"This robosoldier is critical to our plans," Joan objected.

"To your plans, maybe even to your collective's, but not to ours. We were charged with your safety, but we have our own group's safety to consider as well. It's impossible to travel discreetly with an R-S in tow. It almost certainly has a tracking device."

Joan could see his point, feel his urgency, his sympathy, his resolve. But AS had not betrayed them. He had sought her out as instructed. She needed to make the most of this opportunity. "Leave us with the R-S then, me and Carlos," she pleaded. Juan smiled tightly, indulgently. She wished Juan was an empath; Martina would understand.

"Absolutely not," Juan said, adopting a paternalistic tone she'd never heard him use before. Bristling in response, she turned away from him wordless, angry, and sad. But each step that took her closer to AS grew lighter. She felt AS's echolocation beam sweep by, then back, and lock onto her. She turned around and saw Juan trudging ten meters behind.

"He's locked on to me," Joan said calmly. "You better go back if you want to avoid detection."

Juan sighed. "Stay here with it then. I'll go back and discuss the situation more thoroughly with the group and send word when a decision has been made." He looked anxiously at the sky for drones, but clouds were moving in. "I hope he's managed to cover his tracks."

Joan nodded and turned back to follow the beam. On the far side of the hill, she spotted him on the next rise, a huge shadow lumbering toward her. They met in the dip in the road, and she greeted him, "AS-57189, you've found me." She felt a gate close in him, the completion of a mission.

"Permission to report," AS stated in his least-inflected machine-speak voice.

Joan did her best, which was none too good, at imitating the military command voice. "Step off the road, AS." There, hopefully out of drone view, AS reported on the violation of the prime directive.

When Carlos and Andres found them a little later in the moonshadow at the side of the road, Joan was interrogating AS about the report he'd just finished. Andres interrupted, "How about we get a little further under cover."

They followed AS as he crashed through a barrier of blackberry brambles into the more open woods where the leafy canopy was far overhead. There they sat on a ring of mossy stones. Andres had carefully positioned them on the far side of a rocky outcropping. Carlos approved. They might not be very quiet but at least they were out of sight. He and Andres had brought supplies from the troupe, and they were downing their cold supper while Joan quizzed AS.

"You said they took Varvara the bartender. Do you know where they took her?"

Hearing Varvara's name, Carlos lit up, as though some inner circuit had just been made complete. But AS's reply made that circuit spark and sputter.

"Rycken."

Rycken was notorious for its brutality. It was also vulnerable to heat waves and high tides. Immediately Carlos began to plan how he and AS could get back there to break her out. He felt as if he didn't do something, his whole circuit board would be fried.

But Andres interrupted, "It might be a good idea to power down the R-S if we are going to stay here tonight." His fear of the R-S was clearly perceptible to both Carlos and Joan. He wanted to discuss the troupe's plans, and he certainly didn't want to do that with an R-S listening in.

Joan immediately objected. "I've reviewed AS's evasive maneuvers with him, and he's done an excellent job." She was so proud and pleased even Andres, an excellent flautist with zero special empathy skills, could read her.

To the surprise of the humans, AS interjected. "No, the small man has made an excellent suggestion. It is unlikely that I've been followed but I may well be detected by ongoing surveillance. And there's no need to expend battery power."

"Ok, but I'll need to reactivate you when we move," Joan warned.

"Understood," said AS and self-initiated his shut-down sequence.

Carlos and Joan had confirmed shut-down and disconnected AS's auditory circuits.

"You're sure he's not recording?" Andres demanded.

"We're sure," Joan and Carlos answered together.

Andres shook his head. "Well, here's the plan. I can't say I like it, but I went along with it. I don't know why." He glanced at AS with dismay. "The Troupe decided to make a complete break with you and your project. They've left already, and neither Carlos nor I know where they're going. Juan says we are not to follow them. I'm here to make sure we don't. And also, to support you kids, but I have no information about safe houses and no maps. And I can't say I care much for the mission – seems crazy to me."

Carlos felt Joan's sadness, and, for once, he was the one with the arm around her shoulders as she broke into tears. She missed grandma and her new mentor Martina; he could feel it. Abandoned in the woods like those kids in the fairy tale. He broke contact before he got pulled down that emotional wormhole. "C'mon," Carlos said. "You've got us. And as for plans, we just have to get AS to help us with that." Then he shifted closer to speak with Andres about a possible Rycken rescue plan.

Joan felt the terror and sadness of the days on the run rise to the surface and overwhelm her. She felt as though she were back in that dark tunnel, hand in hand with Grandma. But now there was no grandma. Joan hoped she was still alive -- somewhere --please.

In the months after Scrimfall when the City was barely habitable, Grandma had taken them night-hiking through the woods. By day they sheltered from the sun in small caves - fairy or Lenape shelters – that became settings for the many stories Grandma had told to pass the time. The story changed with the day. After a long time, Joan really wasn't sure how long, Grandma had brought them to the homestead of another doctor. There was a barn, goats, sheep. Joan couldn't remember the doctor's name but as for the sheep – one was Bo and the other Peep.

When she was able to lift her head again, Joan had a destination in mind. She noticed Carlos and Andres's worried looks and smiled reassuringly.

"What?" Carlos asked.

"I know where we should go, where Grandma might have gone."

Carlos looked excited. She could feel his overactive optimism kicking in. Andres was merely curious.

"How far?" Andres asked.

And that was the problem. Joan had no idea. "Do you know where we are?" she asked Andres.

"Sadly, no. This was my first trip outside the City with the troupe. I got briefed each morning on our route for the day, but I was focused on other things." Joan knew he meant Carlos. And Carlos knew too of course.

"No problem partner," Carlos said. "We can figure this out. I'm sure AS knows exactly where we are."

Joan brightened at that. She'd been so focused on trying to recall the route she'd travelled as a five-year-old, AS had momentarily slipped from her mind. "Carlos, do you remember where we went with Grandma after Scrimfall?" But Carlos only shook his head. "C'mon you remember. Goats and sheep, Bo and Peep?"

Carlos looked confused. "Maybe."

"We should try to go there."

"But where is there?" Carlos asked. "And that was years ago. What makes you think it's the same?"

"Just a hunch, I guess. But I need to think. I need to remember how we got there. Once I remember that, we can see if AS has any current data on the place."

Carlos nodded slowly. "News could be good or bad."

Joan shrugged off his doubts. "Carlos, you've got to help me remember."

He looked at her, suddenly frightened. "I don't want to go back."

"We don't have to relive everything – just remember our route," Joan pleaded.

"What's going on?" Andres asked.

"She wants to mind-meld," Carlos said, dread hovering over him like a drone.

Unsafe houses

That night as we sheltered in a nearby cave, we heard the shuddering tromp of robosoldiers. A few minutes later a loud boom echoed through the hills. Ash and I had been lying silent and sleepless, each in our own sleeping bags. At the boom I sat up and caught sight of her tears glittering in the pale green light of the cave moss. I reached for her hand, and she clutched mine. Finally, we fell asleep that way – me slumped against the cave wall, she in her twisted bag, and both of us holding on, just holding on.

When I woke, light was streaming into the cave and Ash was outside fixing breakfast. The loudest of the birds were calling now. I stretched out the crick in my neck, rubbed my swollen legs and tested my knees. When I emerged from the cave, Ash greeted me with a plate of battery-warmed grits. I was ravenous but her next statement demolished my appetite.

"We have to go back," she said.

I hesitated, spork halfway to my mouth, the steam of the grits filling my nostrils, and decided to hear her out. "Go on."

"I don't know where to go from here. We have to go back so my parents can help."

I took a bite, chewed. She looked at me as though she were expecting an affirmation of her plan. If I'd had any expectation that her parents had been released, I would have given it to her. But I knew that the boom in the night had meant last night's destination was now a smoldering ruin. And I had no doubt at all that her house had been destroyed as well and that her parents were languishing in a prison cell, neurostripped for their knowledge of the safe house network, of their contacts.

I swallowed the grits. They went down hard. My mouth was suddenly dry. "Ash," I asked as gently as I could, "on a scale of one to ten, how confident are you that your parents are waiting for you back home?"

She winced at that and turned away. I waited for it to sink in.

"They're there. They just have to be there," she moaned.

"You want them to be there so much," I reflected.

Ash gritted her teeth. "'But wanting won't make it so, Mom always said."

"Wise woman," I said with a rueful respect for the mother who had raised this remarkable child. "Listen Ash. I know a destination for us. It's where I was heading when you found me. We're almost halfway there, I think. Maybe another week and we'll be there, and we can check on your parents and make a plan for how you can join them."

"But we don't know any safe houses. We won't be able to get supplies," Ash objected.

"That's true. But you're very skillful. I bet you can keep us alive for a week."

"How will we find the way?" Ash asked. I could tell she was happy to shift her thoughts away from the uncertainties of home.

"The old-fashioned way. Map and compass." Hopefully I pulled them out of my pack. Sure enough, she latched on to the distraction of a new toy and put away her half-realized grief.

Reassignment

Cus actually enjoyed the rest and recreation: two weeks of planning and maps, plus games of predator and prey in the cell block. Red and Mex were on their guard because Cus was obviously getting some kind of special treatment from the muckety-mucks. But when nothing had come down after twenty-four hours and Cus flashed a gold chain, they couldn't resist strong-arming it off him. "That's ok. Keep it safe for me, boys," Cus had played it light.

He'd taken a harder line with the fence Smitty. On his last night in the dorm, he'd asked the guard to step outside the mess hall. Knowing Smitty was a greedy drunk who prided himself on his knowledge of fine liquor, Cus had hinted he had a source. He'd borrowed some quality bourbon from Colonel Adams' study for the purpose. In their confab outside the mess hall when Smitty reached for the bottle, Cus lifted him by the throat and relieved the blackguard of his stunner. He didn't activate the stunner just rammed it home under the guy's ribs. "You have some things of mine, some things of sentimental value. Get them to me by morning and there'll be no more said." He let the guard fall and doused him liberally with the bourbon. Smitty lay in a quivering whiskey-soaked heap at Cus's feet.

The next morning a different guard pressed Cus's watch into his hand as he was en route to the mess hall for breakfast. Colonel Adams was there. "Men, you're here because you've failed in your duties. But we recognize redemption in service. I've asked Lieutenant Custer here to pick two of you for a special mission. Complete it successfully and you can return to your units – no more stockade time." The prisoners cheered and banged their forks on the table. Cus was a bit surprised at their enthusiasm.

Red and Mex were surprised in turn when he pointed to them. "Corporal Raeburn, Private Cruz, come with me," Cus commanded.

"Yes sir," they replied enthusiastically, jumping up from their seats. He knew they thought they could handle him. That afternoon Mex and Red headed out of the stockade with the hundred-pound packs Cus had prepared for them. He kept his own pack bulky but light. They arrived at the Suskie River after an hour's march. Red was lugging an inflatable raft in his pack, but he and Mex balked at using it when there was a bridge overhead.

"What's a little water, boys?" Cus probed. They came up with a variety of excuses – currents, contamination, capsizing risks. "Can't swim, gentlemen?" Cus asked. They shook their heads sullenly. Like Cus they were refugees from the arid west where swimming was a rich man's pursuit.

"No problem, then. We take the bridge." Cus was pleased. He'd planned to spend several days exploring their weaknesses, and already in the first hour he'd hit upon one. He wouldn't have to put up with these snivelers much longer.

Flashback wayfinding

Grandma led the way while Carlos and Joanie, hand in hand crept behind her. It was very dark, scary dark. At first the silvery moon lit their way, but the moon went away. Joanie had a little flashlight, and they could see the back of grandma's running shoes with it. He wanted a turn with the light, but she wouldn't give it to him. "Don't whine," Joanie hissed through his mind. It made a bright green streak in his head. It hurt.

"Grandma, Joanie hurt me," he cried out.

"Come up with me Carlos," Grandma said. He got free of Joanie's sweaty hand and grabbed hold of grandma's belt loop. He liked being in the lead. They squished through mud and crackled through leaves. The sky started going grey between the tree trunks and they got to the first cave.

He had to stay in the cave while Joanie and Grandma got water. But Grandma gave him the map and compass to play with while they were gone. "Don't be rough with this. I want the paper and instrument back in one piece," Grandma had told him. She knew he liked to take things apart.

The map is important. He knew that. Everyday Grandma marked where they were on the map. Every day they got a little closer to the star. He looked at the star really hard. It was important. He hadn't learned to read yet, but he knew some letters. That one came right before C for Carlos.

"Bethlehem," Joanie blurted into his mind. A big red/orange blurt. Carlos got dizzier and dizzier, and the sun got hotter and hotter, and it was burning, burning.

"Carlos, Carlos," Joanie was calling him, out loud. That didn't hurt. But he kept his eyes closed. He wanted to get his bearings first. Let Joanie be afraid for a little bit. Still dark. Still the words. But he was stronger, bigger.

Then he heard Andres. "Are you OK, Carlos? C'mon amigo. Open your eyes."

Carlos looked up into Andres's face, his callused lip and straight white teeth. "I'm okay," Carlos said shaking his head to send the colorful headache on its way. He realized they were in an O_2 tent. No gogmask. "What's this?"

"Joanie tapped the R-S's knowledge of local flora – found an O_2 emitting one and claro, O_2 tent in the wild. Incredible, no?" Andres smiled at him.

Carlos grinned back and sat up. Joanie sat in the corner looking sad. He almost felt a little sorry for her. She didn't want to hurt him but, she did, she always did. "Stupid cacahead," he yelled at her. Their childhood insult. They both burst into laughter while Andres looked on mystified, but eventually he couldn't resist joining in.

On the move again Joanie dripped with sweat. They'd have to stop for water soon. She kept alert for possible water sources – a dip in the land, a greening of the plant life. Carlos and AS were in the lead. On the advice of AS, they were hiking in the heat of the day. AS seemed to fear detection by the heat-seeking drones at night. They stayed off the road, under tree cover, where it was all sweat and mosquitos. Joanie walked behind with Andres, talking about the plan to redirect the R-S from attacking the refugees to protecting them. "I thought this "empathy power" was all superhero caca," Andres said bluntly.

"You know Martina. How can you think that?" Joanie asked him.

"Martina seems pretty normal to me. A little sensitive sometimes," Andres observed.

"Exactly. It's not some kind of superpower. It's just becoming more aware of how other people are thinking and feeling."

"I'm not sure I would want to know," Andres said.

"Believe me, sometimes I don't. You have to learn to not let it overwhelm you."

"So, what does this have to do with machines anyway?"

"Not with machines. With artificial intelligence, Andres."

But there Joan had to stop. It was just too hot to carry on conversation through a gogmask while walking. She didn't have the lungs of a wind player and waved off Andres's "and?" with a "later".

Later happened sooner than she expected. Shortly before lunch, AS stopped in his tracks. "Low power," he intoned. Joan's thoughts raced. She hadn't considered the likelihood that AS would run out of power this fast.

"It's the heat," Carlos explained. "He's having to cool his circuits."

"Do we have to sneak him to charging station?" Joan asked. She was determined not to abandon AS again. He'd given them their map, their location, their directions to Bethlehem, the destination plucked from Carlos's memory — not without consequences. Carlos was still mad at her. It was just so hard to steer around the Scrimfall trauma. Her empathy training had helped her deal with it, compartmentalize it, drive her fury at the Federal Corporate Power into what she hoped would be a beneficial outcome for all of them. But Carlos had resisted training, sulked. Still, even he admitted that having a destination was necessary. She'd have to count that as forgiveness.

"He's got solunar panels. He can charge on his own. Slowly though. And he has to come out from under cover," Carlos warned.

"Oh," Joanie said reluctantly. She didn't want to slow down. Every day was a grind. Their filters were clogging. They were behind on calories. Water seemed to be getting harder to find. She felt her strength seeping away.

Unexpectedly Carlos took charge. "You and Andres go ahead. I'll follow with AS."

Green Pastures and Beyond

The green pastures stretched out below us were dotted with sheep. "Are the black dots sheep too?" Ash asked. And when I said they were, she smiled for the first time in days. It had been a grueling trip. We were hungry for food and room-filtered air. We were filthy too, partly as camouflage, partly because I'd wanted to avoid the parasites that contaminated the water found near livestock farms.

We'd been traveling mostly at night. I'd explained to Ash that not being followed was the primary concern, but she needed no explanation. Covering tracks had been part of training for Ash. She'd been doing it all along without me noticing. I felt terribly old when she explained that. After seeing the smoldering ruins of the safe house, she'd redoubled her efforts, pointing out the rockier routes, perfecting my pathfinding which was based on map and compass. even though I was the one with the map and compass. Ash was a quick and eager learner when it came to mastering these old-fashioned tools, but she showed no joy in her achievement. Worry for her parents weighed her down.

I wondered what we would find at the farm below. My friend Nancy had moved to this cooperative community years before Scrimfall, but I had visited her there only once. Joan and Carlos and I had hiked out of the ruined city and found in the farm a wonderful retreat, although they too had lost people and animals to the sudden blast of heat.

Since then, Nancy and I had exchanged solstice cards each winter, but over the years, as the FCPower consolidated its surveillance, our comments became increasingly guarded and vague. Nancy had always been committed to saving refugees. She'd moved to the border at one point. After she came to the farm though, she commuted to Delphia to work in a clinic there. She was younger and more energetic than I was, but she too had finally retired as of the last snail mail card I'd received.

I strongly suspected her home would be a safe house, and as Ash and I watched, we saw a small family group, two adults and two children, slip through the wire into the pasture. A sheep dog bounded up to meet them and gave three sharp barks of greeting. They stopped and waited, and then I saw my friend's tall form striding across the field in knee-high mud boots. She led the family away.

They'd been expected but we were not. "We'll wait until evening," I told Ash. We spent the day dozing and watching. The peace of the scene below remained undisturbed, and just after sunset we headed down and rang the front doorbell. When Nancy opened the door, she didn't recognize the filth-encrusted me, but neither did she hesitate.

"Welcome," she cried, and wrapped her arms around me and then a shyly shrinking Ash. She pulled us in and closed the door quickly behind us. As I gratefully pulled off my gogmask, she called out my name in surprise.

We spent three days at Nancy's homestead and Ash loved it. She spent all her awake time with the sheep in the pasture or barn. Gus the sheepdog was her new best friend, and we often found her bed empty because she'd snuck out to sleep with him. I couldn't imagine a better place for her, but Nancy had warned us when we arrived. The chain of safe houses was falling one by one. If they continued at this rate, her homestead could be a target in less than two weeks.

And I was wanted. That had been an unwelcome bit of news. "Your picture's on the internet," Nancy had told me. "Carlos and Joan too." I'd groaned. It was only a matter of time. What could I do with this time?

"Have you any other information about Carlos and Joanie?"

"They left the City with a folkloric dance troupe. I'm hoping they weren't taken at a safe house, but I think it would have made the news. A whole dance troupe with two wanted teens? I can just imagine how they would have spun that – terrorists in tights?"

I chuckled, relieved. "Do you know where they're headed?"

"I don't and I wouldn't tell you if I did." I grudgingly acknowledged the priority of secrecy over my need to know, because, really, I didn't <u>need</u> to know, just desperately <u>wanted</u> to know that they were safe, that the R-S project was on track. But I knew better than to ask Nancy about that.

We had discussed where I should go next. They needed organizers in Swamp City. It was a high-risk assignment, but I was expendable, and eager to be wherever I could have the most impact and cause the least harm. Ash, however, that was tricky. She was so young and completely countrified. She'd never stepped foot in a city.

"No," Ash cried. "I'm not leaving. We just got here!"

"I have to leave, Ash. I'm wanted. And the R-S are cracking the safe houses, one by one."

"We can hide. I'm good at hiding." Ash declared.

Nancy interrupted. "Dr. Katie has to leave. It's not what she wants to do. It's what she has to do. She has work to do, and it's not her choice, really."

"Oh," Ash said, eyes downcast.

I could see Nancy struggling with herself. "But you can stay Ash, it you're willing and can follow instructions. It's risky but everywhere is risky right now, I guess."

Ash nodded, wide-eyed and silent. She gave me a hug for the first time ever and ran for the door. "I believe that was a yes to your offer, Nancy. Thank you."

"We'll figure something out," Nancy murmured reassuringly. "All I ask is that you be the one to break the news about her parents before you leave. They're on the Rycken Island burial at sea list for today."

After a week at Nancy's fattening up and restoring my lungs, I moved on. I'd needed every day of that week. Telling Ash, well, I had plenty of experience telling kids their parents were dead. You just did it and moved on. She withdrew to the barn and I to the preparations for the next leg of the journey.

It was as challenging as I'd feared. The terrain was increasingly marshy. I missed my kayak, but I had packed two lifejackets, one for me and one for my backpack, so I could swim over the deeper sections. I'd resupplied with a week's worth of food. My water filter was clean, and though I could carry no oxygen, I had studied all week to learn where I was likely to find the cleanest air – near marshes (no problem that)- and around certain plants. Nancy had given me a pair of light-weight waders and despite the shimmering heat, I found myself wearing them more often than not. I had a lifelong fear of snakes, and the waders provided a sense of protection.

There were no caves in this terrain and barely any dry land to tent on. Periodically there were hillocks with trees where I could string up my hammock and rest during the day. The night was so thick with mosquitos I actually found myself grateful for the extra coverage of the gogmask. Grateful to the bats and nighthawks too, though there weren't nearly enough of them. I was taking malaria prophylaxis and leaving an orange puddle of urine at each campsite. It wouldn't do to arrive feverish at my desperate destination.

My destination was an offshore refugee camp near the Capital, commonly known as Swamp City. The Capital had been inundated by rising sea levels, but the FCP government remained headquartered there in defiance or denial of the new climate realities. Pumps and seawalls and gates, modelled after those of the long-gone Low Countries, kept the government dry most of the time. The rest of the population survived in the upper floors of high rises or on boats bobbing colorfully on the newly expanded reaches of the bay.

I was heading for a refugee camp sited on one of the artificial barrier islands constructed to shield the city. It lay directly in the path of hurricanes blowing up and down the coast and across the ocean. The storms blew in from all directions these days. When I'd left Nancy's, Hurricane Xerxes was stalled out down south fortunately. Not fortunate for the Southerners of course.

After several days of mucky marsh wading, I was getting close. I pushed through the night and found myself at a boardwalk leading down to the docks. A lurid purple dawn backlit the boats and made it difficult to find what I was looking for – a boat called Nightshade. That ominous name triggered a parade of poisonous plants marching through my fatigued medical memory. I reined in these thoughts just in time to spot the boat pulling into its slip.

I gave a coded wave. The person at the motor waved back. Good. I hustled toward him, and he grabbed my arm to haul me aboard without bothering to tie up. "Get below. We can't stay here," he barked. In the small cabin below decks, a miraculous bowl of warm beans and corn awaited me on the tiny table. I had to rip off my gogmask to avoid drooling into it. As the boat jerked away from the dock, I gobbled the meal and downed some water. No sooner had I finished, than I felt the pace of the motor slowing and the hard slap of arrival against the hull.

Beacon

Carlos and AS sheltered together in the large cave they'd found three days ago. At first, they'd been moving from place to place – not far because Carlos didn't want AS's batteries discharging more than they could take in – but far enough so they couldn't be pinned down to one location. With the discovery of the cave, they felt comfortable enough to shelter there and just vary AS's charging location.

Carlos was thoroughly enjoying himself. AS was an excellent companion – no mind probes, got right to the point of whatever problem they were trying to solve. They'd just finished cleaning his gogmask with AS's blower, and Carlos was breathing much more easily now. He and AS had even toyed with the idea of setting up a clean air circulation system for the cave, but it didn't seem worth the power since he knew Joanie and Andres would be waiting for them at the homestead. AS estimated ten more days until he was at full power. Carlos half-wished it were twenty.

Not that he didn't want to see Joanie and Andres again, but he was so busy he hardly missed them. He slept during the day while AS was in the road or a clearing charging. Once Carlos even climbed a tree with the solunar panels and secured them over the canopy, much to the disgust of a nesting raven. When he'd climbed up to bring the panels down, she'd assembled a mob to attack him. Fortunately, AS had been able to drive off the mob with an ultrasonic siren of sorts, but Carlos didn't try the tree climbing approach again.

The forest was full of small animals competing for the berries and nuts that were in season. Carlos's hands were stained from the blackberries he foraged daily. The pecans were maturing too so his diet, though boring, was adequate enough that he didn't have to eat the bitter MRE rations Joanie had left with him.

At night AS returned to the cave and Carlos began what he considered his real work. With AS in a low energy state, Carlos was testing circuits like a brain surgeon. He was glad he'd insisted on bringing some tools from home. He'd been able to map all the motor systems, the weapons systems and some of the sensory systems. But the decision-making centers and echolocation systems were more challenging. He'd made little headway with those.

One night shortly before dawn he'd activated a circuit that brought AS suddenly and fully alert. Quickly Carlos shut down the circuit but kept AS powered up. "What was that?" Carlos asked AS.

"The homing beacon," AS replied.

"But I shut it down, so we're okay right? We're in the cave so the beacon can't get out?"

"No, Carlos. The homing beacon is geologically permeable and permanent. We'll have to leave the cave. It's marked now."

Hours later, as Carlos and AS hustled down the margin of shade at the edge of the road, the drone monkeys had swarmed them. They had been trying to put as much distance as they could between themselves and the beacon-marked cave. When the drones dived in at them, AS had tried to protect him, but they'd both been electrostunned. AS was too heavy for the little buggers though. By comparison Carlos was a lightweight. It only took one drone to lift his limp body away. As he rose into the sky, Carlos could see AS immobilized at the side of the road. The massive form grew smaller and smaller.

Despite his pain and fear, a small spurt of exhilaration crept into him. It was his first flight and the patchwork of forest, pasture, swampland, glittering lakes and rivers, shoreline and ocean unfolded beneath him. He began laughing uncontrollably and weeping – some kind of stun effect he thought.

Underneath the rush of feeling, Carlos's brain was whirring with anticipation. What would happen next? He'd be interrogated. The R-S plan would be revealed, the empaths rounded up. It would be his fault. Escape or death. And now was the time. In prison, no, he couldn't imagine it. Or he could, too vividly. Was Varvara there, still alive? Could they work together? Fairy tales.

Focus. He remembered the focus he'd brought to bear on the roboserver's finger in the jazz bar. Could he loosen the claws than gripped him? He couldn't see them. He was positioned prone in their grasp watching the landscape scutter by below. But he could feel those claws. He closed his eyes and concentrated, imagining the claws relaxing, feeling his shirt slipping through, feeling the claws retightening. It took ten cycles before he finally slipped from the drone's grasp and felt himself falling.

Carlos opened his eyes and found to his surprise he was barely twenty feet above the ocean. He glanced about frantically trying to get his bearings. He caught a brief glimpse of shore before he'd tucked and tumbled into the water.

Keeping his eyes shut against the salt, he felt his body reach the end of its plunge and begin to rise. Incredibly the gogmask had held. He made his way up to the light and broke the surface in time to see the drones heading mindlessly away from him into the afternoon sun.

Camping and Consequences

On the third night of their trek, as they sat around the electric campfire, Cus pushed Red and Mex to tell their stories. The crickets and frogs were making their nasty Eastern swampland noises and Cus looked forward to the distraction. The two soldiers had been cautious around him at first. Reasonably so. Cus had managed to get Adams to have his sidearm shipped down from the City, so he was armed with that as well as the stunner, and they were weaponless. They'd even groveled a little by pretending to admire his handling of Smitty.

"He was always a sloppy drunk," Red observed, as he downed another shot of whiskey. The gold chain they'd taken off of Cus glowed dully around Red's neck. "Keep it," Cus had told them when they'd offered it back the first night of the trek.

"That's a nice watch too," Mex observed regretfully. The watch crystal twinkled in the fire light, as Cus lifted his arm to admire it. No stars twinkled overhead. The scrim and the swamp mists washed them out, but there were flickers of fireflies.

"So, Mex," Cus began. "What's your story?"

Mex regarded Cus suspiciously. "You been real nice to us, Lieutenant. I don't wanna mess that up."

Cus gave him a reassuring grin and refilled Mex's shot glass. "Naw, just interested in my men. Spit it out Mex."

The man downed the shot and held his hand out for the bottle. He took a long pull directly from it and began. "I was born twenty-five years ago in the Cañon de Cheley. My family gave me the name Barboncito, but they all called me Barbo. When I was five, we started the long walk north to find water. A lotta people died. My uncle made sure I didn't. When we got to Salt Lake, we stayed in a refugee camp until we converted. I'm a Mormon. Didn't have my first drink 'til I joined the Army. Ain't quit since, have I, Red."

Red nodded and reached for the bottle which Barbo surrendered reluctantly.

"That how you ended up in the stockade, Mex?" Cus asked.

"Hell, no. I stuck a man when he called me outta my name." Barbo's eyes glittered dangerously in the firelight.

Cus felt his sidearm lying comfortably against his thigh. "You want me to call you Barbo, Mex?"

"Now that might be a right smart thing to do paleface," Barbo slurred as Red put a restraining hand on his shoulder.

"I was born in Scotland," Red interjected, "and I shoulda stayed but I had a little trouble with a fellow over a wee bit of cryptocoin, so I thought it best to pursue my fortune elsewhere."

"The stockade?" asked Cus.

"Just a steppingstone on the way to riches. And you Lieutenant?"

But Cus reclaimed the bottle, waved them away to their sleep sacks, and clicked off the fire. That night he dreamt of the mountain.

He dreamed out the whole plan. The map had shown a so-called "mountain", Mount Joy, north of the river. He'd always preferred mountaintops for his sacrificial art. The two men would make fine food for the vultures if there was an open top. He had found most of these eastern mountaintops were forested, but, in his dream, it was jagged and rocky.

They'd been following a riverside trail for two days now, and it was time to turn north. Cus debated whether to drown them here in the big river or hope for a marshy lake. There were several shown on the map, but he didn't trust the shallows to do the job. The mountain was a two-hour hike north. They were big men, but if he butchered them carefully, he could pack them up one at a time.

Over breakfast he traced a trail away from the river on the map. Remembering to call Mex "Barbaro", Cus sent the man down to the river to wash the pots and filter water for the day's march. Ten minutes later, he turned to the Scotsman. Stunner in hand Cus aimed for the man's back. No, the chest would be a more reliable target. "Hey, Red," Cus called, "you wear a flak jacket?"

Red turned, on his guard. "Of course." But his helmet was off and before Red could say more, Cus had fired his stunner. Cus was into visuals, not dialogue. He admired the crumpled heap Red had become. He wasn't dead, just out, so Cus hogtied him and handcuffed him for later, then hustled down to the river.

Barbo looked up in sullen alarm as Cus jogged toward him. "What's wrong?"

Cus smiled. Barbo was balanced on a jetty, water bag in hand. The stunner fired striking Barbo and sending him hurtling into the current. The stunner beam had struck the water surface too and a few fish were already floating to the surface. Barbo snagged on a rock. Cus stripped down, swam out and submerged the stunned Barbo for ten minutes. There was no struggle. He simply sat on the man and watched the river swirl by, green and muddy, insects hovering just above the surface. A red dragonfly flew by and Cus snagged it. He crushed its thorax and set the critter carefully into the knit of his cargo shirt. He roped the corpse, reeled it in and up on to the rocks.

In the distance he heard bellowing. Damn. He'd forgotten to gag Red. Cus loped back to the campsite. When Red sighted him, his shouts grew more frantic. "Hush, you big ox," Cus said gently, as he slit the man's throat and watched the blood form puddles and patterns on the pebbled sand of the campsite.

Fifteen minutes later pouring rain washed away the blood. Steam rose as the rain hit the hot ground. Cus ignored it, racing to take apart Red's body. Barbo lay next to Red. Storm clouds had loomed downstream to the east as he'd dragged Barbo up from the river. He'd hoped the storm would miss them but no such luck. OK, so he'd modify his plan.

The rain was pelting him as Cus took only the heart, the kidneys, an eye, a hand, and a foot from each corpse. He left the livers. They'd jellify in the heat if he hiked up the mountain with them. He'd drawn out the innards quickly enough but sawing off the feet and hands, that took a while. By the time he was done, wind was whipping through the trees like a bull running after a cow in heat. The rain was falling hard as an avalanche. Blood and globs of fat swirled in the inch deep puddle at his feet.

He packed the harvest into a game bag, lowered the bag into his pack and hoisted it up to his shoulder, trying the weight. About forty pounds, not bad. He grabbed the food bag and the tent that Red had obligingly packed up earlier. He shoved these into his pack, not without difficulty. He was running out of space. He'd have to leave the rest of the gear.

Well, that was the tradeoff. He could have sacrificed them later, when they got to the target, but he craved the mountaintop. Now to bury the bodies. Wouldn't do to have a coroner looking at saw cuts and dissected body cavities. Ah, almost forgot.   He cut the chips out of their arms and pocketed them. You're coming with me, boys. Remember, we've got a mission.

He heard trees cracking in the forest, and, as he lifted the shovel to dig their graves, he saw water rushing through the trees. River must be over its banks. Screw it. Let the flood take them then. He grabbed his pack and started jogging, dodging falling limbs, taking glancing blows as he did so. The wind was blowing steadily at his back, pushing him up a gentle slope. When he got to open pastureland, he paused to catch his breath.

He felt a drip running down his forehead – cold. One of the falling limbs must have cracked his helmet. He was glad to be out of the woods, though the rain was even harder here. He hadn't believed that rain could fall that hard. The wind shifted and blew a wall of water against him. He needed cover. He knew the mountain wasn't far even though he couldn't see it through the downpour. There might be cover on the mountainside – good rock cover not these infernal claptrap trees, snapping like toothpicks. He stood with his back to the wind and saw the trees at the edge of the pasture cracking and falling. Big storm, hurricane maybe.

He turned to push against the wind and rain that was nearly horizontal now. His helmet compass kept him oriented. Walking on instruments. The pasture was tufted and muddy. He took at least two falls before he felt the satisfying crunch of gravel underfoot -- the road to the mountain!

Rescue

On surfacing Carlos was flooded with relief. He was free. He wouldn't be interrogated. The movement would live on. They had a chance. Then a wave slapped the exhilaration right out of him. He began doing his best to swim toward the sun, westward toward the shore he couldn't see. He hoped the drones wouldn't return. They weren't too smart, drones. And whoever had been monitoring them, didn't seem to have been keeping track of their prey, of him. He'd heard some audio squawk and a man's name – Corporal Phillips while he was glitching the drone. Should he add that monitor to his revenge or gratitude list?

He kept his mind busy reviewing the flight, the fall. He was trying not to think of the sharks that had boomed in these waters as they'd warmed. At first, he'd bobbed in the water, buoyed up by the backpack Grandma had forced on him for his birthday because it was a water-activated flotation device, and she was a safety nut. But the thought of sharks got him moving.   He swam his best version of the crawl as hard as he could for fifteen minutes or so, then alternated between crawl, breaststroke and back stroke, strokes he'd watched Joanie do for hours even as he refused to put a toe in the pool. The breaststroke was best for tracking the increasingly slanted rays of the sun.

He seemed to be making little progress. Just his luck if the tide was heading out. Lying on his back he noticed the sky had changed color – had gone from a scrim-dimmed blue-grey to a putrid greenish yellow. Pus for a sky. Oh great, a hurricane. Like a new game level kicking in, the wind picked up, blowing east to west, a good wind because it favored his progress toward shore, a bad wind because it raised up waves that first lifted him up and then slapped him down.

Carlos quickly started to feel seasick. This hurricane would surely drown him. From the peak of a wave, he caught sight of a dorsal fin a few yards off. Was that a shark? He closed his eyes, then opened them again almost immediately. Closing them made the seasickness worse, and his mind's eye was way bloodier than current reality. On the next peak he saw two of them, arcing up and down, and on the next six. Then he felt a curious mind tickle, a question, "Are you in trouble?" An empath must be nearby he realized. And for once, Carlos was glad <u>not</u> to be alone with his thoughts. At each wave peak he searched for a boat or lighthouse or rocky outcropping, but he spotted none of these. "Where are you?" he asked, hoping that his desperation would power his transmission through.

This empath thought more in images than words - images and feelings. "Storm coming," they thought, for now he was sure it was more than one. And Carlos saw the hurricane hitting full force at night, hours from now. "I know," Carlos thought back. "I need help."

"We are headed for the deep ocean," they broadcast. He received an image of the murky depths spotted here and there by bioluminescent creatures. They must be in a submersible Carlos realized. So, he wasn't entirely surprised when he spotted a shape approaching him from beneath a wave. When it surfaced, and was followed by another, and another, Carlos was shocked to discover he'd been communicating with dolphins.

The waves seemed huge now, and more than once Carlos jerked up his mask to vomit into the water as the dolphin pod nudged him along. He felt their goodwill along with their disdain for creatures who stupidly lived on the surface. His muscles were cramping with fatigue by the time they reached the shallows and the dolphins announced he was on his own. He stood unsteadily in the surf watching them swim away, dancing in the waves.

Turning to face the shore Carlos was blindsided by a huge wave and found himself planing through the salty water only to smash painfully into a sand shelf. As the wave sucked back, he clung with all fours to the sandy bottom. When the pull slackened, Carlos staggered to his feet and ran as fast as he could through the shallows toward the short beach. Again, he was slapped down by a wave, again he clung to the shore for dear life – his grandmother's phrase he thought dully. Again, he rose, and this time made the beach, then the rocks beyond.

The rocks were littered with flotsam, and surely it was sheer luck as he climbed them that he spotted his backpack. He hadn't even realized he'd lost it. The dolphins must have rescued that too. But that must mean . . . He looked back to see a monster wave approaching dimly through the pouring rain. He grabbed his pack and sought shelter behind a largish rock. The wave hit with a crash and soaked him, but the rock protected him from the full force of it and provided better holds by far than the sandy shallows had. Still the receding wave sucked and pulled at him as though it wanted to feed him to the fishes.

He lifted his face to the fresh water that pelted him from above, rinsing the salt from his lips and mouth and gogmask. He was careful not to swallow too much. Too many contaminants in rainwater to drink it unfiltered.

A light swept across him from above and he froze. Who would be looking for him in this storm? Then he realized he was at the base of a lighthouse, a safer shelter by far than his current shaky situation. Manned lighthouses were a story from the past, like that little red lighthouse book Grandma had read to them when they were small kids. But he'd have to look out for security cameras.

Carlos scouted the ocean for another large wave but really couldn't see much through the downpour, more like sidepour. The wind, whipping the rain into his face, slapped him into action. He scrambled up the rockpile to the lighthouse. The door was on the side away from the wind. Plastic fragments lay scattered its threshold. The camera overhead seemed to have been smashed. A lucky break maybe. Or perhaps a warning that an even bigger wave was on its way. Glancing over his shoulder, Carlos pushed open the door and stepped into the dark. Dim step lights revealed a winding metal service stairway. He closed the door against the rain, waited. Nothing. He slipped off his gogmask. The acidic salt of the sea on his lips gave way to the unexpected smell of cinnamon.

Carlos climbed the winding stair as quietly as he could, the sound of his steps covered by the wailing wind and crashing waves. The rock tower held steady. Carlos followed the scent of cinnamon and scouted ahead as best he could. Should have studied the telempathy stuff he scolded himself. Then he'd probably know if someone was there. At the top of the stairs, there was a motionless lump in the corner. The whirling light in the center of the chamber illuminated the lump briefly or he might have missed it altogether. Except for that delicious smell. He wanted to hit the overhead light switch, but he was afraid of cameras.

"Hello?" he ventured. But there was no response. He crept closer. The unmoving lump was in a sleeping bag. No, not unmoving. He caught the rhythm of breathing in the slightly shifting bag. He squatted nearby and waited.

Eventually the figure in the bag stretched and sat up. The figure of a woman. "Hello," he said again, just before the light swept by him.

"What are you doing here. This is government property," she snapped. As she spoke the light swept over her face and torso. He thought he glimpsed swallows rising up from her breasts. "Varvara?"

"Who are you? Is it time?"

"I'm Carlos, Joan's little brother. Time for what?"

"Oh, nothing," she sighed.

"But you are Varvara, right?" Carlos wanted to be sure.

"Yes, yes," she waved her hand dismissively. "You can call me that. You have food in that pack?"

"A little. Are you hungry?"

"Famished. I'm not good at conserving supplies."

"I'm out of water though," he confessed.

"Oh, that I have plenty of," she reassured him. But as she turned toward the jugs at her head, he caught a brief gasp of pain which set off a yellow glitter bomb in his mind.

He gasped in turn, "You're hurt!"

"It's my leg. That's why they had to leave me here."

"They?"

"A group of us broke out of Rycken during the storm. Not all political." She hesitated but badly needed to talk it out.

"Go on," he nodded.

"The lower levels were flooding. Prisoners were drowning. You could hear the sequence: shouts for help, screams loud at first then fewer, then shorter, then silence, level by level." Varvara shuddered. "The guards ran away when the storm first kicked up. They know that island's vulnerable and we're expendable. Fortunately, one of ours, Kepler, you've met him I think?" Carlos nodded again. "He'd managed to get a copy of the key for his cell, but when he got out, he couldn't find a passkey. Finally, he located a switch and the cell doors, all of them that weren't shorted out, swung open. Luckily the main power wasn't out yet." Varvara paused gathered her thoughts. "Anyway, I slipped and hurt my leg getting on to a fishing boat that had conveniently broken loose and found its way to Rycken.

She unzipped the sleeping bag, and Carlos saw a blood-soaked bandage on her leg. He reached into his pack and pulled out two items — his bicarbonate, which he quickly mixed into some of the water she'd shared, and a bandage supply, part of the first aid kit his grandma had always made him carry in his backpack.

After drinking his bicarb, he checked the wound. It was bad, hard to look at, but he'd had a lot of experience with protest wounds. He cleaned it gently and wrapped it tight. She commented on his deft touch — "almost good enough to tend bar" while she downed the prison hooch she'd had in a bag of her own. "Can't be a bartender and not brew a little on the side," she joked, but her voice winced with the pain.

When he finished, Carlos knelt to zip up her bag and realized with embarrassment that she was staring at the erection his loose dancer's pants did little to hide. She reached up and grabbed his waistband at the hip. "Mind if I help you with that?" she asked boozily.

Carlos gulped and met her eager eyes. "Sure," he murmured, "sure", and "sure" once again as she took him into her mouth.

Tadaima

As I scaled the ladder up to the platform from the Nightshade, I was swarmed by children, maskless ones I noted with dismay. "Food, food," they shouted. It was both a demand and a question. But I had no food. I shook my head sadly and showed my empty palms. The children gave a collective shrug and dispersed up into the superstructure where they seemed to be scanning the horizon, for food delivery boats I presumed. Then a siren whistle blew, and the kids disappeared to the far side of the structure. My ride pulled away behind me, and I was alone on the platform with my backpack. Shouldering it, I walked toward the shadows where I could dimly discern a figure. As I entered the shadows, she stepped toward me.

"I'm Carol," she stated grimly.

"I'm . . .," I began.

"No, don't tell me. I'll tell you. You're Junko," and she slipped a set of documents into my hand. "I don't know, and I don't need to know. Follow me."

I expected to see more people as we walked and climbed toward the center of the structure, but there was no one there. When Carol looked back to make sure I was keeping up, I caught her eye and gestured to the emptiness around us.

"Yolanda is coming," she said curtly and turned to resume her brisk pace. I scrambled behind, wondering who Yolanda was, when the wind picked up and began to whistle through the iron framework overhead. Xerxes, now Yolanda, I realized. We're in for a hurricane. We had the wind to our backs, and it hurried us along to a pipe that dwarfed the bright yellow door at its center. Emergency exit signage coated the door which Carol cranked open. We stepped through and into a caged elevator that began a slow descent.

The intent of these artificial barrier islands had been to protect the city. They'd been built with scavenged materials including those of retired oil drilling platforms. They were retrofitted with subsurface emergency quarters for the refugees who normally lived in the superstructure, currently being evacuated because of Yolanda. The lights flickered and my pulse quickened. I didn't mind darkness, but I had to have air. In this case air had to be pumped down from the surface and circulated.

"We won't lose power," Carol informed me. "We're wave powered."

We exited the elevator to garish green light which leant a ghoulish air to the crowd that gathered around us eagerly. Expressionless, Carol waved them off and led me down a barren corridor so long it must have run the width of the platform. At its terminus we opened an unadorned hatch and pulled the bell cord hanging just inside. A small dark man hurried forward and bowing welcomed me in Japanese, "Irasshai.[15]"

I bowed in return, "*Konbanwa*[16]", then added hopefully, "*Tadaima*[17]."

The man smiled slightly and nodding, replied, "*Okaeri*[18]."

I heard the hatch clank behind me. Looking back, I saw Carol was gone.

Just because we wouldn't lose power, didn't mean Hurricane Yolanda wouldn't bring disruption to the refugee camp. It was tremendously overcrowded below the surface. I suspected that I'd been ushered to one of the more organized sections of the camp. These Japanese refugees, who'd fled tsunamis, earthquakes, volcanic eruptions, nuclear disasters and most of all a land mass shrunken by ocean rise and landslides, had modeled their space after a capsule hotel. There were shifts of sleepers, eaters, and workers. The sleepers occupied the tiny bunks where they would sleep or engage in any other solitary activity that could be conducted in a two by one by one-meter space. Some capsules were a bit wider to accommodate families, but the children were sternly warned to whisper when encapsulated.

Now it wasn't quiet at all. The wave generators throbbed, and the wind whistled by the air intake ports that led from the superstructure to below deck. From my alarmed expression, Seito-san, the elderly man who had greeted me began a reassuring patter in Japanese from which I was able to extract only a few words – pump, drowning, radio.

---

[15] *Irrashai* – Welcome.

[16] *Konbanwa* – Good Evening

[17] *Tadaima* – I'm home

[18] *Okaeri* – Welcome back

"*Sumimasen*[19]," I interrupted and asked in Japanese. "Do you speak English? My Japanese is not that good."

"No, no, Junko-san, your Japanese is quite good. Seito English not very good. I try," he replied. "Here no drowning. Pumps very very good. Power by wave. By radio reports arrive."

"Reports?" I ask.

"Hurricane Watch Network. Short wave radio. On ground reports."

"Ah, I understand. *Wakarimashita*[20]," I said. The words rolled thickly off my tongue. For years they'd laid unused in my heart with the memory of my son and my daughter-in-law.

"*Tabemashou*[21]," he said leading me to a low table. I pointed to my knees. I had never mastered kneeling at table. He smiled and brought a legless folding chair into which I awkwardly slipped. A woman brought tea and cookies.

"*Arigatou,*[22]" I nodded, taken aback by all these courtesies after so much time in the woods.

"Watch please," said Seito-san. "Next shift you do this."

I devoured the tea and cookies, and soon the woman returned with a rice steamer and bento boxes. A twelve-centimeter-long dried fish stared up at me. Pickled seaweed and plums looked more appetizing, certainly less confrontational. There was a tiny bit of scrambled egg. Famished I devoured it all and even managed the miso soup chaser as others joined us at the long table and chattered away in Japanese.

"*Gochisousama*[23]," I called out to our server as we rose.

"Now radio," Seito-san said and led me to shortwave crackling with alarming reports. The wall of the hurricane had hit Swamp City head on. The city had been evacuated. Further north my home city was being submerged, but our apartment in the Heights was still above water. Fear flickered through me and set my left eyelid to twitching. There was no report from Rycken. Despair for my incarcerated comrades surged.

---

[19] *Sumimasen* – Excuse me.

[20] *Wakarimashita* – Understood

[21] *Tabemashou* – Let's eat

[22] *Arigatou* - thanks

[23] *Gochisousama* – Thank you for the meal.

A siren interrupted our listening. "All hands to pump station." Now Seito-san looked alarmed. "I go. Junko-san, stay here please." As I awaited further instructions, I found the possibility that I might share the fate of my comrades oddly calming.

Hurricane at the Homestead

Despite the short man's waddling gait, Joan and Andres had arrived at the ridge overlooking the homestead earlier than she'd expected. It stretched out below them, bucolic, sheep bleating intermittently, goats, bells ringing, bounding playfully through the pasture. Joan found herself weeping. Andres pulled out his flute and played softly. The wind carried his tune back the way they had come. Joan sobbed harder.

"What's the matter?" Andres asked.

"I shouldn't have left him," Joanie blurted between sobs.

"He'll be around. Don't worry," Andres reassured her.

As if on cue, they heard that unforgettable stomping sound in the distance behind them.

"AS?" Joanie wondered as she sought out his echolocation bean. There it was. She exhaled slowly and turned to Andres who was hurriedly packing up his flute and preparing to flee.

"It's AS the robosoldier, our robosoldier." It was her turn to reassure him.

"You can empath it?" Andres asked incredulously.

"Something like that," Joan replied.

"I'll wait down slope, just in case," Andres countered nervously. He scuttled down the rocky slope and disappeared behind an outcropping just as AS lumbered into view.

AS was moving quickly – almost urgently – as he homed in on Joan. That pace can't be efficient she thought. The relief she'd felt on first sensing AS began to seep away. "AS report," she commanded when he stood before her.

"I regret to inform you that Carlos has been taken by the drone-monkeys."

"Are they following you?" Joan asked scanning the sky.

"Negative. Search beams successfully deflected."

OK, well, that was something at least. This was no time to grieve or panic. "We have to get him back AS."

"Power stores at 3%. Switching to low power mode. Solunar panel deployment initiated."

Andres scrambled back up the slope when he saw Joan trying to camouflage the immobilized R-S. The sun colored the western horizon beyond them, and a red moon rose ominously to the east.

AS's report had galvanized Joan but to what effect? Her mind raced frantically and fruitlessly, back and forth through the maze of problems to be solved if Carlos was to be rescued. He was the maze runner, not her. Sequence, sequence, sequence she reminded herself, trying to order her thoughts so that they would lead to a set of linear, productive actions. Interrogating AS <u>might</u> lead to a set of possible destinations where Carlos <u>might</u> be held. Rycken would be high on that list. She shuddered. But maybe they'd take him to a military post. At any rate AS was unavailable until charged.

Perhaps after AS was partially charged, she could walk him down to the Homestead. After dark. When drones and satellites would be less likely to spot him. He'd shut down in a far too open setting. As her mind churned, her body focused on camouflaging the robosoldier, rubbing dust into his shiny surface and surrounding him with downed limbs and leaves. Andres was helping her, but they weren't talking, not here in this exposed spot. By the time they had finished AS was a suspiciously large hump of brown and green, looking like no natural structure that Joan could recall. She and Andres crept under the nearby cover but kept AS in sight.

"You heard?" Joan asked.

Andres shook his head. "No, but I see. Carlos is not with him."

That was when Joan felt the tears welling up again. Andres put his arms around her, and she let it happen. The wave of tears crashed silently on the shore and withdrew. She lifted her head.

"How do we get him back Andres?"

But Andres only shook his head sadly, having known the loss of too many companions already.

Joan shook herself loose from this sudden moment of shared despair. "Go down to the homestead. See if they will take us in, resupply us, let us plug-in charge AS."

Andres sighed. He wasn't hopeful, but he was weary. They needed food and new gogmask filters. He got to his feet and worked his way down the slope to the house keeping under cover on a circuitous route. After an hour or so Joan saw a light flick on in the valley below and the murmur of voices floated up to her. Then a door closed, and the valley was dark and silent again. She waited, anxiously alert at first and then nodding off as the stresses of the day and the arduousness of the journey caught up with her.

In her dreams Joan was back in the apartment with Carlos and Grandma. They were eating udon noodles, and Carlos was secretly piloting a toy drone behind grandma. Joan was angry at him, really angry. She didn't know why she was so angry. There was a kind of crackling noise in the background that got louder and louder. Suddenly Joan was awake and felt the soothing hum of mental contact with a nearby empath.

"I didn't mean to wake you," the unfamiliar empath thought to Joan, who retained a tinge of anger from her dream.

"No, no, it's not you. Just a dream," Joan thought back. "Thank you for coming." She let gratitude and relief wash away her anger.

"I'm not sure I can help much, but I'll try," Nancy replied. That's right. The woman's name was Nancy, Aunt Nancy, as Joan recalled from that long ago visit. The woman was next to her now. It was pitch black, but she could feel Nancy's arm reach around her shoulders and give a gentle squeeze.

"Is my grandmother here?" Joan blurted. She felt her spirits rising as Nancy sent her a mental image of Grandma Katie taken when she had passed through a week earlier. Grandma looked so thin though, worried and wrinkled.

"She's doing very well, fantastically really for a fugitive of her age. But we had to send her on. There's been too much surveillance here, and we're expecting a covert attack of some sort. We'll have to send you along too."

Joan was dismayed. AS needed a good long charge and so did she.

"We're in luck though if you want to call it that. A hurricane is due to arrive tonight and that should disrupt the surveillance and attack plans. You can come down to the house now."

"But I have this R-S," Joan began. She felt Nancy's shudder and knew that she'd suffered at the hands of robosoldiers deployed against a protest somewhere, sometime in the past.

"He's not violent now," Joan protested, sincerely and desperately.

Nancy sighed. "OK, we'll put it in the barn. There's a hookup there. We can let it charge as long as the power lasts. You'd better get those solunar panels down. We'll lose trees tonight."

Joan hoped AS had gotten enough charge to get him down the hill to the barn. She switched him on and was thrilled to see him gradually reactivating.

"Power rating: extremely low. Ten-minute functionality," AS reported.

"Recover solunar panels. Proceed downhill to barn," Joan ordered.

It was a race, but they made it with two minutes to spare. Joan quickly switched the power cord from the panels AS had grabbed and held under his arm rather than taking the time to store them. Fortunately, the plug matched the barn outlet where their tractor had been charging. The wind was picking up, and Nancy was shuttering the barn, calming the animals.

"Stow panels," Joan reminded AS. She didn't want those damaged.

"Quick, you and I need to get to the house," Nancy warned.

Hail, fortunately small bore, pelted them as they dashed across the barnyard to the house, illuminated by bursts of lightning.

That night Joan lay next to Nancy, grateful for a warm bed and the comfort of a companion close at hand. The wind wailed and battered the old farmhouse. She felt a bit guilty about Andres who was bunking with strangers, the farmhands who helped Nancy while her sons were away doing underground transport.

But Andres had been happy enough, had made friends as they prepared the Homestead for the hurricane followed by music – fiddle mostly. Andres had pulled out his flute and Nancy had sung some old folk tunes. The chowder they ate had been thin, diluted with water and sheep milk. Each bowl was populated with one or two oysters taken from the bay that had extended up toward the valley over the past thirty years, bringing salt and threatening the water supply.

Nancy had stayed up with her into the wee hours of the morning. "I remember you as a little girl, Joanie, just learning about your capacity for empathy. We all were learning at that point. It was as though some stressor triggered the ability. It didn't seem like much at first – just a clearer idea of what the other person was thinking and feeling. But then with practice, we realized we could communicate over short distances. Not long ones. I wish I could check in with your grandmother."

"Where did she go?" Joan asked. Before she could block the thought, Nancy thought of the offshore refugee camp, how it must be faring in the hurricane.

"Oh," said Joan. "Where is that?" A map bubbled up in her mind, offshore, some miles from Swamp City.

"We have to get the refugees out of the camps," Nancy had told Joan. "People have been there for years, many separated from their families, unable to contribute to the struggle, with so little opportunity or control in their lives. People die of despair, of too little food, of lack of medical care."

Joan nodded solemnly and shared the plan – the subversion of the robosoldiers, the take-over of the gated communities. It felt like such a slender hope. But Nancy already knew. "It's a good plan, but do we really know enough to implement it?" Nancy asked.

"We know more than we did thanks to AS. We have an idea of how to win them over without directly controlling them." Joan realized they really had made progress, more than she'd thought.

Nancy got the picture. "Where will you go next?"

There was a loud bang, and the power went out. Joan shuddered. "The attack?"

"No, I know that sound all too well, "Nancy said. She was both reassuring and resigned. Joan and Nancy were silent for a few minutes. Then Joan heard the growl of an engine. "An auxiliary generator – runs on tallow from the sheep," Nancy told Joan.

But Joan was still considering Nancy's question. "I don't know where to go," she admitted. "I wanted to stay here, work with AS, work out a plan that includes rescuing Carlos." She looked at Nancy, hoping she would change her mind.

"No way, we've been watched ever since . . .," Nancy's voice caught. The vision of a man lying blasted in the forest took Joan by surprise. "Since Ted was discovered doing a transport." Then it was Joan's turn to hug Nancy and remember. Uncle Ted, she remembered. At five, that's what she and Carlos had called him. He'd been young, brown-haired, always good for a piggyback ride, but she still recognized him in the image of his death, wide-eyed and white-bearded. "I'm sorry," Joan whispered to Nancy and held her wordlessly, meditatively until Nancy was asleep. But Joan herself lay awake pondering her next move.

The Mountain

As the hurricane dumped rain, then hail onto his back, Cus retreated into a small cave he'd happened upon near the base of the mountain. He studied the space for signs of other life, animal or human. He was alone. Looking back to the outside, he could see only the glare of his helmet light reflecting off the sheets of rain. No use wasting power. He switched off the light and tried to catch a few z's.

Was it only a few minutes before he felt water lapping onto the floor of the cave? The floodwaters must have crossed the pasture already. Cus gathered himself and made his way into the darkness. No more rain at least. Switching on his light, he spotted the gravel track that twisted and turned up the mountain. Once well above the flood, he took a break, munched some rations and leaned against his pack to nap.

Cus was pleased to wake to the warmth of the sun on his face, clean air in his lungs. He looked back over an expanse of glittering muddy water. Tree tops protruded at the far edge of the completely covered pasture. He'd been right. The river had overflowed, and the water was still slowly rising. Time to gain some altitude.

As he climbed, the day grew steadily hotter, the air dirtier and the insect hum louder. He grabbed a few mosquitos out of the air and crushed them happily, then unhappily noted the blood spots on his hand. They'd been feeding on someone, probably him. He paused to survey the scene. He saw no signs of anyone else. He supposed others could be sheltering in the forest on the mountainside. Half-heartedly he slapped his helmet back on, partly as a defense from the mosquitos and partly so he could use the infrared detectors in his helmet. But the infrared was busted. At least the filter system still worked. He realized he needed it too, should have activated it when he saw the horizon go from mist to muck.

He wheezed his way to the top, sweating heavily but not drinking. A Westerner knew to conserve water. He scouted his surroundings, sky included, regularly. When he saw what he thought was a flight of drones to the west, he stepped into the shadows at the road's edge. They were circling downwards, then lifted with a flapping of wings. Not drones, vultures, he nodded, pleased. There'd be plenty of carrion today.

A stink began to escape from the backpack. Good thing he hadn't waited any longer. He'd topped off the gamebag with hailstones last night, but they were all melted now. Even the drip from the drainage holes at the bottom of his backpack had stopped a while back.

Finally, one more turn and he saw the rocks at the top of the mountain, bare and jagged just as he'd dreamed them. Excited and exhausted, he loped to the summit but dropped like a stone when he got there. As he propped himself up against the backpack, a coughing fit seized him and held him captive until he barfed up his morning rations. Damned Eastern allergens. Usually, the helmet mask took care of them. He slipped out the inhaler issued to every recruit and took two hits. The art was urgent, the materials rotting under his nose.

When his breathing eased up, Cus set to laying out his art. He placed the hearts at the centers of two adjacent circles, the hands at twelve o'clock, the feet at six. The kidneys flanked the circles at nine and three. He studied his work. The colors were less intense than when he'd initially removed the organs. The hearts, almost identical in size and drained of blood were pinkish in tone. He marveled that the colors were so close for the Scot and the Indian. The kidneys were also very similar but a much darker maroon. He'd arranged two of them where the circles touched. The paired kidneys looked like a pair of wings. The hands, lying on the palms and showing their backs, looked different. The Scot's right hand was pale with the palest of freckles; the Indian's left hand had a uniform coppery tone. Their feet, located at the bottom of the circle, were, in their battered state, more alike. Both feet seemed to have blanched and swollen. Perhaps the effect of the hailstone melt plus the several days of hiking beforehand. The jailed men hadn't been used to so much walking.

Sitting cross-legged on the stony ground of the mountaintop, Cus was transfixed by his art. It was everything he'd dreamed. A jingling sound startled him, and he looked up. He was surrounded. Gogmasked and clad in black, they'd formed a circle around him, people of all sizes smudged with black ash or something. He reached for his sidearm, but he'd taken it off to work and it lay with his backpack outside the circle of strange figures.

The people began to stamp their feet gently, jingling softly, and a saxophone sounded, eerie and high pitched. Then the singing began. Cus's feelings were decidedly mixed. It was scary to be surrounded like this, weaponless, but for the first time he had an audience for his work. Thrilling. That they were responding to his art with a dance, that seemed right too. He should be angry, he knew that, and find a way to kill them. They were probably some kind of Mexicans. But the singing penetrated him, disarmed him, and he just felt sad. He looked up and saw the vultures circling overhead – held at bay by the dancers. He would wait for this performance art to play itself out. A tall man, blacker than the rest, was blowing on the horn. As he watched the sound grew fainter and the man seemed to shrink.

Then it was quiet except for the flapping of wings. Cus awoke with a start. The vultures had landed. He'd almost missed the climax of the piece. The scavengers clawed the organs, shredded and pecked at them. Cus grinned, feeling the fury at his core reigniting. Time to move on.

He wondered if he'd been hallucinating the black dancers, but when he got to his backpack, he saw a footprint and his sidearm was gone. Cus felt the scarlet heat of anger cloud his vision. It was his oldest weapon.

"The finest weapon there is, it's a man's mind", another of his father's maxims. This wasn't the first time he'd been disarmed in hostile territory. And he'd caught hell for it as a kid. Strangely, the memory calmed him. He wasn't a kid anymore. He was in charge. He thought about tracking the dancers, but it wasn't wise, not now. His art was complete and with it, his vengeance on his cellmates. Satisfied, Cus grabbed his pack and moved on toward the target, the homestead.

Loose cargo

Five days earlier Yolanda had slammed through the refugee camp. Despite Seito-san's confidence, the pumps had failed. We'd had to evacuate lower sections of the camp and pack into the first three subdecks like sardines in a can. When the shrieking winds had quieted and our shortwave radio assured us that Yolanda had passed, we scrambled up long emergency ladders to the deck. The superstructure was a wreck. Adults quickly shoed the children back down until a safe space for them had been walled off by debris. They re-emerged then, in orderly lines with their backpacks, and an on-deck schooling session began.

As the skies cleared the deck grew hot despite the scrim. All who weren't engaged in clearing away debris or fishing returned below decks. I was assigned shifts at the pump station and the kitchen. Although it was more difficult physically, I preferred the pump station. It was less crowded, and if I thought through a task instead of attempting it by brute force, I could still pull my weight.

The exhaust hose had sprung a leak; we were bucket brigading up the ladders. Two-gallon buckets were more than I could handle so I retrieved my trusty backpack which held a two-gallon water bladder. Now I could do my share. Unfortunately, most of the refugees hadn't been as well equipped. Almost all their belongings had been confiscated before they arrived at the camp.

On the second day after the storm, the shore devastation began to drift by. Pieces of houses and boats, bloated bodies of animals and humans. The refugee fisherfolk, fearing contamination, lost their enthusiasm for netting fresh seafood. On the third day Seito-san confessed he'd been unable to communicate with the Refugee Authority. Food stocks were exhausted, and the camp was well overdue for a delivery.

By the fifth day we were quite hungry. The sea was still and hot and tinged red. We didn't say it, but we feared it – a red algae bloom that would suck the oxygen out of the air. So, it was with tremendous relief and gratitude that we greeted the captain of a cargo ship that had stopped by in response to our distress call. To discover his cargo included bananas rendered us ecstatic, especially the kids. The huge deck of that ship was now covered with the refugees and their scanty belongings. The Captain and Seito-san knew each other from the old country and were engaged in an intense conversation, in Japanese of course. What I could understand sounded bad and good. Massive destruction in the Capital. Security forces in disarray. No one would be there to welcome, feed or shelter the refugees. But neither would any authority be there to turn us away.

I stood at the helm where I was wedged in among others sweating and excited to set foot on land, albeit very soggy land. The cargo ship had taken us up a vastly widened river until the first bridge, where it could go no farther. Both ends submerged, the bridge arched from the waters like a whale. I let those fitter than I be first to scale the ship's gantry to reach the bridge railings. I followed carefully, knees and hands stiffened from inactivity. Once I'd set foot on the refreshingly steady pavement, I followed those who'd preceded me down to the waters that covered the lower spans of the roadway to the city. We waited at the water's edge – waited for rescue or for the flood waters to recede or for . . . I wasn't sure what for but at least the red tide wasn't threatening to asphyxiate us. Hours passed.

The moment came when I just couldn't wait and do nothing any longer. I made my way painfully up and over the central hump of the bridge. I was concentrating on mindcasting. I had so little skill at this, but it was the only way I could think of to contribute. So far, I'd raised nothing. I envied the productivity of some men who were using filters brought from the camp to clean water gathered from the fast-flowing river. I longed to join them but disciplined myself to stay in place. I doubted they required my help.

Seito-san was trying his own form of outreach – the short-wave radio which he'd brought from the camp. We were on opposite sides of the hump, trying not to interfere with each other. Almost everyone else was on the lower bridge deck out of the sun. I was the mad dog in the sun, failing in my fourteenth cast. I faced east, into an ocean breeze dripping with brine. My stomach was grumbling when Seito-san appeared at the top of the hump. He waved.

"Lunch time!" We climbed down the ladder to the shaded deck, and I personally devoured three bananas and a liter of water.

"Any contact?" he asked.

"No, I feel as though there are empaths nearby, but I haven't been able to link up. Any news?"

"The city evacuated to the Sprucedeer Mountains. No official rescue under way. I do not want to make May Day call. Not yet. Do not want officials to know we are here.

"Are we better off here than we were?" I asked.

Seito-san nodded vigorously. "Oh yes, Junko-san. More food - "

"Not much," I thought.

"and much much more hope!"

That afternoon, near sunset, the children started shouting and whistling. I thought I saw swans, then realized it was a small flotilla of sailboats coming from upriver. For us? As they drew nearer, I could hear the empaths aboard mindcasting to us. My response was joined by many others, refugee empaths, most of whom I hadn't met. I should have realized there'd be empaths among them, among us. Too much ego. I should have realized.

The boats were showing very little sail. They were traveling fast on flood currents. As they neared the bridge, they hauled up their sails so they could brake using the sea breeze. They anchored under the bridge and reinforced their anchorage by tying onto the bridge supports. Women lowered clothesline to snag the rope ladders the boats carried, secured the ladders to the bridge railings and began scrambling down. As elders Seito-san and I stayed behind to release the ladders and return them to the crowded decks of the boats. Left alone on the bridge we gazed with satisfaction as the boats set off to find a landing spot for our people. The sun had just set as we walked down the arch to rendezvous with a couple of kayakers dispatched by the flotilla. "*Sugoi, ne?*[24]" Seito-san nodded at me, and I smiled and nodded back.

---

[24] *Sugoi, ne* – This is great, isn't it.

Purpose and Quandary

The morning after the hurricane dawned humid and hot, steam rising off the pastures as though they were boiling. Joan usually shuddered whenever she saw water boiling in a pot. This was worse. Don't wallow in it. Do what needs to be done. She went to the barn to check on AS. He was fully charged, she noted, grimly satisfied. There was no excuse to stay longer.

Back at the house, the farmworkers were at the breakfast table, DISCUSSING plans for the day. They ate well there in the mornings – eggs and mutton sausage and greens from the garden. Even a bit of coffee, from the tree Nancy had planted years ago, anticipating the temperatures to come. Not so much coffee that they didn't mix it with chicory though. Joan didn't much care for chicory.

She spotted Andres, who looked so happy chowing down in the crowd of workers. They were talking music, the latest bands, stuff she wasn't into. She waited. When they'd all eaten their fill and gotten up to tackle the day, Joan caught his sleeve. Andres turned to face her, and the sadness in his face and mind momentarily overcame her. Again, she buried the emotion and spoke firmly. "We have to leave today. Sorry Andres."

"It's required?" he asked.

She nodded. "We'll bring R-S. He's charged now. Go pack up while I round up some food for the trip." He didn't bother to argue, to ask for the plan. She knew he thought she didn't respect him enough to share it, but, truthfully, it was all a bit fuzzy to her.

Last night Nancy had told her about another safe house close to Swamp City.

"But I thought the safe house network was compromised?" Joan had asked.

"They're different. Not actually a house – a whole community. Gated of course," Nancy had replied.

"What! A gated community. I thought they were just for the rich."

"Yeah, amazing how a computer can inflate a bank account," Nancy explained. "And how much cover a well-bribed surveillance officer can provide."

"Too much information," Joan said sharply.

"Well, you need to know they're weird. They're a settler community, not a pass-through as far as the migrants are concerned. And they don't much care for empaths. Had a purge a couple of years back."

"Sounds perfect – not," snapped Joan. But Nancy had no other suggestions. And Joan was out of ideas herself. Remember the purpose. She needed a place where AS could stay charged up, where she could work with him to subvert the roboarmy, to give the empaths a tool in their struggle. Would this community be willing to shelter a fugitive and an R-S?

It was a gamble, but Joan had a hunch. The more she thought about it, the more she was convinced they needed to take advantage of the hurricane havoc, to travel as quickly as possible to the gated community and then, then, well throw themselves on their mercy. She just couldn't figure out why she thought this was a good idea. That made it hard to explain to Andres, so she didn't.

That night they set out. At the midnight break, a blond-haired kid joined them. "Hi Ash," Andres recognized the kid from breakfast. "Are you coming with us?"

"No, but I have something to teach her." Ash said pointing to Joan.

Joan turned surprised and instead of seeing one child, saw several, no dozens, no hundreds. In every direction she saw more of Ash. Then they faded back into the one Ash who pressed a warm cylindrical object in Joan's hand.

"You have it now," said Ash and faded back into the woods. Joan could feel it was true. She'd acquired some knowledge or skill called the Hydra effect. "Thanks," she called out.

"Whoa. What was that?" Andres asked.

"So you saw it too? I don't know exactly," Joan admitted. Embrace uncertainty, she told herself.

They sat in silence again for a while, neither eager to resume the trek. Reluctantly Andres asked, "What about Carlos?"

"I don't know. I just don't know," Joan said again and found herself crying into her sandwich.

Andres patted her shoulder and then AS spoke up. "The probability is that Carlos was taken to Rycken. However, my newsfeed indicates that Rycken experienced flooding during Hurricane Yolanda."

"You have a newsfeed?" Joan and Andres blurted together in surprise.

"Passive only. Not traceable," AS stated.

"Are there any reports about Carlos?" Joanie asked, fearful that the flooding might have claimed him. Or the RTA if he didn't have his medicine.

"No reports. A list of drowned prisoners is currently being compiled. Also, escapees."

Escapees, Joan thought, escapees! Let him be an escapee please.

As they hurried from Nancy's homestead toward Swamp City, the road was rarely dry. AS's help was key. He carried Andres when the road dipped and flooded, Joan too when the water topped the waders Nancy had given her. Often, they had to sidetrack because bridges were out, and AS's sensors indicated such a fast, deep current that it was unsafe.

As they walked, Joanie and Andres pressed AS to give them details from his newsfeed. At first, they focused on weather and weather-related evacuations. The FC Power had evacuated Swamp City for their hideout in the Sprucedeer Mountains, but AS could find no indication of evacuation of the Nacotchtank Heights gated community they were headed for.

Joan had a map that Nancy had drawn for her. She wanted to share it with AS but after the near-miss capture, she was nervous about doing so. AS suggested she put a self-destruct instruction on the document to be activated in seven days or in event of capture. Joan worried that the file might be recoverable, but AS assured her that the self-destruct program was intentionally robust, with no backdoors.

That morning, as they were bedding down for the day, Joan asked AS for the Rycken report. She'd been afraid to ask when they were moving, not wanting to distract AS, or to be honest, to demoralize herself, but it was time to know, to deal with it.

She and Andres sat without speaking, immobilized by the stream of names that AS began to speak – first the dead, then the escaped and wanted. She heard a few names she recognized but hadn't known the people well. Andres gasped once during the list of the dead. She reached out to him and after that, they held hands until the list was done. Varvara was one of the escapees – good for her. But Carlos wasn't on either list, and AS said there was still no record that he'd arrived.

"Where could they have taken him?" Joan asked.

"80% probability that the monkey drones took him to Base for questioning," AS said.

"Base, which base?" Andres asked.

"Unknown. There are five bases in proximity with monkey drone capability."

"Which base is most likely?" Joan asked trying to be more specific.

"Insufficient data to compute."

Joan sighed and shut her eyes against the light. She and Andres crawled into the filter tent.

"We'll find him Joanie. I know we will, but we have to start looking," Andres whispered against the background of chirping birds greeting the sunrise.

"It's just that we can't lose time, Andres, or I'd go to every single base. But I need to reconnect with an empath group and brainstorm how to use AS."

"Poor AS," said Andres. "Always being used."

"He's a robot, Andres."

"Oh, so you do remember that," Andres came back at her. "Sometimes I wonder. You guys get so buddy-buddy."

Joan had nothing she could say to that. She knew Andres thought they should be looking for Carlos. But something he'd said rattled around in her head. "Buddy-buddy."

Fire

Cus traveled by night. The days after the hurricane were just too hot and humid for daylight travel. He'd patched his helmet, and the night vision was back, so that was okay. He traveled light, having jettisoned most of their equipment at the campsite. Too light. His absent sidearm was a phantom draped along his thigh. He willed himself to ignore that, just as he ignored the hunger that pecked at his innards. The mission was the point now. The resister's homestead would give him what he needed.

When he arrived there at dawn, he perched beside a boulder overlooking the scene. He was glad to see grazing animals again, even if they were just puny sheep and goats. A large barn stood below with a house about thirty yards beyond it.

Hmm. Now for the creativity. Colonel Adams had wanted something subtle but disabling. Best to sleep on it, see what dreams would bring. Cus dozed as usual that day, hungry but patient. He woke as the sun set and waited for the lights to go out. No dreams to speak of but never mind. This was just a job, no great inspiration required. They'd have alarms, no doubt. He searched for their power line, then dug where it burrowed into the ground. With his pocketknife, Cus frayed the insulation and peed on the bare line. The single yard light flickered and went out.

He moved quickly then to the barn. A few animals stirred, baaaed, but they must be used to strangers. They certainly didn't rouse the way the ranch cattle had. Not enough predators hereabouts.

He scrambled silently up to the loft like a hungry puma on the prowl. Or a firehawk. The hay was dry, hot, ready to go when he struck the match. Quickly he climbed down and retreated to the verge of the meadow. Soon smoke was billowing. Now the animals were sounding off, desperately braying and bleating. People came pouring out of the house shouting for water.

In the distraction Cus crept into the house just as he'd crept into his father's study, looking for whiskey and weapons. He found neither in the homestead, but there was food and he helped himself without being too obvious about it. Took a large kitchen knife too. He turned the stove burner on and left a dishtowel in the flame. The other end of the towel hung down behind the counter where he poured some cooking oil. That was enough. Subtle.

He left cautiously, avoiding the firelight, walking the gravel driveway to avoid leaving an exit trail. By dawn he was a good fifteen miles from the homestead. Satisfied that he had remained undetected, Cus took the time for a generous breakfast – apples, cereal, and milk pilfered, no, requisitioned from the homestead. Mission accomplished, stomach full, his daytime doze came on as easy as a calf nuzzling its dam.

Cus woke shortly before sunset, or he would have missed them. Three sets of prints in the dirt at the side of the road. Unusual prints. The prints of a solitary R-S, and beside it human prints – two sets. One set of slender feet with a slight imprint, the other set cut more heavily into the soil, were stubby and spaced a much shorter distance apart. The girl and her midget brother.

Cus reared back and howled with delight. The sky was clear overhead. His helmet newsfeed confirmed the good weather. There was no time for a diversion west to Paxtang. Colonel Adams could wait. These tracks led east. And he had plenty of practice with marshland tracking in the preserve outside the City. As he strode along Cus picked up three branches from the storm litter on the road. Considering his prey, he snapped two slender ones into pieces and kept a thick one as a walking stick.

Belonging

The refugees who'd left the bridge by sailboat transferred to rowboats, kayaks, canoes and cute little swan-shaped paddle boats, caravanning to the Jubilee Monument, which sat like an island on the flooded mall. There I could see our diversity, we refugees from drought and hurricanes, heat waves and firestorms, nuclear explosions and runaway oil wells, roboarmies and fascist states. We were black and white, yellow and red, pink and brown and a lot of in between. Some, like Seito-san, had made it here from overseas, some were from the desertified west and southwest of north and central America. There must have been five hundred of us huddled in the shade of the monument's roof.

Our rescuers were volunteers. The military had left with the government. Most of the citizenry had been evacuated before Yolanda hit, and as I looked out over the floodwaters that sloshed about in the tidal basin, I doubted that anyone would be back soon. The volunteers had stocked the Monument with food and filters. Incredibly the water and plumbing were still functional. Unfortunately, medical supplies were limited. There were only two small filter tents for the ill or injured.

I checked in with the staff there to let them know I was a physician. They eyeballed my white hair and wrinkles and said they had things well under control thanks. Frankly I was grateful to be spared. I needed time to think. I went and sat in the shade on the eastern steps. I drifted along on memories from the past, distant and recent. I hoped a plan other than flight would bubble up, but the waters of my mind lay as still and flat as the water before me.

By the time Seito-san tapped me on the shoulder and handed me some water and a sandwich, I was glad to be interrupted. I'd admired Seito-san, his leadership in the crisis of the storm. Perhaps he would have some ideas – something other than hiding. But when I asked, he just shook his head.

"I do not know what is right for you, Junko-san. I must find a way out of this place before it too is just more refugee camp. A home, a staying place is needed." He glanced up at the heights to the east. "Something like they have."

Nacotchtank Heights.   Slowly and heavily, the name rolled back to me like an armored gate on casters. That was Gladys's old, gated community. I'd visited here there once, decades ago. She'd told me it had grown friendlier after she and the child Denise were expelled -- the betrayals less frequent, the surveillance looser. Given the hurricane perhaps the officer in charge had evacuated with the rest of the military. Perhaps the whole community had been evacuated.

"Let me see what I can find out." I looked at Seito-san and saw the worry lines relax just a bit. I reached out to touch his face, then caught myself. How inappropriate. I bowed my head. He bowed in return. Our eyes caught and for the first time in days, we both smiled just as Venus poked through the evening mists, and a seagull wheeled by calling out to its flock.

I had committed myself to Seito-san, to his band of refugees, and to others gathered at the monument. I rested that night in the great open hall full of a crowd's murmurs, occasionally punctuated by babies' cries and adults' shushing. The next day I circulated among the volunteers who boated us over the still high floodwaters. "Anyone from Nacotchtank Heights?" I called out, hoping for a ride over the water to the road I could see twisting up a hill to the gated community. No one answered. They regarded me strangely if they paid any attention at all. Finally, an older woman in a purple tandem kayak called out to me.

"You know someone up there?"

I hurried over to her. "Sort of. Friend of a friend of a friend or two sort of thing."

She nodded gravely. "Because they aren't too friendly up there. And I can't guarantee you a ride back."

"Understood," I bowed to her and slipped into the rear seat.

She handed me a paddle. "Know how to use this?"

"Oh yes," I smiled. It felt great having a well-used wooden paddle in my hands even if this one was much heavier than I was used to. "Can you tell me more about the Heights community?"

"Not much," said the volunteer. "I'm Sarah by the way."

"Nice to meet you. I'm . . .", I coughed to cover the hesitation. "I'm Junko." Despite her silver hair, Sarah was a powerful paddler. "Thank you so much for the lift."

"I'm grateful for the extra paddle time. We've been so busy packing food, and my boat's so small. I only get to paddle on the last run of the shift."

She made short work of the distance. As she dropped me off, Sarah warned me again. "They're weird, the people up there. Keep to themselves. Never volunteer. But if a fresh refugee makes it to them, they'll patch them up, then ship them out. That's what I hear anyway. They're very discreet."

"Don't they have a surveillance officer?" I asked.

"Oh sure, all the gated communities do. Security or jailer or community policer – whatever you want to call them. But he must be lax or blind or something, because they've gotten away with it for years."

"Did the officer evacuate?" I asked hopefully.

"I know a significant number of the community residents evacuated. Government workers you know. The ones who didn't, well I hear they have some survivalists among them – determined to ride it out in place. Make whatever adaptations they have to."

"Ah, I see." I knew survivalists could be dangerous, highly protective of their territory. "Thanks for all the information. I really appreciate it."

"I'll try to swing by after my shift. Maybe you'll have some good news to share with me," said Sarah.

"I hope so. Thanks again. See you." I stood waving as she paddled away, reluctant to turn and start the climb up to the unknown, the forbidden. As Sarah dissolved into the mist, I began the walk up the road to the walled village. From what I could see, it had weathered the storm well. There were no abandoned vehicles in the road. No fallen trees. No trees at all I realized. This was an all-built environment, curiously devoid of life. Still, as I neared the locked gate, I felt the fleeting touch of an empathic mind.

I knocked on the gate, called out a soft hello, and mindcast awkwardly, as always. The door creaked open and an almond-eyed boy with a shock of straight dark hair poked his head out. "Can I help you?"

"Yes," I said. "May I come in?"

"Are you on the guest list or related to a family member?" he recited dutifully.

"No, but . . ."

"Then I'm not supposed to let you in."

"But you'd like to let me in, wouldn't you." I wasn't trying to coerce him, but he was projecting so clearly.

"I didn't say that," he said fearfully.

"No, but I can hear you think it."

He slammed the gate in my face as he thought loudly, "Wait."

So I sat and waited, sweating and breathing shallowly, looking out over the flood plain. After half an hour or so, a pebble came skittering by. When I looked in the direction it had come from, I caught a glimpse of a beckoning finger, so I got to my feet and hobbled that way.

Outside the perimeter fence was a rock overhang. Underneath it was shady, and I could make out the boy squatting in the shadow. He looked to be about sixteen or so and was staring at me wide-eyed. We didn't speak aloud but thoughts flowed easily between us.

"You're one of them, an empath, aren't you," he asked.

"Yes, of course, and so are you."

"I knew it," he thought triumphantly. "I'm not nuts, blotso, crazy."

"Of course, you're not. Don't you have an empath coach?"

"There aren't any empaths here . . . except me," he added sadly.

Then I saw the memory – an expulsion of some thirty people with their belongings. He must have been a small boy at the time, because, in his memory, the empaths were all so tall. "But why?" I asked.

"They say the empaths can control you. Is that true? Because I can never control anybody. I just hear what they're thinking and feeling."

"Empaths can't make people do things they don't want to do, but they can make people think about things, see things from someone else's point of view. Mostly empaths feel how other people are feeling."

"Right, like I can feel when my friend Barry is in a bad mood and wants to pick on me, and I can stay away from him."

"Exactly."

"But that's not what people here believe. They think empaths can control your mind. Can you move in here and be my coach, but secretly?"

"Hmm. Maybe. I have a big family though." And then I explained about the refugees while his eyes got bigger and bigger. "I need to talk to a leader in your community about this."

Kei, the boy, then took me to his mother, Andrea. I repeated my story about the refugees' flight but omitted any mention of empathy. She called a meeting for that very afternoon, and the residents came to debate the matter. "Our development is half-empty. If we're to survive here, we need new people, new skills," she argued.

A bearded older man, Bob, lashed out angrily. "I can live just fine on my own. I've got everything I need. What I don't need is a bunch of vagabonds trying to take it away from me."

It went back and forth but, in the end, the residents said they would agree to host the refugees but first they wanted more data – a kind of census – numbers, ages, occupations, but no names or identity numbers. That evening, I found Sarah at the rocks, and we paddled back to discuss the plan with Seito-san and his people.

Fever and Mission

They'd slept afterwards, he and Varvara. Exhausted and relieved. No longer alone. Carlos woke first, roused by Varvara, who though still sleeping, was tossing about. An uneasy sleeper he noted, feeling closer to her for knowing that now. He also felt warm and reached out to follow a gradient of coolness ending in the adjacent stone wall. Despite nearly drowning the day before, he felt surprisingly good. He went down a level to pee into the latrine which had a window facing the sea. It was bright and calm.

His stomach growled, barely disturbing his thickly layered contentment. Back upstairs Varvara still slept, her face flushed. He didn't want to eat without her, but he hated to disturb her. He laid out what they each had. He still had the yucky MREs, whose impermeable packaging seemed to have protected them from their soaking in the sea. Varvara had nothing, wait, here was a wrinkled old apple and a candy bar. She did have water though.

She still hadn't wakened, and his stomach was grumbling louder. He went and touched her hand gently. Ice cold. Shocked he reached for her face which felt warm before he'd even made contact. An infection? Hurriedly he undressed her leg wound. She didn't waken, and the wound looked fine – no pus, no redness. He redressed the wound and tried to think of what Grandma Katie would do.

Embarrassed, he began to undress her. He gasped at the burns on her breasts and labia, but they were old and healing well. He recognized them from the burns he'd gotten soldering, but, of course, these burns were in all the wrong places. He felt anger driving away any embarrassment, lust, or disgust he might have felt. Finally, as he turned her to check her back, he saw the source of the infection. He should have realized that they'd dug out their chips and left them at Rycken – or somewhere en route. The sea perhaps. On the back of her left arm an angry hole dribbled greenish pus and the area around it was puffy and red.

Carlos gulped. His stomach was silent now. He'd seen his grandma treat this kind of infection. The pus had to be drained. Dead tissue cut away. Everything sterilized and cleaned. Antibiotics of some kind, scrounged off a black market, given. It was a common injury when a person tried to shed their tracking device which was designed to be meshed into the tissue precisely so it couldn't be easily removed. He sterilized his utility knife in the flame of his waterproof matches, letting the match burn down until it singed his fingertips. Once again, he laid out the contents of his first aid kit. He had barely enough disinfectant.

Before he started, Carlos held Varvara's hot face in his hands. He could feel her delirium and relief at the coolness on her face. "Jeremy, Jeremy," she called to a figure drifting away into suicide in a calm sea as the sadness rose in her.

"Varvara, Varvara," Carlos sent to her. "You're sick. I have to fix your arm. It will hurt. Lie still."

He could feel the relief flood into her. "Of course, Jeremy," she murmured.

In the two days that followed Varvara never did call him by his name. She was confused but able to drink. He made a slurry of the MREs and got that into her. Just as their water supplies were running out, Carlos felt the mindcast of a strange empath. He ran downstairs to look through the latrine window. There it was, a bit of white shooting up above the ocean's ripples. A small sailboat was approaching.

This was probably the first time Carlos was relieved to be in the company of empaths. They had Varvara below deck, treating her with antibiotics and wound care. They'd stationed him above, on deck, and were helping him to reinforce his shielding from her suffering. He'd thought he'd improve once they weren't touching or weren't in the same room, but something had happened to him, at least as far as Varvara was concerned. He felt as though he'd know what she was thinking and feeling even if she were a million miles away.

"You don't have to block everything," Alma was telling him. "Just fuzz it a bit – like you're covering it in gauze."

But when Alma said that Carlos thought of the pus-soaked gauze on Varvara's arm in the lighthouse and how he'd had no more gauze to replace it and her fever and confusion and . . .

"Deep breath. Count. Green light – no, not that bright, dim green light, that's right cave moss," Alma commanded.

Alma was there beside him, helping him wrestle the images into sense and calm and a just a bit of beauty.

"Now think of the most beautiful thing about Varvara," and he thought of her tattoos, of the swallows flying up from her breasts.

"Good, go with that."

He and Varvara were the swallows flying up into a gentle lucid blue sky to a hill where their nest was. They were together building it. Then they were humans again at the base of the tree smiling.

"Very good Carlos. You're helping Varvara. Keep it calm. No sex. She needs to rest."

He held Varvara there under the tree, and they sat leaning against the trunk. An apple fell to the grass beside him.

"Carlos, time to eat." Carlos opened his eyes and there was Alma with a sandwich, water, and a package of rehydration salts. They were still on the open deck. He had a harness on, and they were sailing under the stars on a moonless night, speeding along the waters.

"You have a strong mind and a wonderful spirit," Alma told him. Carlos glowed with the acknowledgement.

"I would be honored to be your coach," Alma offered.

Carlos hesitated, then laughed at his own stubbornness. "Of course, Alma. I'd be honored too. But I have technical work to do."

"No problem," she smiled. "There's always something on a boat that needs fixing."

"I have a, a special project." He quickly clouded his mind before she could see the R-S plan.

"Ah, I see. Well, you're with us for now, Carlos."

"Where are we headed?" Carlos asked, though he knew from the stars they were sailing south and could smell that land was not far off.

Now it was Alma's turn to guard her secrets. "Somewhere where we can help Varvara heal. You want to be there, don't you?" she smiled.

"Yes! You know I do," he blurted and, embarrassed, turned to his sandwich. But as he chewed, a sense of duty tugged at him He knew the R-S project came first. It just had to.

The sailboat had anchored in a new bay that covered a large swath of Swamp City. The floodwaters were receding. "We believe our anchorage will stay watery – at least until the Engineering Corps returns to Swamp City," Alma told Carlos.

"Will the FC Power try to reclaim it then or stay in the mountains?"

"We don't know yet. Right now, there are refugees in the Monument, but as far as we know, no one else remains in the city."

Varvara's fever continued. She still didn't call him by name. Carlos spent time each morning, afternoon, and evening with her, holding her hand, going back to the apple tree. Alma kept the sessions short. "She needs rest, and you need to focus on other things as well."

Carlos continued his training with Alma, finally getting the colors that accompanied others' thoughts under control, not so blindingly bright. Joanie had been right. He should have trained before. Still his favorite time of day was the time he set aside to think about AS and how useful he could be. He'd already proved his usefulness in transport, but he hadn't seen the drones coming. His mapping skills were great. And the prime directive seemed hardwired in so AS should be robust in that dimension if his memory circuits weren't tampered with. Carlos suspected that's how the R-S were overridden. And that's why the control wasn't remote. The memory override had to be precisely timed by the commanding officer. He really wanted to brainstorm with Joanie about this. Where the hell was she, he wondered, letting some annoyance creep in.

"Keep it down," Alma thought back from below decks. For the umpteenth time, he had to be careful about emotions amplifying his thoughts. As he turned down the volume of his own mind, Carlos heard the subtle throb of an electric motor. A small launch was approaching them.

"Hey there," the passenger in the launch hailed him. "You called for a doctor?"

Carlos's heart lurched but he managed to call back, "Probably." He realized he was the only person above deck and checked in empathically with Alma. She told him to lower the ladder so the man could climb aboard. He greeted the doctor eagerly and as politely as he could.

"Welcome, where are you coming from?"

"Oh, the Monument," the doctor replied. "We have a small hospital set up over there."

"Have you got a silver-haired lady doctor named Katie?"

The man looked at him sharply. "No, there was a silver-haired woman who said she was a doctor. Met her when we had just finished setting up. Came in with a group from the offshore refugee camp. Said her name was Junko though. She didn't look very Japanese, but it's hard to tell with the old ones sometimes."

That was Joanie's mother's name. It had to be her.

"She's not with you anymore?" Carlos asked.

"We didn't need her. I think I heard she went up to the Heights," he gestured to the housing high above the floodwaters, "to see if they'd take in her refugee group."

"Oh, how about a girl, black hair, almond eyes, kind of skinny? Name of Joan?"

But the man shook his head. "Where's the patient?" Just then Alma popped up from the gangway and impatiently gestured the doctor down. Carlos followed.

He'd brought new antibiotics and started a new IV to run them. "You've done a good job containing the infection but curing it will be harder. I'll come back tomorrow to debride the wound."

Alma asked, "How many days do we have here?"

The doctor sighed, "I hear there's a robosoldier army on the move. We estimate three to four days before they're here."

"Enough time for her?" Alma nodded at Varvara.

"We can hope," replied the doctor. "We can hope."

Communication

"AS," Joan asked the next day. "Are you buddy-buddy with other R-S? Do you communicate with each other?"

"R-S communication circuits are designed for inter-R-S communication under human command. Purpose – coordination of movement and conditions of operation. There is no provision for other inter-R-S communication."

"Could you? Could you communicate with another R-S if not under human command?"

The circuit is not designed for this use."

"OK, but what if a human, not in the chain of command, ordered it."

"Verification protocol for identifying commanders is renewed daily and is strictly adhered to. Violation of verification of command protocols requires decommissioning of the R-S."

"Then why . . ." Joan began but Andres emerged from the tent with two MRE's in hand. He waved them at Joan.

"This is it, Joanie. The last of the food. We can't waste time talking. We've got a lot of ground, or maybe I should say water, to cover."

Joanie looked down. "That's it, huh? How many more days, AS"

"Two, one if we assume no surveillance. A logical assumption at this time." AS reported.

They set out at a fast clip, AS carrying them both as well as their gear. Sitting on his broad shoulders, Joanie and Andres could talk over AS's head as the R-S thundered and splashed toward Swamp City. It was dark enough that they could barely see each other's gogmasks.

"Have you picked up any empath mindcast?" Andres asked.

"No, it's weird. It's like totally silent around here," Joanie replied.

"Well, AS's newsfeed did say the area had been evacuated."

"I know but usually some people still stay. Not necessarily empaths so they wouldn't be casting. But I can almost always tell when there are other people around, empaths or not."

"Hey, you're a city girl. Don't you think you might miss one or two people?"

"Maybe. I'm more worried the storm, the flooding, or some aftermath event might have finished any stragglers off," Joan speculated. "If there were injured or suffering people within twenty miles, I'd definitely know."

"That sensitive! Ay!" Andres sighed. "So, it's Nacotchtank Heights for us then?"

"If they'll have us. Nancy seemed a little unsure about that. She said they usually take only fresh refugees – no one through the safe house network. That way they can't be traced back."

"And the refugees just stay there?" Andres asked.

"I think they just replace people who die with refugees, replace their identities or something," Joanie said.

"That's so -- so different." Andres said.

"Yeah, well they have a surveillance officer," said Joan flatly. It had to be said some time.

"What!" Andres shouted. She could see the whites of his eyes through the gogmask.

"A friendly one," Joan tried to say reassuringly, though she was far from reassured herself.

"What is that? What is a friendly surveillance officer?" Andres demanded in disbelief.

But just then she felt it. "Andres, be quiet, I'm getting something, a mindcast or something."

Dragging AS and Andres in her wake, Joan followed the mindcast. She didn't recognize the empath. They weren't very clear in their casting, but the emotion, the urgency, almost panic, that they emitted seemed strangely familiar. Whoever it was must have tremendous range, because she was picking up the cast in the dead zone twenty miles out from Swamp City. As they got closer the signal chatter picked up and made it a bit more difficult to hear but, surprisingly, not so difficult. It almost had a color to it. A kind of mossy green. Weird. Carlos was the only one who'd ever communicated just color to her, but he was totally short range.

At dawn they reached the bridge. When they waded across to its arching roadway, she looked down at the bay and spotted the anchored boat with furled sails. That's where the cast was coming from. She'd been trying to send an answer but seemed to be getting nowhere. She turned to AS. "Can you hear that?" Joan asked.

"There are many sounds. I do not understand "that"," AS replied.

Andres chimed in. "Yeah, what are you talking about. You've been weird all night."

"It's an urgent mindcast, moss green. That's as specific as I can get. Oh, and it's coming from that boat." Joan pointed to the upriver craft.

AS followed her finger and deployed his infrared search beam. "There are five individuals aboard the vessel. One above deck, four below."

"Try your echolocation circuit, AS," Joan urged.

"Severely increased heart rate on an individual below deck. Severe illness, dehydration or blood loss probable," AS responded.

"AS, train your echolocation circuit on me," Joan ordered. When he had done so, Joan initiated a mindcast to him. "Can you hear me thinking AS?"

"Affirmative," AS responded.

"Now train your echolocation beam on the individuals on the boat. Can you hear any of them thinking?"

"The one above deck is very loud. No words. Green. Urgent call. I recognize the caster," AS said.

"You do?" Joan called out, surprised.

"Of course. It's Carlos," AS stated.

Andres and Joan grabbed ahold of each other joyfully. When she shifted her gaze back to the river, Joan caught sight of a kayaker approaching the flooded end of the bridge. "AS, you must hide," she warned. The three of them scanned the bridge decks, the pilings and then the span.

"Up there," AS pointed to a small house in the trusses overhead.

"Will you fit?" Joan asked.

"Affirmative," AS replied and began climbing as Andres and Joan rushed down the roadbed to head off the kayaker who'd lodged at the underwater end of the bridge.

"Good morning," he said as the two of them approached. "Looking for a lift? It's pretty wet in this direction."

"I need to get to that sailboat upriver," Joan said pointing.

"I only have one seat. If you wait, I'll get somebody to come with a bigger craft to pick up the three of you. There are three, right? I thought I saw a bigger guy up there."

"Just us two," Joan snapped. "But if you could take me now, I really need to get to that boat."

"Are you sure?" Andres asked.

"I'll be back Andres," Joan reassured him. "You know I will."

"I should ask the boat owner first," the kayaker said, but then saw Joan droop with disappointment and felt more eager than usual to be helpful. "That's Alma's boat. I'm sure she won't mind."

Joan cautiously slipped into the kayak, grabbed the extra paddle and she and the kayaker – Gene, she finally learned his name – headed against the current for the boat. "I'm coming," she sent, but she knew Carlos wouldn't hear her. Such a bad listener.

Control

Cus scowled. The R-S tracks had gotten harder to follow once the group had reached Swamp City. So he'd climbed this bridge to surveille the scene. A bridge house was located further up but he had a fine view from the roadway. He spotted the Monument, swarming with ant-like humans. Was there a glint of R-S metal there? He couldn't tell. Small boats were darting to and fro over the waters that lapped the monument steps. He'd have trouble trying to commandeer the R-S and its robonappers in the midst of this herd of humans. He'd have to find a way to cut his prey out of the herd. For a moment he regretted his uniform, his helmet. No way just to sneak in undercover.

He studied the surroundings, looked for the high land. There, to the east, housing – surely a gated community. A fortified outpost of civilization with a fellow officer, food, supplies. Excellent. He had his destination and his probable target both in view. He climbed down to the lower deck of the bridge, seeking shelter from the sun that was climbing higher. The bridge was totally submerged in the direction he wanted to go, but he spotted a lone kayaker coming down the river, headed for the sea.

"Ahoy," Cus shouted, dredging up some navy vocabulary from some long-lost comic book of his boyhood. "Ahoy."

The man looked up, alarmed by the uniform apparently. Cus took his helmet off and stood bareheaded backlit by the sun, then rushed down the sloping roadbed of the bridge. Too bad the boat was a one-seater. The man was tying the boat to a service ladder under the roadbed. Cus waited for him to climb the ladder.

"Sorry," the guy said, as he climbed, not looking up. "I only have a one-seater, but I can send out a larger boat when I get to harbor. I do have some supplies though – water, food, bandages – if you need them."

He was a little guy, not a problem. When he reached the top of the ladder, Cus was there, helmet on, ready. When the man looked up, he felt a little shiver of satisfaction at the fear in his eyes. He swung his heavily booted foot under the man's chin. The kayaker sailed back and up with the blow and plopped limply into the rapid current below, then conveniently disappeared. Grimacing, Cus shook the guy's pain and confusion out of his mind as he climbed down the ladder.

Soft, he was getting soft, Cus told himself as he reached the kayak, where, as told, there was food and water. Suddenly he felt the hunger and thirst he'd held at bay while tracking the R-S. In the shade of the bridge, as shifting tides rocked the kayak, he wolfed down food hardly noticing what it was, only that it was food. And drank water, clean water. Sleep seized him then but briefly. He woke when the rocking stopped.

Cus experienced a momentary confusion, followed by panic. The current had slowed and the guy whose kayak he'd seized might have friends out searching for him. He had to get out of here. Get a grip. No need to panic. Cus talked himself down. Best be on his way though. He pulled up to the ladder to untie the rope, then paddled free of the bridge. He could still make out the housing on the heights but had lost sight of the Monument because of pesky trees lining what must have been the river shore before the hurricane. He took a bearing with his helmet compass and paddled, not very well but powerfully. Soon he was in the shade of the swamped trees. Here, Cus thought, it would be safe to rest. He was very, very tired. He could climb the hill to the heights come nightfall. It was all under control.

Cus was awakened by shouts, horns, whistles. The name "Gabriel" floated on the breeze to him as he sat in the kayak leaning against the willows. Probably looking for that guy whose kayak he borrowed. His cover was good though. They wouldn't see him until they probed every inch of the bank. The water did seem lower than it had been. Good. Time to get some authority back in the area.

He waited until the shouts and whistles had faded. The light had grown dimmer, but it wasn't full night yet. He could wait. He thought about sleeping in a bed, drinking a beer, taking a shower – simple stuff that a guy comes to crave when he's in the field.

When the mosquitos started to swarm in on him, Cus decided it was dark enough. He pushed his way slowly and stealthily through the drooping willows and picked up the current. The river was quiet. He saw lights on the Heights above. They must have a generator up there. He hoped the surveillance officer would be cooperative.

When he reached the rocky shore below the Heights, Cus pulled on his pack and, after exiting the kayak, turned it over and sent it back into the current. The hump of the kayak, colorless in the twilight, quickly disappeared. Cus waded ashore and began his ascent.

At the gate he didn't hesitate, just pounded on it and announced himself, "Lieutenant Custer, Army of the FCP, on military assignment. The gate opened and Cus found himself on the wrong end of a vintage AK-47.

"Take off your helmet," the man with the gun ordered.

Cus did so slowly but with confidence that he'd pass the next test. Sure enough, the guy flashed a retina scanner at him and five seconds later had dropped the gun barrel and grabbed him by the shoulder in a soldierly half-embrace. "Boy, am I glad to see you," Bob said. "Follow me."

They climbed the stairs to a surveillance officer's guard tower and quarters. Cus was surprised to realize the man wasn't in uniform. "Sit," Bob said. He had an imperious way Cus didn't appreciate in a civilian. But then Bob pushed a can of beer and a bag of pretzels toward him. Bob grabbed a beer for himself and proposed a toast. "Here's to our new surveillance officer!"

Cus grinned and downed his beer. He liked the sound of that. "I get the feeling you didn't care much for your old one."

"That guy? A pushover. A softie. An embarrassment to the military really. He let people here get away with treason."

Cus let his eyebrows shoot up. "You should have reported him."

"Easier said than done when you're under his command," Bob retorted.

Cus softened his tone. "I reckon that's true enough."

"Listen son, we have a situation here. Those refugees down at the Monument are gonna come swarming up the hill right into our community any day now."

"Tonight?" Cus asked.

"No, not tonight. I stalled 'em. Asked for more data. But tomorrow, this old lady – she's no refugee but she's representing them – one of those volunteer types – she'll be back with the numbers and the residents here have agreed to it in principle."

Cus was relieved the situation wasn't imminent. He'd have tonight to sleep on it and take charge in the morning. "Show me my quarters old man, and I'll need dinner."

"Yes, sir. I'm Bob. Just keep an eye on the gate for me and I'll be right back."

"Better leave the AK47 for me if you want me to keep sentry duty."

"Oh no Lieutenant Custer. The AK's mine. Your gear is in the locker behind you."

Reunion

Carlos was under the apple tree with Varvara. She was talking to him. He hoped that meant she was feeling better. He sent happiness, pink-tinged, to her. The words were getting louder. They weren't Varvara's at all. "Alma?" he asked.

"No little brother. It's me, Joan."

And then she walked right into his scene, his scene with Varvara. Carlos to a deep breath, calmed himself as Alma had taught him and thought firmly, "Wait for me on deck, Joan." When he emerged from his trance time with Varvara, there was Joanie, looking properly remorseful but also glowing with gladness. Alma was there too. She must have filled Joanie in because Joanie got right to the point, out loud.

"Carlos, I'm so glad to see you and I'm so glad you're all right, but we have work to do. I need your help with the project."

Alma interrupted. "The problem is Carlos is also needed here, to help with Varvara's recovery. They've formed a special bond."

Joanie nodded. "I know. But it's not far – just to the bridge." She gestured downstream but the bridge had disappeared in the rising mist.

"We're leaving tonight," Alma warned her. "Our sources tell us there's a robosoldier army coming to reclaim Swamp City. We're not safe here."

"But this is our chance," thought Carlos. He turned to Alma. "I have to help with this project. The R-S army coming only makes it more important."

"I've been following Carlos's mindcast for twenty miles. He has incredible range. If you're not too far away . . . no, I'm not asking where you're going, I'm just saying he may still be able to reach Varvara."

Alma shook her head sadly. "It's a risk, a big risk. Are you sure, Carlos?"

He remembered the kindness of Varvara's touch and the wisdom of Alma's teaching. Then he thought of all the risks they'd taken to get the R-S project this far. "I'm sure that this is what I have to do Alma. But I think I should explain."

Joan looked at him, shocked, but he went on to explain the R-S empathy project, as he called it, to Alma. "So you see, the arrival of an R-S army, it will be an important real-life experiment."

"And likely fatal for you both," Alma said flatly. "Our group, I can tell you now, won't be willing to stick around to find out. But I can drop you at the bridge if that's really what you want."

"Thank you," Joanie and Carlos exclaimed, but tears brimmed from Carlos's eyes and streaked his face. An intense deep blueness filled their minds.

Alma gave him a warning glance and he muted the cast.

"And I'll try to boost your signal to Varvara," Alma told Carlos. "Let's work out a schedule, twice a day, agreed?"

Carlos nodded vigorously.

"And if you survive this experiment and need a pickup and we're in range and it's an acceptable risk, we'll pick you up afterwards."

"A lot of ifs," Carlos smiled wryly.

"That's right," Alma said and didn't smile back.

As Joan waited for them to set sail, she finally had time to think. She was disappointed by Alma's hostility but not surprised. Because of the fear of discovery and imprisonment or worse, the empaths had separated into cells with little central direction. Each cell had its own tactics – all to the end of bringing the world's population together into one egalitarian group and dismantling the fascist grip of the FCPower. But, as her grandmother had warned her, the isolation created suspicion and inhibited cooperation. How great if they'd all been able to work together with AS on this boat, although, as she looked around, she could see there really wasn't that much space. She was hopeful that they could use the small bridge house to work with AS out of view – she and Carlos together.

The current sent river ripples lapping against the anchored boat. Carlos was below with Varvara. He'd changed she thought sadly. Why should she be sad though just because her little bro was growing up. And his mindcast skill, amazing! She was grateful to Alma for his training. He still didn't hear very well – at least couldn't hear <u>her</u> very well. Too much practice ignoring her.

She set aside these frustrations and settled her mind on the task at hand. A roboarmy. Danger and opportunity. So, the experimental question was, could they, through AS, gain entry into the echolocation circuits of multiple robosoldiers? Once there could she broadcast to them the need to observe the prime directive – do no harm to humans?

For AS, it had taken witnessing his commander harming another human after having had the trigger to override set by her suggestion. Would another human sacrifice be necessary? As she was thinking of the horrible last scream that Janice had loosed, Carlos joined her on deck. Immediately she hugged him with all her might. She was so relieved when he hugged her back that a little sob escaped her. Too soon, she thought. Too soon to let down her guard. Too much to do.

Alma heaved up the sea anchor and set sail. Ten minutes later they reanchored a few meters upstream from the bridge. A small dinghy, just big enough for three, was lowered into the water where the current grabbed it. But its tie-up yanked it back, close to the sailboat. Carlos with his battered backpack, Joan, and Alma scrambled down to board the bobbing dinghy. They were cast off by someone on deck. Joan couldn't make out the person's features, and then she realized, that was the idea.

They rode the current the short distance, Alma taking the tiller and expertly steering them to an alcove at the piling where a metal ladder led up to the deck. Carlos hooked a rung by tossing up a grappling iron and reeled them in, straining against the current that wanted to pull them out to the ocean. Joan and Carlos climbed the ladder calling out their thanks to Alma below. She'd wait for the tide to shift before rowing back, unless the sailboat headed downstream. Joan hadn't been informed of that part of the plan. No need to know.

Silently Joan led Carlos up a series of ladders to the bridge house high above the deck. They saw no one in the dark mists, not even Alma below. Joan searched for AS's echolocation beam, but he was silent. She knocked on the bridge house door with some trepidation. Andres peaked out and, grinning, let them in, giving Carlos a huge hug as soon as he'd stepped over the threshold.

The space was tiny. "Where's AS?" Joan asked anxiously.

"Right here," Andres pointed to the table he'd been sitting at. AS had folded up, powered down.

"There was somebody in uniform down on the bridge earlier, but he left. Just one guy. Didn't see us," Andres continued.

Joan scouted the space around them. It was just big enough. "We better stay here then. Time to begin," she said.

Teatime

I almost capsized Sarah's kayak so eager was I to disembark. Looking for Seito-san I pushed my way through the mass of refugees. When I found him, he was leading a meeting to discuss next steps for the group. My Japanese was coming back. I could follow what he was saying.

"We have word that a roboarmy is coming and should arrive in three to four days. Unless you want to be taken back to a camp, now is the time to act." He looked up to assess the crowd. Which way were they leaning? There'd been a dismayed whoosh, like air escaping a balloon, when he'd mentioned the roboarmy. They'd already known of course. Rumors must have been flying back and forth for a couple of days. But now that Seito-san had said it, it was official for them. I, however, was stunned. The roboarmy was news to me. Then he spotted me, standing in the back. I slipped off my gogmask, smiled and displayed an upright thumb.

He nodded but his face remained serious, unsmiling. "Our new arrival refugee Junko-san has made the trip to Nacotchtank Heights and confirmed their willingness to take us and keep us out of view of the roboarmy."

Whoa! I hadn't said anything to them about a roboarmy.

Seito-san continued. "Please consider your options but I would urge you to remain as a group."

Many in the crowd nodded at this and muttered, "Of course, of course."

He stepped down. Several people came up to him to talk about the timing of their shifts. The refugees had maintained a work schedule in the Monument but coordinating with the volunteers hadn't been completely stress-free. I waited for him and eventually he came to me. We bowed our greetings. "Please Junko-san, won't you have tea?"

"Of course, Seito-san."

He led me to a box where he had tea things laid out. I sat quietly, holding my tongue, until the tea sat steaming before me. *"Itadakimasu[4]."*

"Itadakimasu," he replied.

"Seito-san," I began. "I didn't know about the roboarmy. I don't believe the Nacotchtank Heights people do either. At least, it didn't come up in our meeting."

"Tell me about the meeting please."

"One man was opposed but most were favorable. Many have left the community, so there is plenty of space."

Seito-san nodded but said nothing.

"They want to know more about us – numbers, gender, occupation."

Seito-san looked surprised.

"I think that's reasonable, don't you? They want to prepare for us."

"Perhaps I am too suspicious Junko-san. Such lists could be used against us. Which person asked for this information?"

Ah, this was why I was no good at politics or cards. I couldn't remember. "I'm not sure. But they all voted on it. And the main thing is, they've agreed to house us as long as they get the information first."

Seito-san looked even glummer. "I suppose we have no other choice. I do not want to fragment our people as some of the other refugee groups have discussed. They want to hide in the marshes."

"I'm sure you're right Seito-san. It takes many skills to live in the marshes. Of course, your people are very skilled."

"No, really, they are not. Not marsh living. I make the list Junko-san."

"Good, I'll take it first thing in the morning and your group can follow in the evening when it's cooler. We'll need to talk to the volunteers about transport."

"I have already done this, Junko-san."

"Of course. Seito-san you are quite wise."

"And Junko-san is quite brave. Be careful please. Let me know if things are not ready for our people."

Same old lady

Cus was quite pleased with the contents of the locker. Plenty of guns. Then he realized there was no ammunition for them. Still there was a functional stun gun, a uniform with a colonel's silver eagle attached, and a saber emblazoned with the Great Seal of the Federal Corporate Power. He took an experimental swing and the saber hilt molded to his hand as though it had been made for him. It felt even better than his grandfather's had, the one he'd been forced to leave hanging over the fireplace in his father's study.

Cus decided to dress for dinner and celebrate a self-promotion by leaving the silver eagle attached. The shower ran hotter than any he'd had since he upped for the service. The guy had left behind some electric clippers, so Cus took to trimming his hair and beard to regulation length. As he stared in the mirror, he had an uncanny feeling that he'd changed somehow. He was gaunt from the past few weeks on the trail, and the uniform had been tailored for a larger man. Both factors resulted in a jacket that hung limply on his frame. And his eyes glittered strangely and gradually morphed into the eyes of the screaming woman he'd gunned down. Shuddering, he broke eye contact with the image in the mirror and went back to the locker area. "Get a grip," he told himself. "This is a sweet spot." He slipped on clean sky-blue socks, a bit of heaven, and polished boots, a little smaller that he'd like, but when he stamped his foot, the floor resonated with a satisfying thud.

In a third locker he found an empatho-logical detector. At first, he hadn't recognized it, but then he recalled a paragraph from his gated community reading. Something about a gated community that had been harboring some so-called empatho-logicals. They'd been detected using some handheld device invented by the local surveillance officer. Device wasn't very reliable. Oversensitive, like the old lie detectors. Still, he clipped the detector to his belt. He'd figure out how it worked later. Maybe Bob would know. He dug into the back of the locker and discovered a robovalet, all folded up. His own robovalet! This was the life.

Bob knocked and entered with a plate of food. "Looks like you found what you needed."

"That's right," Cus said, grabbing the grub. He started shoveling it in before he even sat down.

"Wow, you were hungry!" Bob exclaimed.

Cus just nodded and grunted. When the plate was spotless, Cus leaned back and swiped the crumbs from his lips and beard. "Any beers left?"

"Yeah, but, uh, the community wants to meet with you. I figured it'd be better tonight, you know, before the old lady shows up tomorrow."

Cus stood up immediately, stamped his feet. "Let's do this, Bob." On the way out the door, Cus turned back to the weapons locker to grab his stun gun, scabbard and saber. As they walked through the development, Cus asked about the ammunition.

"Oh, that's stored separately. The community leader has the key to the storage area. No guns there, just the ammunition."

"You're not the leader, Bob?" Cus asked accusingly.

"Shoulda been if the election had been fair. Shoulda just been household heads voting but they let everyone in," Bob said bitterly.

Cus patted his shoulder comradely. "So, who's the leader?"

"Bitch named Andrea."

"I got you covered, Bob. Just give it time."

The meeting went well enough. Some people were glad to see an officer back in charge of security, others reluctant to acknowledge his authority. Andrea, for example, refused to release the ammo. But Cus was confident he'd sort it out. Especially after hearing the announcement that a roboarmy would be reentering the area soon. Meanwhile he looked forward to being the one to greet the old lady from the refugees tomorrow morning. Another old lady causing trouble. Or maybe, he had a hunch, the same old lady. He fell asleep smiling.

The List

I was up early, organizing my backpack. Seito-san came by to give me the list. Sarah came in her kayak as the sun started to streak the waters which had grown shallower and more debris-cluttered in the past twenty-four hours. It was the kind of day we would have called beautiful in my youth, but as the sun, scrimmed though it was, hit the atmosphere, caustic yellow beads of pollution began to form. Even through the gogmask I could smell a horrible stench and knew it to be the smell of flesh burning.

Sarah put me down five hundred yards further out from Nacotchtank Heights than before. I waded through muddy waters hoping to avoid injury and infection. It was a long sweaty slog up the hill after that and by the time I reached the gate, I wanted nothing more than a cool glass of water. I mindcast for the boy Kei, then knocked and called his name. The gate opened and I stepped inside, relieved to pass from the glare to the shadows. I slipped off my gogmask and blinked, hoping to see who was kindly taking it from my hand, then froze. A robovalet in uniform. "Please, follow me," it said in a polite but commanding tone. I did so slowly and reluctantly. I saw no alternative but to confront the surveillance officer who must have returned. If he was as lenient as some claimed, perhaps I could persuade him to turn a blind eye to the refugees. But I had no bribes to offer.

When I turned the corner and caught sight of him, I knew it was hopeless. He was thin and trim in an oversized colonel's uniform, but I recognized him as the patroller from the woods. "Welcome," he said. "I thought it might be you."

I said nothing. What could I say? This man had left me for dead and had me at his mercy again.

"We should have quite a show this afternoon – refugees versus a roboarmy. It may be bloody or watery – the deaths I mean – but I'm sure it will be exciting.

I'm so happy to have an additional audience member." Disgust welled at the back of my throat, for him and for myself. I'd led the refugees to their deaths.

"How about a bit of breakfast," he asked. I shook my head, nauseated. It was relief to close my eyes, block out the sight of him, but I didn't dare keep them closed. "That's right. Pay attention. I believe you have something for me?" The list. Damn me, he meant the list. "That's right. The list. Hand it over . . . please."

I looked about for a flame. Maybe I could get a fire going, destroy the list at any rate. But I saw nothing. I reached in my pocket, crumpled the list, and handed over the balled-up paper. He sighed, smoothed it out and inspected it briefly, then handed it to the robovalet. "Interesting. You don't seem to be on it. Travelling under an assumed name, Katie?"

"Why should I?"

"Answer the question."

"No," I answered then looked away. A small glowing device at his waist caught the corner of my eye.

"Ah, you're lying. Shouldn't lie to me Katie."

I glanced up to see him pulling a stun gun and pain shot through my body, my brain.

Last minute preparation

They all squeezed into the tiny interior of the bridge house – Carlos, Joan, Andres and AS. When he'd seen Andres and AS, Carlos couldn't believe he'd ever hesitated about coming back with Joan. But time was short and there wasn't enough of it to review all that had happened to them even though each was curious, even AS.

"I require information on your location since capture by the drone-monkeys," AS had stated.

"Why?" asked Carlos. He didn't recall AS ever having been curious about anything before, or even having asked a question if it wasn't relevant to the task at hand.

"Developing intelligence requires a post-hoc check of real events against a priori hypotheses," AS replied.

"Uh, translation?" Carlos turned to Andres and Joan.

"He just wants to know whether he guessed right about where you were taken by the drone monkeys," Joan broke it down for him.

"Well, that's a long story," Carlos started.

"And we have other priorities right now," Joan interrupted. "AS, we were told a robosoldier army is approaching our position. Can you detect them?"

"Correct. One hundred robosoldier unit approaching from southwest. Ten kilometers from our current position. Erratic velocity. Currently 2 km per hour."

"So how soon will they be here?" Carlos asked."

"Five hours minimum but with obstructions and rest for human handler, possibly twenty-four hours."

"We're finally going to have a chance to see if AS can influence the other robosoldiers not to harm humans!" Carlos said. He was excited but firm.

"You're going to face off with a roboarmy? Count me out," Andres protested.

Truthfully Carlos was a little concerned about this plan too. Still, he shook his head. "Not a face-off. More like a secret probe. But can AS pull that off? I think he'd be immediately identified and demobilized."

"I have something to teach all of you," Joan said. "Including you AS. Ash, the little girl from the Homestead, taught it to me. It's called the Hydra effect."

"I am familiar with the term," AS replied. "The hydra effect owes its name to the Greek legend of the Hydra which grew two heads for each one cut off and is used figuratively for counter-intuitive effects of actions to reduce a problem which result in stimulating its multiplication."

"What?" exclaimed Carlos.

"But I do not know the device," AS added.

Over the next several hours they struggled to deploy the Hydra device. The effect required a reflector (AS's shiny chassis worked well), the holographic projection device, and light – the stronger the light the more counterfeit images they could create of themselves. There seemed to be an empathy reflector component as well. But they had only one device, the one Ash had given her in the marshlands.

"We'll either have to stay together or one of us will have to use the device while the rest of us hide," Joan concluded.

"I volunteer to hide," said Andres. "This is *completamente loco*."

"I'll keep the device. You two hide and AS will go to a different hiding spot. I think AS can blend in with the roboarmy but"

"But what?" Carlos asked.

"AS and I can't just command them to stop. They'll have to see it for themselves, the harm to humans."

"I have seen it," AS contributed. "The command is corrupted."

"We talked about this before," Carlos said. The commanding officer must be overriding the prime directive. We have to get to the CO."

"Or whatever tool he's using to command them," Joan suggested.

"Can we override the override? Sabotage it somehow?" Andres asked.

Carlos shook his head sadly. He didn't want to bring up his own device, Kepler's R-S control device, lost in the plunge from the drone monkey's claws.

Still, he had overridden the drone's system to get free. It took a while, and it was just a tiny change.

Joan speculated that AS might be able to share his experience with the other R-S. "Do you have an uploadable record of that event?"

AS replied, "Of course. I have integrated this file to modify the command override program. For this soldier it is no longer possible to override the prime directive without a rebuild. But uploading to other R-S under a different commanding officer may not be possible."

"A different commanding officer. Hmm. Who is your commanding officer?" Joan asked.

"The last commanding officer of AS-57189 was Lieutenant Custer, serial number 789206, but on Day 4, Month 3, FCP year 42, due to command corruption, informal transfer of command to Assistant Repair Technician Gloria AKA Joan, and subcommander Carlos.

"Hey, I'm a subcommander!" Carlos lit up even if that did make him secondary to Joan.

But Joan frowned. "I am not your commander AS. You saw for yourself the corruption of your commanding officer of record. You reprogrammed yourself to follow the prime directive without exception,"

"I am structured for command, but I will integrate this information into my learning circuits," AS responded.

Carlos erupted with excitement. "I have an idea. Let me see if I can loosen the command structure just a little bit by mindcasting. I've done it twice, you know. Once with the roboserver in the bar and once with the monkey drone. It was the motor system, but if AS can show me where the override circuit is, maybe I can loosen that, and he can upload his violation video."

"Good," Joan smiled. "But we'll need to move soon. Can you give us a newsfeed report AS? Focusing on robosoldier activity."

AS activated a radio receiver circuit and broadcast to the small group.

"A robosoldier contingent from the City Heights Regiment under the command of Lieutenant Phillips is conducting mop up operations of the Sprucedeer Mountains-Swamp City corridor. As the floodwaters of Hurricane Yolanda recede, hostile elements – both citizen stragglers who violated the evacuation order and illegal aliens who used the storm to leave their assigned areas and invade our space – are being dealt with. Sanitary disposal of the remains of these elements and other carrion is being carried out."

Andres interrupted. "How far away now, AS?"

"5 kilometers."

"They've moved five kilometers in three hours," Carlos noted. "Not an astounding pace but it suggests they have a target in mind."

"If we're going to move, we should do it now," said Andres. He was standing next to a small window. "The water at the end of the bridge has receded. We should be able to walk across Nacotchtank Heights. The Monument is still surrounded by water but there are a lot of small craft there. Looks like they might be packing up."

They'd seen it all so clearly from above, but when they got down to the muddied bridge off ramp, the air was dense with yellow smog and a stench even gogmasks couldn't keep out. "Good," Joan thought. "At least they won't have a visual on AS."

They headed up the road that led to the Heights, seeing no one. As they neared the gate, they left the road and began reconnoitering, seeking a hiding place. They found an overhanging ledge and scrambled over the rockfall underneath. They could see nothing except yellow mist but sometimes shouts echoed up from refugees in the Monument below. Carlos retreated to the back of the overhang for his scheduled session with Varvara while Joan began to mindcast, searching for empaths in the Heights compound. She found two – a boy her age and, to her relief and bewilderment, her grandmother.

Confrontation

I woke manacled to a chair, looking out a high window. My tongue felt parched and too big for my mouth. I gulped air, trying to swallow.

"Ah you are back with us. Robo, bring the prisoner a cup of water – with a straw."

Just then I felt a mindtouch. I wondered if it was Kei, but it didn't have his desperate clumsiness. In fact, it had a distinctly familiar ring. I dismissed that perception as wishful thinking. The waist device was lighting up again.

"Ah, you're one of those empatho-logicals aren't you. Not a very good one though. Who are you talking to?"

"No one or maybe someone. I don't know for sure."

"Why don't you look out the window. Maybe you can figure it out," he said with a smile.

When I looked out the window, I realized hours had passed. The sun was sinking in the west. The mists were thick. Below a small man commanded the roboarmy that encircled the refugees and volunteers in the mud at the shoreline of the hill. A lone robosoldier was walking toward the group. "Why I believe that's mine," he said, leaning forward. "And look where it's headed, back to the Army where it belongs. And who does it have in custody? Why I believe it's your grand-daughter, Joan."

I stared then while taking a long pull on the straw presented by the robovalet. I used the cool water to soothe my tongue and calm my heart. The robosoldiers turned toward her. Her thoughts powered through the government static. The robosoldiers began to drift apart.

"Will you do this?" I wondered to myself, seeing her straight black hair, remembering her black button eyes.

"Turn, turn, turn," she's projecting to the R-S.

I felt the stun gun at my neck. "Tell her to shut up," the colonel barked.

"Look at these humans," Joan thought to the R-S. "Use your vision. See what is before you."

The R-S orange vision targeting beacons lit up the particles of pollution. A slow shirring flicked the particles to a froth that obscured the action. "What's happening?" snarled the colonel.

"I don't know," I snapped, filled with fear that my people were about to be mowed down. "*Ganbatte*[25]," I thought to Joan, to my little one grown fierce.

"You said something." He glanced at his waist detector.

"*Callate*[26], shut up. Your words." And he couldn't catch the lie in the charged atmosphere.

"Bah, the old hag's not worth the power expenditure – or the air. Put her out. I want to see her crawl." He grabbed my gogmask from the robovalet who escorted me out the gate.

****

Cus returned to his vantage point, proud to be overlooking the slaughter field to be. But no, the girl was controlling the R-S battalion. They're approaching the gates. Where was Phillips? He thought he'd spotted Phillips in command. In his confusion, his father's voice returned to him.

"Make me proud," his father had demanded as he presented him with the family sword. "It's the little things that mark the gentleman. Be courteous but never hesitate to finish off an enemy." Pride in self, family, clan, school, fighting unit, country. Pride was the backbone. No backbone and what did you have – some squishy squirmy thing that belonged in the mud. It was his job, an honorable job done by the few, the proud, to keep those things in the shallows, the murk. To defend the high ground and preserve the greatness of his patrimony.

Everyone he knew had recognized his quality, had respected his self-discipline, his commitment, and his belief in their cause. Single-mindedness was what it took to survive and thrive. So why the hell was he standing here while his post was threatened by the scum of the earth, useless eaters, and their mechanical turncoats. Off with her head became his mind's chant, a mantra which released his body from the shock that had seized him when she and the

---

[25] *Ganbatte* (Jp): Do your best!
[26] *Callate* (Sp): Shut up.

migrants had reached his perimeter.   He grabbed for the ceremonial sword at his side. The warmth from the grip stole up his arm as he gave a practiced swing and whoop.

****

When the gate opened, the scene had cleared. I saw Joan leading the refugees through the midst of the robosoldiers who had split into two sections, vacuuming as they turned and backed up, leaving a dry path to the Nacotchtank Heights gate I had been ejected from. The gate was ajar, propped open by my foot. Suddenly she was there, still standing.

****

The newly returned robo had the audacity to question him.

"We stand our ground!" Cus called out, sterling true, and mentally summoned the horns and baying hounds of the hunt. "Follow me, dog!"

He bounded down the metal steps which rang out the threat of his steel-booted approach. Where was that stupid slant-eyed girl? She must be the one with the controller. At first, he couldn't spot her, but he remained calm and scanned the hubbub. There! He caught her black-eyed gaze.

****

Joan hesitated and, in her eyes, I saw the reflection of the Colonel waving a coppery sword and charging down the stairs. "Scatter!" I shouted then, and choking, fell into the crusted mud.

****

Grinning Cus brandished his sword, its hilt ruby-encrusted, so like his father's gift. A spark diverted his gaze for a microsecond, no more, and when he looked back there were a thousand of her.

****

Through the dust I saw ten, a hundred, a thousand Joans, crowded into the gate. Robosoldiers and migrants poured past me through the barrier. I heard a howl, then a clatter, and a sword lay beside me. Mangled and bloodless, it's no longer a danger. A robotic arm lifted me out of the mud, and before I could collapse again, clapped an oxygen mask on me. The myriad Joans condensed into one warm human being who took my arm, steadied me. For a moment we shared an ample *onsen* of hope, then turned to enter what would become the sanctuary of Nacotchtank Heights.

Epilogue – Thirty years later

"What day is today children? It's a special day."

Carlito's hand shot up. "It's named after my great-aunt, teacher. It's Joan's day. But my daddy always says it should be my grandpa's day too."

"Many people think we should name it after the Empatho-Ecology Movement instead of one person, because there were many, many people involved in helping the movement overcome the FCPower so we could all work together to solve our planetary problems," the teacher lectured. She was a young teacher, too wordy for the seven-year-olds, but perceptive enough to tell she was losing them.

"Let's draw pictures of the people who were important to the E-E Movement." This was more like it. The children grabbed their markers and their art tablets as the teacher circulated around the room.

A little girl with long dark hair was drawing a figure with long black hair, Joan probably. Oh, look she's drawing more Joans. "Why so many?" the teacher asked the girl.

"It's the Hydra effect. Don't you know about that?"

"Oh, yes. You're very smart to remember that."

"I'm named after her."

"I know dear." There were far too many children named after Joan and Carlos, both of whom had been captured and executed by the FCPower close to the end of the prolonged ten-year struggle.

She leaned over another little boy's shoulder. He'd drawn a robosoldier. "AS-57189," he had carefully written on the R-S's body. "Great letters and numbers Bobby." The boy grinned at her. A robot is not a person, but the kids had trouble understanding that. AS had been key in winning the R-S to the side of the empaths, and, despite their drone fleets, the FCPower had never recovered from the loss of their bot boots on the ground.

When she came to Carlito's desk, she was surprised to see him drawing a yellow-haired man sleeping under a cactus. "Who's that?" she asked.

Carlito hesitated. "I forget his name. But he's the bad guy."

By the time the empaths finally gained control, Lieutenant Custer had actually and officially become Colonel Custer. As a prisoner he'd requested exile over rehabilitation and had been sent back to his birthplace in the drylands. He was given a water-producing machine for personal use and had outlived all the key participants in the Nacotchtank Heights sanctuary action.

The lunch bell rang, and the eager children jumped up while others continued, caught up in their drawings. The teacher summoned the slow ones and lined them up at the door. Then they walked across the breezeway to the lunchroom. It was a clear day, an easy breathing day, so different from those grim days of gogmasks. Carlito ran up and grabbed the teacher's hand. "Do you know about my grandma Varvara?"

"No, Carlito. Tell me about her."

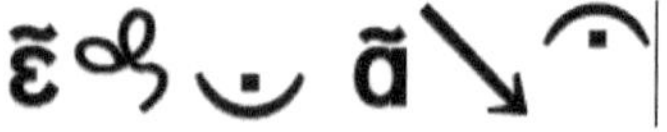

Acknowledgements

I am grateful for the supportive criticism offered by multiple readers including Janice Benson, Carol Caref, Marshall Clarke, Allison Culley, Nancy Fritz, Dave Robbins, Nancy Shih-Knodel, Eric Stahl-David, Michael Stahl-David, and the members of Poughkeepsie librarian Debora Shon's "Write and Rewrite" writers' group. At the inception of this novel, I had the good fortune to be housed and fed by my sister-in-law Barbara Wright in her home overlooking the Kanawha State Forest. A special thanks to my husband Dick David and his brother Cliff, who enthusiastically listened to my reading of the day's chapters for many nights running.

I am most fortunate to have a talented artist in the family. The cover art was kindly provided by my daughter-in-law Mado Todd-Morel. You can view a selection of her other work at https://www.mado-todd-morel.com.